TORMENTED DREAMS

TORMENTED DREAMS

by

Maddison Greer

SCAR TREE
AUSTRALIA

SCAR TREE
AUSTRALIA

Tormented Dreams
ISBN 978-0-6488029-4-5

First published in 2019 by Scar Tree Australia

Editing by Ashley Greer

Disclaimer

The material in this publication is of the nature of general comment only, and does not represent professional advice. It is not intended to provide specific guidance for particular circumstances and it should not be relied on as the basis for any decision to take action or not take action on any matter which it covers. Readers should obtain professional advice where appropriate, before making any such decision. To the maximum extent permitted by law, the author and publisher disclaim all responsibility and liability to any person, arising directly or indirectly from any person taking or not taking action based on the information in this publication.

For my family, who encouraged me to follow my dreams, and for my mother and sister, without whom this book would not exist.

CONTENTS

PART ONE

CHAPTER ONE

The Letter

IT WAS A LARGE, beautiful realm, the Kingdom of Dresden, bordered on one side by the sea and the other by rolling mountains and thick dense woods that were home to many creatures. The air in the surrounding plains was clear and fresh, but the royal palace, situated in the heart of the city's capital, was heavy with the bitter scent of civilisation: burning coal bursting from the smithies; fresh manure wafting from the cattle; the full, rich and slightly tangy trace of hay lurking about the stables; and the taverns, cooking the mouth-watering evening meal—not to mention serving copious amounts of alcohol. The streets were teeming with people, no matter the time of day or evening. Still, Dresden and its surrounds had all the things that made a city pleasant.

Artisan halls were dotted around the kingdom. Timber and stucco houses were covered with dusky, leafy vines hanging like beautiful draperies. Birds tweeted and cawed to the tune of their own song. Sea vessels lined the expansive harbour, sails pointing to the heavens above. The port was one of the busiest places in the city and reeked with the harsh odour of fish and seaweed.

A mystical charm emanated from the city, and Maldwyn felt this was one of the most alluring places on which he had ever set eyes. The curvature in the grey stone archways and the sculpted figures in the battlement walls lent the city a certain fierce romance.

Despite Maldwyn's love for Dresden, he remained vigilant and all too aware of the darkness living in the hearts of its citizens, especially their king. The King of Dresden ruled with an iron fist under the delusion that he was protecting his people from the mysterious influences of magic.

Magic was prohibited in the Kingdom of Dresden and the sentence for using sorcery was death. Standing in the expansive royal chambers and waiting for Prince Harlan to finish reading the letter Maldwyn had delivered, he felt a familiar buzzing surge and struggled to conceal his discomfort.

His whole life Maldwyn had been different. He had been born wrong. His mother raised him to be ashamed of the truth. Every day was a fight to hide any sign of abnormality.

Maldwyn had magic.

Magic was a power the gods granted, and it existed all around, binding together the fabric of life. Using spells, potions or rituals, anyone could tap into this power and use this gift. Unlike all other people, Maldwyn didn't need spells or potions to use magic. He was born with it. If anyone discovered Maldwyn's power, he and everyone he knew would be hunted and killed. The only person who knew about Maldwyn's magic was his mother and—for good reason—she instilled in him a great sense of fear concerning his abilities. She taught him to always keep it hidden.

Having spent his life denying the magic he harboured within, Maldwyn never mastered his power. Every now and then, he lost control and Maldwyn's magic escaped his grasp, like a caged beast waiting for its chance to pounce.

Prince Harlan cleared his throat, bringing Maldwyn back from his thoughts. His yellow hair glowed like a halo over the prince's head and his strong arms were constricted by his tight-fitted shirt. Prince Harlan was a tall, powerfully muscled man. Still, Maldwyn could see from his expression, the prince was upset.

Prince Harlan looked back over his shoulder, resting his weight on the heavy timber desk in front of him. There were no tears in the prince's blue eyes, rather his face was shrouded with helplessness. Maldwyn was quick to look at the floor so as not to cause offence by making eye contact with the Crown Prince of Dresden.

'Who gave this to you?'

Maldwyn noted the quiver in the prince's voice as he asked the question.

'Your Grace, what does the letter say?'

'That's not your concern,' Prince Harlan snapped and turned back to the letter, flipping it over on the table. 'What I want to know is, who gave this to you?'

Maldwyn shifted his feet making a quiet scuffing noise. A lump formed at the back of his throat as his curiosity about the letter left him filled with apprehension. He swallowed, wondering if giving the name would cause more harm than good.

'Well,' Prince Harlan pressed.

'It was Ser Mikel Tanzer of Karana Downs, sire.' Maldwyn remained very still; his hands clasped in front of his torso. 'When he handed me the letter, he asked that I deliver it to none other than yourself. Ser Mikel told me it was very important the contents were to be read by you and you alone, sire.'

Prince Harlan stayed quiet and resumed his usual impassive disposition. Maldwyn waited and fixed his gaze on the beaten variegated floorboards of the prince's private chambers. The warming fire crackled. A cold gentle breeze swept through the room from the nearby window, carrying the bloomy spring perfume on the night air. Maldwyn shifted his gaze to the window. It was a clear evening and the stars sparkled, glimmering like flecks of moonlight reflecting on the calm surface of the rippling ocean.

Lifting his head a little, Maldwyn glimpsed the prince and checked his demeanour. There was no change.

Maldwyn had been a servant in the palace for some time and, although he didn't know the prince well, he had never seen the prince appear this defeated, even saddened. In the past, Prince Harlan had always seemed smug, arrogant and a little aloof. Having never witnessed anything from the prince to contradict his opinions, Maldwyn had always considered him to be conceited, always overestimating his abilities and spoiling himself in spite of his father's despotism. He couldn't begin to imagine what information might be causing the minute traces of his expression to betray his regular poised royal façade.

Finally, Prince Harlan turned back to Maldwyn.

'Thank you. You're dismissed.'

Taking a deep breath, Maldwyn bowed politely and moved to leave the room. He paused as he reached the small door leading to the servant corridors, resting his palm on the handle. He considered talking with the prince and reassuring him, but that would be improper and contradict the prince's orders to leave.

Maldwyn pushed on the handle and opened the door. He felt the prince's eyes on him, and he disappeared out into the hall, clicking the door closed behind him.

The air was stuffy in the servant halls from the lack of windows. The corridors were poorly lit by the sparse number of torches lining the stone walls, mottling them with shades of orange and casting black shadows that swallowed the light. Maldwyn let out a breath of air as he considered that his life as a servant was similar to his life with magic; both required him to be invisible.

As a servant, Maldwyn was not allowed to walk the greater corridors without permission from either a member of the court or the Master of the Staff of Servants. The palace servants were to enter rooms through smaller doors and moved about the castle using lesser halls and tunnels, going about their work unseen and unnoticed.

'Hey, servant,' a familiar voice called.

Ahead, Maldwyn could see the empty corridor. Turning back, he peered down a side hall from where the voice had originated. A man stood in the middle of the hall, cloaked in a hooded robe. Maldwyn stepped forward and the man pulled his hood down revealing his face. Uneasy, Maldwyn cringed a fraction as he recognised the slimy sneer and greasy black hair of Ser Mikel Tanzer.

'Ser Mikel Tanzer,' Maldwyn addressed the knight and bowed, as was expected for a servant to address a nobleman. Although it was odd for a member of nobility to enter the servant halls and wander the palace cloaked, it wasn't unheard of. Sometimes the servant halls were the best way for court members to have privacy away from the prying eyes of others.

Ser Mikel's dark eyes searched the halls, ensuring they were indeed alone. He struggled to remain still as if he were anxious about something and he stroked his smooth chin with his hand.

'How did you go with the letter? Did you deliver it to Prince Harlan?'

Maldwyn's palms began to sweat as his concern for the contents of the letter rose. He resisted the urge to ask what the letter said. A nobleman did not have to answer to a servant, and Ser Mikel was one of the least polite and respectful knights Maldwyn knew. To him, Maldwyn's words would be worthless.

'The letter was delivered, and the prince has read the message, my lord.'

Ser Mikel let out a breath and slapped his hands to his face as if he were relieved. Something about his presence made Maldwyn's skin crawl.

'Good… he needed to know.'

Maldwyn drew his brows together. Ser Mikel stepped close. Maldwyn felt his breath on his face and saw beads of sweat form on Ser Mikel's forehead. Threatened, Maldwyn looked down.

'If you tell anyone about this conversation, I will kill you.' Ser Mikel placed a firm hand on Maldwyn's shoulder. 'Remember servant, you're not a man, you're a thing and you answer to members of the court. No one would question if you were killed.'

Maldwyn met his cruel stare with an intense look of his own. Ser Mikel pushed him back a step.

'Return to your work.'

Staying still for a moment, he watched Ser Mikel rush down the dark corridor and out of sight. He exhaled. Pushing his shoulders back, he stood tall and continued into the night down the musty halls which were his home.

* * * * *

Going about his normal routine, Maldwyn spent the next morning making beds with crisp fresh sheets, collecting the dirty clothes and linen that had been strewn about the royal private chambers for the laundry staff, washing and polishing the dirty floors, and clearing the breakfast trays from the rooms. No matter how much or how hard Maldwyn worked, he couldn't stop thinking about the letter he had delivered to Prince Harlan and the aggressive encounter with Ser Mikel in the hallways.

While cleaning King Viktor's room, Maldwyn thought about the sadness that Prince Harlan's face bore and how he had left him alone with his thoughts. Feeling guilty that he hadn't tried to speak with the prince before walking out the door, Maldwyn felt a knot form in the pit of his stomach.

He sighed. Having been scrubbing the timber floors on his hands and knees, Maldwyn sat back to rest his bodyweight on his feet. He rubbed his forehead with the back of his hand, exhausted and wishing he could quiet his mind. Maldwyn checked the area.

Clean white sheets covered the thick mattress of the huge four-post bed. An embossed royal blue bed cover with a fine pattern of golden thread lay atop the flat sheets. The curtains were pulled back on the two tall windows filling the room with brilliant sunlight. There was a rug on the floor in front of the massive fireplace that had been swept clean and a desk on the far side of the room situated on a raised dais.

Maldwyn stood and smiled at a job well done. He moved to leave and knocked the bucket of water he had used to scrub the floors. The bucket wobbled and water splashed up the sides, spilling out onto the floor. The droplets spread out in a wide radius around the bucket.

Annoyed, Maldwyn scratched his nose and got back down on his knees. The floorboards creaked as he shifted his weight, lowering himself to the floor. He had just begun wiping the spills with the damp rag when he heard heated voices outside the main entrance to the king's room.

Quick as he could, Maldwyn wiped away the water splashes on the floor, tossed the cloth over the side of the bucket as he picked it up and darted through the servant door. When he pulled the door behind him it caught in the jam. Maldwyn could hear the king enter the room, having an argument with someone. He didn't want to slam the door to close it, so he held it as closed as he could with his hand while he waited for them to leave.

'Keep your voice down!'

'Why? The rest of the kingdom already knows, don't they? It seems like it was a public execution!'

With one hand gripping the handle of the bucket, Maldwyn carefully placed it on the floor as quiet as he could, taking in a breath of the mildewed halls. It was then that he realised the cloth was no longer hanging over the bucket's side. He had dropped it somewhere in his dash from the king's bed chambers.

Gently, he slipped his hand along the coarse door and pushed it ajar just enough to peek inside and locate the missing rag. Maldwyn didn't want to think about what the king might do if he found the cloth in his quarters or became aware of his presence lurking in the halls. Through the small gap, Maldwyn saw Prince Harlan confronting his father.

'The rest of the kingdom knows, but Cassara doesn't and if she finds out because of you...' The king was pointing at Prince Harlan, his index finger almost touched the prince's nose. Prince Harlan's eyes flashed furiously. 'Let's just say your mother won't be the only one in the family to lose her head!'

Prince Harlan took a deep breath and looked down. His face was distraught. Despite his imposing stature and strong physique, Prince Harlan knew his place, and that was beneath the king. Maldwyn believed he was afraid of his father.

'How could you, father?'

King Viktor was a broad-shouldered man with trimmed, well-kept, greying hair that had a streak of black on the left side of his head. Even with the gold laurel wreath for a crown, the distinguished streak made King Viktor identifiable from a great distance. 'Your mother asked for it. She knew the risk, and what the consequences might be.'

Maldwyn tried to be polite and ignore the conversation. He scanned the room and saw the scrunched-up rag a few feet inside. He just needed to wait for them to leave the area before he could grab the cloth and properly close the jamming door.

'That makes it okay?'

'Don't be stupid,' the king told Prince Harlan. 'Your mother committed a crime. For that, she was executed.'

Prince Harlan turned away from his father, moving toward the dais. 'You didn't have to kill her.' He rubbed his forehead as if to soothe his rage. 'You could've banished her,' the prince suggested.

King Viktor looked disgusted.

'Banished her? You're being a sentimental fool. She disgraced herself. Death was the only option.'

'How could you have kept this from me? For all these years?'

'I never wanted you to find out the circumstances surrounding your mother's death. I wanted to preserve her memory for you and your sister.' The king hissed as he stalked closer to Prince Harlan. 'The palace staff, the nobles and all those in service of the crown were instructed never to mention your mother's execution. Who told you?'

'I received an anonymous letter.' The prince's voice gave no hint that he had lied. Confused, Maldwyn supposed Prince Harlan's fib was a feeble attempt to protect Ser Mikel. 'Does it matter now that I know? Did you ever love her?'

'Love is for the weak-minded,' King Viktor spat. He waved his hand, shooing his son's query aside.

'You're a coward!'

Maldwyn froze. Paralysed with shock, he heard the crack of the king's forceful fist meet with his son's jaw. Prince Harlan, a strong man, staggered back from the force of the blow. His hand came up clutching at the wound.

Maldwyn checked his magic, worried it would escape. A part of him wanted to rush into the room, but knew it wasn't his place and that it would do more harm than good. He considered what sort of father the king was. Maldwyn knew his fair share of abusive people but had expected better from royalty.

'Remember who you're speaking to.' King Viktor lowered his voice. 'I am the king, and your father. You will respect me.'

Maldwyn, peering through the door, saw the king circling the prince like a wolf rounding its prey. Silent and cold as a statue, Prince Harlan, knowing his place, made no objections.

Three wraps sounded on the main door on the far side of the king's chambers. His circling ceased. King Viktor took a deep breath, composed himself, and walked over to the heavy timber door. A low creaking resounded through the room as the king answered the summons.

Maldwyn couldn't see who it was, but he was able to make out the muttered conversation. The voice beyond the door mentioned something about the king being needed in the council chambers regarding the contested border along the Anhalt Mountains, and a sorcerer being held prisoner in the palace dungeons. He thought they mentioned something called the Valuwan prophecy.

Nodding, the king finished the hushed conversation and closed the door.

'I am needed elsewhere. You are not to show your face at the banquet tonight. I will have the servants bring your supper to your bed chambers where you will spend the rest of today and where you will remain until I feel you are calm enough to return to your duties. Do you understand?'

Prince Harlan nodded.

'You will not breathe a word of what we have discussed in this room today.'

'Yes, Your Majesty.' Prince Harlan replied formally as he bowed.

'Good, now go.'

Prince Harlan scanned the king's chambers with his eyes. For an instant, Maldwyn thought the prince's gaze rested on the rag and he wondered if he noticed the door wasn't closed. Then, the prince turned and left the room, without so much as a word about the cloth. His father followed close behind.

When the room was empty and Maldwyn could be sure it would stay as such, he opened the door and let out a huge breath, relieved to have not been caught eavesdropping. The air was clearer than in the servant halls, yet the room held an intense aura making him want to leave as soon as possible. He picked up the damp cloth and threw it in the bucket. Then, he left, pulling the servant door closed behind him with such force the bang echoed down the empty corridors. He would have to come back later and fix the door with the right equipment.

Right now, he wanted to be as far away from the king's chambers as possible.

Unsure about what he had witnessed, Maldwyn wished he could forget everything he had heard. A knot in his stomach told him this was his fault. He had delivered the letter to the prince which had told him of the queen's execution.

Running his hands through his thick hair, Maldwyn considered that his mother was right. For some reason, he had been born wrong and was destined to doom all those around him, including the prince. His magic rose within, humming like a hive of bees, and Maldwyn knew he was cursed. Trying

to forget what had just occurred, he busied himself with his
endless list of tasks.

CHAPTER TWO

Kindred Souls

MALDWYN'S STOMACH RUMBLED. The scent of slow roast goat, creamy, buttery mashed potatoes, sticky plum and cherry sauce, and steaming loaves of fresh-baked bread caught his attention in the kitchen. He hadn't eaten all day and was very hungry.

The kitchen staff rushed around. A matronly woman was grabbing pots and pans hanging overhead. Others chopped fresh fruits and vegetables and butchered mounds of meat, pulling trays of food from the fiery hearth, and preparing the bowls and platters for the banquet.

Ordinarily, Maldwyn was not permitted in the kitchen, but Master Damyan, the Master of the Staff of Servants, had instructed Maldwyn to collect supper for Prince Harlan and deliver it to his private chambers. Of course, Maldwyn accepted the task and told no one of the events he had witnessed earlier.

'What are you doing in my kitchen?' the head cook shouted to Maldwyn. He was a short, pot-bellied man with beady, sepia-coloured eyes and a high forehead.

'I'm here to collect the prince's supper.'

The cook eyed him a moment, then stepped away and grabbed a silver platter loaded with a plate of food, utensils, a goblet and a jug of wine. He brought the tray of food and drink to Maldwyn and offered an apologetic expression.

'Sorry boy, there's a banquet on tonight and you wouldn't be the first servant to come here and try to steal food.'

Maldwyn had seen other starving servants try this before. Food could sometimes be an expensive commodity in Dresden, and the hungry palace staff were poorly paid, struggling to find the funds to purchase a meal. Many of the servants would hunt or forage the city surrounds to find sustenance, and the little food that they gathered was usually shared. When they weren't able to collect food, they would often spend money on alcohol from the tavern. It was cheaper than buying food, and offered enough warmth and calories to sustain them for the short term. The servants who stole food in the castle were imprisoned for theft against the crown. At least they would be fed in the dungeon, Maldwyn told himself.

'I understand,' Maldwyn said to the cook kindly and in a soft tone of voice. 'Thank you, I'll take this to the prince and get out of your way.'

The cook let out a nervous chuckle and Maldwyn headed back to the servant halls. It was a cold evening and the air was damp.

Maldwyn stopped when he reached the door to Prince Harlan's room. Though it was a small door, it never felt more imposing than it did in this moment.

Clearing his throat, he checked his posture and fixed his placement of the tray on the flat palm of his hand. Lifting his other free hand, Maldwyn pressed his shoulders back and knocked on the door. He waited for a response and readied his grasp on the handle.

'Enter.'

Maldwyn pushed open the door and walked into the lavish room. The last time he was here with the prince, Maldwyn had delivered the letter from Ser Mikel Tanzer. Keeping his gaze down, he noticed the striking form that was Prince Harlan, standing on the far side of the room, staring out the window, his back towards Maldwyn.

'Leave it on the table.' The prince's voice was distant and cold. His straight posture seemed proud, but the way he remained so perfectly still was telling that he wished to be invisible.

Silent, Maldwyn strode through the room and put the tray down. He unpacked the tray, placed the plate on the table top and set out the cutlery. He took up the ornate goblet and filled it with the deep, rich, red wine from the jug and set it by the plate. He returned the jug to the tray, making sure everything was in its place.

The prince hadn't moved, nor had his manner changed. Maldwyn glanced around the room and noticed the large bed was still made up, the lounge by the fireplace appeared not to have been sat on from the lack of indentations on the cushions, the windows were unopened, and the drapes remained pulled back despite the late hour. Maldwyn thought the room looked untouched since he prepared it earlier that morning. He wondered how long the prince had stood unmoving by the window, watching the world outside.

Again, Maldwyn checked his posture and clasped his hands in front of his body. 'Your Grace, may I be of any further assistance to you?'

'No, that will be all.'

Maldwyn headed back for the door and, when he put his palm on the handle, he had a perfect moment of déjà vu. Maldwyn had felt guilty about leaving Prince Harlan to struggle with his thoughts the last time he was here. Now he believed he had a second chance to reach out to the prince.

'Permission to speak freely, sire?' Maldwyn said in a quiet voice, ready to be denied the chance to talk openly with the prince, and to be dismissed yet another time.

'Sure,' Prince Harlan agreed as he let out a bothered breath, gazing out the window, into the night sky.

'I'm afraid I must confess I overheard your conversation with your father—the king—in his chambers earlier today.' Maldwyn kept his gaze down and held his hands out, palms facing upwards.

'You did?' Prince Harlan, still looking out the window, didn't give the impression that he was surprised by Maldwyn's confession, but he did sound disappointed.

'Yes, Your Grace.'

'I wasn't sure who it was, but I knew we'd been overheard.' The prince gently tilted his head a fraction, as if he had noticed something in the courtyard below. 'I saw the cloth… and the door.'

Maldwyn had been afraid this might have been the case and he felt the knot return to his stomach. A lump formed in his throat and he swallowed. The ball seemed to stay caught.

'Sire, I apologise. I meant no offence by being there.' Interlocking his fingertips together, Maldwyn straightened his back. 'I had been organising the king's bed chambers when I heard your voices. I needed to rush out of the room but the door jammed and wouldn't close completely. I had to hold it closed and when I realised that I'd dropped the rag in the king's quarters I needed to wait until the room was clear so I could retrieve it. So, I was stuck holding the door and waiting for the room to empty—'

Prince Harlan held up a hand to silence Maldwyn. 'It's alright Maldwyn. You have nothing to apologise for.'

Mouth slightly agape, Maldwyn stood transfixed. He hadn't known the prince knew his name. As a servant, he was invisible and without value. As Ser Mikel said, he wasn't a person to those whose station was higher than his own, he was an object. A thoughtless emotionless thing that completed tasks.

Yet, the prince knew him by name.

Prince Harlan made no move toward his food. Maldwyn could tell his thoughts were consumed with the news of his mother's execution.

Emboldened, Maldwyn's shoes clicked on the wooden floor as he made his way over toward the prince. He stood beside him in the window, looking out at the paved courtyard below. There were guards patrolling in formation, winding their way around the wide-open space.

Standing beside the prince, the cool night air emanated from the glass. He suppressed a shiver. Prince Harlan stared at him and Maldwyn remained careful not to meet his gaze, continuing to examine the courtyard.

'What was your mother like, sire?'

Impassive, Prince Harlan went back to looking out the window, ignoring Maldwyn's closeness. He let out a heavy, saddened breath.

'I don't know and that's the problem. I was about three and Cassara was one when she died. I have no memory of her; not her face, her voice, her laugh, her values, nor her fears.' The prince squinted his eyes a little, mulling over his memories of his mother. 'She's nothing more than a figure in my head.'

Maldwyn understood. He never knew his own father. Staying beside Prince Harlan, Maldwyn remained silent, hoping it was enough for the prince to know he wasn't alone.

Maldwyn watched the stars. He imagined reaching out with his magic and making the stars dance and grew saddened at the thought that he had no control over his abilities. Ever present, his power constantly simmered within, and just thinking about it was enough to make it excite and almost reach boiling point, desperate to escape his grip. Maldwyn tightened his hold on it before it broke free.

'More than anything, I wish I knew her face.' Prince Harlan's tone was thick with the desperate yearning to know his mother, as if knowing her might help him to understand himself. 'I've had a bad day. I could use a distraction.' The prince glanced in Maldwyn's direction. 'Tell me about yourself.'

Maldwyn, his grip on his power tighter than ever, was uneasy. He preferred his invisibility in the servant halls, it felt more comfortable, and he almost regretted hanging back in the prince's chambers. Prince Harlan's eyes were watching him, waiting for him to speak.

'I'm not all that interesting, Your Grace.'

The prince scraped his foot and turned to face him. Maldwyn didn't move a muscle. 'Really? I doubt that.' His deep voice was smooth and hushed.

'I am a servant, sire. I assure you my life is less than compelling and very insignificant in comparison to yours.' Maldwyn didn't mean to sound bleak; he just stated the truth. Everyone in the palace always reminded him of his lowliness.

Prince Harlan cocked his head to the side with a concerned expression. 'I don't believe that,' the prince told him.

'Your Grace, I am less than a person.'

'We are all people, Maldwyn,' Prince Harlan pressed in a kind tone, stepping a fraction closer. 'Look at me.' Maldwyn let out an awkward laugh. Prince Harlan held out a welcoming hand. 'There's no one else here—no need for formality. Look at me.'

Maldwyn let his gaze shift up to face the prince. There was a familiarity Maldwyn felt when their eyes met, like a tune he had known his whole life. Flawless and composed, the prince was like a painting. His blue eyes shone like jewels. The awful bruise on Prince Harlan's jaw was inflamed, and, Maldwyn noted, the only imperfection marking his otherwise perfect features.

'That's better,' Prince Harlan told him and offered him a gentle smile. Turning his head to the side, the prince put the wound out of view.

'Sire, have you had that looked at by one of the court physicians?'

Prince Harlan scoffed. 'No, it's fine and I'd prefer fewer people know about it.'

Maldwyn bit his cheek. He had suffered many wounds himself and knew that, although the wound was mostly superficial, the prince would be in quite a bit of pain. He considered this was the reason he had made no move to eat his dinner.

'May I, Your Grace?'

Prince Harlan conceded, Maldwyn reached up with a gentle touch and he turned the prince's striking, chiselled face to better see the bruise. The raised bluish-purple skin faded to red around the edges. It was an angry wound. He could tell it hurt.

Wishing he could take away the pain, Maldwyn felt his magic course through the hand that touched the lump. He tried to stop it escaping and was gladdened when nothing appeared to happen. Prince Harlan's hand came up to the wound and he took a step back looking surprised.

'What's wrong, sire?'

'It's strange, the pain is gone.'

Maldwyn swallowed. He didn't know what he had done. He hadn't healed the wound—the bruise was still visible—but he had somehow managed to numb the pain.

'Perhaps it is just numbness settling in, sire.'

After a brief moment, Prince Harlan's hand dropped to his side and he looked across to where his plate waited for him. He agreed it must have been numbness, and Maldwyn was relieved he didn't seem to think it was in any way sorcery.

Prince Harlan walked over to his food, scraping the chair on the floor as he pulled it out to take a seat. He sat down and his cutlery made a clinking sound when he picked it up to start digging into his dinner. Maldwyn remembered his hunger and wished his stomach would stay quiet a little longer. Prince Harlan pushed his food around the plate, and the waft of the roasted goat and the plum and cherry sauce made Maldwyn's mouth water.

'You're relatively new to the palace staff, aren't you? Where are you from?'

Prince Harlan piled food on his fork and filled his mouth with the juicy, sweet goat meat. Maldwyn was a little jealous watching the prince eat food that smelled so divine, especially when he was so hungry.

'Yes, sire. I've been working in the palace for a few months now.' The guard's boots pounded around the courtyard below, as they marched through the grounds. 'I'm from Alander. It's a small town on the edge of the kingdom.'

'That's quite a while away. How did you end up here, working in the palace?'

Maldwyn felt his stomach rumble. He was glad it was a silent reminder he hadn't eaten, rather than a loud roar.

'There was a bad harvest a while back and my mother grew ill.' The guards below congregated in the centre of the courtyard, assembling together in rows. The officer at the front of the regiment wore finely detailed metal armour and bellowed a few orders. 'We didn't have money to buy food and trade in the town was failing.' The officer turned and waited with his contingent. Their shift was ending. The new guard would be arriving soon to continue patrolling throughout the night. 'No one had anything to offer. I needed to work to support my mother.' On the far side of the courtyard, the new guard filed into view. 'So, I came here where I found work as a servant.'

'What about your father?' The prince's fork scraped along the base of his plate. 'Could he not support your mother?'

Maldwyn felt his shoulders hunch ever so slightly as he intently watched the changing of the guards outside. 'I'm afraid I never knew my father, Your Grace.' Maldwyn gazed over towards the prince.

Prince Harlan paused, stopped eating and stared back at Maldwyn. 'I'm sorry to hear that.' His tone was soft and calm. The prince remained still, watching Maldwyn, waiting for him to lead the conversation.

Maldwyn headed toward the table and stood beside Prince Harlan. Even seated he was quite a presence to behold. The prince gestured for him to take a seat. Maldwyn reluctantly pulled out a chair and joined Prince Harlan as he picked at his food.

'It's as you said, sire, I have no idea who he was or what he was like. My father is a fiction placed on a pedestal reality couldn't possibly meet. In truth, I know very little about him other than that he was gone before I was ever born.'

Prince Harlan offered a knowing smile telling Maldwyn he understood the turmoil of never knowing a parent. Maldwyn watched with envy as the prince took in another mouthful of food, chewing loudly. Prince Harlan locked eyes with Maldwyn and, as a force of habit, he looked away.

'Did you have any other family?'

'I had an uncle, but he passed away a while ago.' The prince looked apologetic, as if he had stumbled on another sore point of discussion. 'He was an awful man, I don't mourn him,' Maldwyn reassured.

Maldwyn wiped his hand along the smooth surface of the heavy table. The prince picked up his goblet and took a sip of the velvety, red wine. The silence in the room had a lulling effect. Prince Harlan's goblet clunked as he placed it back on the table. Maldwyn felt his hunger rise.

'I should leave, Your grace.'

Prince Harlan gave him a saddened expression, as if the open conversation between them had been the better part of his awful day. 'Of course, you have other work to do.'

Mostly, Maldwyn wanted food. He pushed himself up to stand and then tucked the chair under the table. 'Is there anything further I can do for you, sire?'

'No, you may go.' Prince Harlan waved him away and turned his attention back to his plate, picking at his food.

Maldwyn headed for the servant door, no longer feeling guilty for having ignored the prince's mood. Before he pulled the door open, he looked back and saw the bruise marking the prince's face. Maldwyn thought about how he had been able to take the pain away, and wished he could take away the emotional ache the prince suffered too.

'For what it's worth, sire... you were right. Your father didn't need to execute your mother, and I'm sorry I ever delivered that letter to you.'

Prince Harlan's intense eyes watched him, but he offered no response. Maldwyn left the prince's chambers and returned to his dark, cold and musty halls. His opinion of Prince Harlan as being self-absorbed and aloof was beginning to change, and Maldwyn couldn't shake the sensation there was something familiar about the prince.

CHAPTER THREE

The Raven

'WELL, WHAT DO YOU THINK?' Ailaya asked as she flicked her long, auburn hair back over her shoulder. Her moss-green dress highlighted the olive flecks that were marbled through her large, dark, chestnut-coloured eyes, which sparked with mystery. Her arched brows were raised at Maldwyn as she waited for him to answer.

He laughed, smiling at her. 'I think you're crazy.' Spinning his mug of frothing ale around on the smooth heavy benchtop in the tavern, Maldwyn shook his head. The older man behind the bar was rough looking and had narrow lips that emphasised his overbite, and a stubbled jutted chin. He smirked at their tête-à-tête as he wiped spilt ale from the bar. The tavern was full of people that were enmeshed in loud conversation.

'Maybe.' Ailaya said in a teasing tone. 'Maybe not.'

'You're talking about a knight!' He drummed his fingers on the timber bench. This was not the first time she had mentioned her fascination with Ser Theodor Martell. Maldwyn was beginning to grow a little annoyed with her persistence. People of their station should never entertain such hopeless thoughts.

'Yes, I am.' Ailaya winked, knowing full well that she was beginning to irritate him. 'Ser Theodor isn't like the other knights in the palace.' She reminded him as she leaned closer to Maldwyn. 'He's kind and respectful, and I can't help the way I feel.'

'You shouldn't let yourself be overheard talking like that,' Maldwyn scolded and laughed at her lovesickness, taking a sip of his foaming ale. The warming beverage caught at the back of his throat and he swallowed the need to cough.

'Ugh, it's just a dream, Mal.' Ailaya turned back to the bar, picked up her own drink and took a sip. 'It's not like anything is going to happen. I'm a servant. He would never notice someone like me.' Ailaya slumped over her drink.

Feeling guilty, Maldwyn suppressed his frustration. 'Ailaya, he would be crazy not to notice you… even if you are a servant.'

Ailaya perked back up. 'Okay, I'll stop talking about it.' She waved her hands in the air, swatting the topic aside. 'What about you? Anyone I should know about yet?'

Maldwyn rolled his eyes. He didn't want to talk about such things. He hadn't let himself be intimate with anyone for quite some time, ever since his lover had died. It was yet another reason Maldwyn had come to Dresden. It pained him too much to think about moving on and letting go of his beloved.

'Nope, my life is much simpler that way.'

'Really?' Ailaya neared him. Her disappointed expression zeroed in on him. Maldwyn shook his head, wishing she would let it go. 'Fine. You're a mystery to me, Mal.' She took another sip of her drink. Maldwyn figured she knew he hadn't wanted to talk about it. 'I'll change subjects then. What's with Prince Harlan knowing you by name?'

'I knew I shouldn't have told you that.' Maldwyn threw his head in his hands. 'How should I know?' His voice was muffled.

'I don't know. It seems a little strange.' Ailaya kicked her foot against the counter. She swore under her breath and winced. Readjusting herself in her seat, she continued. 'From what I've heard from the other servants, Prince Harlan is usually very distant and difficult to comprehend. I guess I was just wondering if you know what you did to get noticed by him.'

Maldwyn felt his magic come alive. He tried to distract himself from the worry of losing control over his power by thinking about what Ailaya had asked. In truth, he hadn't known why the prince had noticed him. Prince Harlan had somehow known him by name before he had consoled the prince in his chambers, perhaps even before Maldwyn had delivered the letter informing the prince about the queen's execution. Prior to that, Maldwyn didn't think the prince had ever seen him.

'I have no idea. I'm newer to the castle, I guess.' Ailaya gave him a suspicious look. 'I'm serious, I don't know at what point he became aware of my existence.'

'Maybe you should ask him.' Ailaya shrugged. 'Of course, as a servant you never could speak out of turn.' She sighed. 'To be honest, the prince would probably just ignore it if you asked him.' Maldwyn looked away from her dissatisfied expression, trying to hide that he had already spoken out of turn, and the prince hadn't seemed to mind. Maldwyn's power was still simmering.

He huffed at her as she hunched her shoulders. Her dejected state of mind was a little depressing. 'Can we change the subject please?'

'Fine,' Ailaya threw her hands up. 'What do you want to talk about?'

'I dunno,' Maldwyn slurred. He tried to think of something that might lift both of their spirits. 'How about the rumours about the princess's nightmares?'

Ailaya's eyebrows shot up with excitement. 'It's so interesting, right?'

'I haven't actually heard all that much about it.'

A loud clanging sounded as a plate hit the hard-wooden floorboards. For a moment, the startled crowd became quiet. Then, one group near the incident broke out into laughter and conversation resumed.

'Well, apparently Princess Cassara has been having these awful, vivid nightmares. There are rumours her dreams are visions.' Ailaya's hazel eyes glittered with intrigue.

'You mean they're magical visions?' Maldwyn's interest grew. Supposing that the princess might be a seer made him feel less alone in Dresden.

Like Maldwyn, a seer's power to dream was their own. They were the direct descendants of the Norns, the rulers of destiny. As all things are subject to the endless rigours of time, all beings, including the gods, are subject to the ruling of destiny. Seers were able to dream time, picking up on the Norns' decrees.

Scratching his scalp, Maldwyn thought how sorcerers were not like seers. They did not have their own magic; rather they channelled the divine power of the gods through spells, potions or rituals. He thought about how seers could also learn the craft of sorcery and tap into the power of the gods. His understanding was that all seers could be sorcerers, but not all sorcerers could be seers. To dream time was a gift with which one was born.

'Who knows?' Ailaya lifted her hand to her cheek. 'That's why they're rumours, Mal. Maybe she's a seer who was born with the magic of the Norns and her father will want her executed, or maybe she's just a person who's having nightmares.'

'You're right, of course.'

'Supposedly, her latest dream was that Queen Sonia's triple horn pendant will be stolen from King Viktor's personal chambers and cursed by a man with a raven birthmark. Strange, right?'

'Very odd.' Maldwyn considered the way the king was rumoured to contemplate issues as he held Queen Sonia's pendant close in his grasp, stroking it mournfully as if he missed her presence. It was strange that the king might do this, especially since Maldwyn now knew King Viktor had executed the queen. 'Although, that is supposed to be one of the king's most prized possessions.'

'Yeah, but it's not missing.'

'Yet,' Maldwyn retorted in a tantalising way. It was amusing catching up on all the gossip that surrounded the royal family. Still, Maldwyn didn't dare share the news of the letter, or the conversation he had with the prince in his chambers. There was something that felt deeply private about their discussion, as if they had some strange understanding of one another. Not to mention, the informality of it all would see Maldwyn disciplined by either King Viktor, or Master Damyan. Neither of which was preferable.

'Oh, Mal. Life is boring when you're not around.'

Maldwyn laughed and took a sip of his drink. He and Ailaya had been close since he began working at the castle. She prepared the rooms for the princess and her ladies-in-waiting. Ailaya was the only person in Dresden Maldwyn that had let see the best and the worst sides of himself, and, even then, he held back, keeping his powers secret and censoring his past.

'Have you heard the latest about Ser Mikel?' Ailaya asked. Maldwyn shook his head. 'Seems he's missing.'

He nearly spat his drink across the bar at the news. Maldwyn hadn't seen Ser Mikel since the night he had delivered Prince Harlan the letter about his mother's execution. The thought occurred to him that he was probably the last person to see Ser Mikel in the castle.

'Really?'

'Yes, for a few days now.'

Unsettled, he finished his drink and let out a heavy sigh. 'We should get going before it's too late.'

Ailaya scowled at Maldwyn. She gulped down the rest of her drink. 'You're right, as always. A servant's work is never done, especially in a castle.'

Together they paid the barkeeper and left the other patrons to their drinking. The cool night air outside reinvigorated Maldwyn after a long, hard day. He breathed in deep and allowed the fresh air to clear his lungs. His power eased in its vivacity and he strolled through the quiet streets toward the palace.

*   *   *   *   *

Maldwyn grinned at the way the castle hugged the craggy seaside mount, shining under the moonlight. The ancient walls were a patchwork of furry moss. Standing tall and proud, the turrets gave the impression of an army of statues standing guard over the city, watching the horizon. In the background, Maldwyn could hear the soothing low tide crashing against the mount's rocky base and a gentle breeze carried the salty ocean scent.

Up on the battlements, he noticed a tall feminine silhouette observing the castle grounds. He considered it might be the princess, Cassara, avoiding her nightmares. The figure stood alone and remained still as he watched for a moment. A cold chill overwhelmed him and his magic flared as if it were trying to warn him about something.

'Are you coming?' Ailaya shouted from further ahead. Maldwyn shook the worried feeling away and jogged to catch up with Ailaya, gravel crunching under his feet.

The entrance to the servant halls was via a small timber door, decorated with swirls of wrought iron, on the other side of the wide-open courtyard. A large tree in the centre of the square reached out with its long bulbous arms, forming an umbrella blocking the moon's radiant beams. Vines wrapped around the stone archways like delicate cobwebs providing cover for the outdoor walkways.

The door creaked when Ailaya opened it. Beyond was a set of steps leading down to the servant halls. At this time of night, there were few guards around and everything was quiet.

'What were you looking at back there?' Ailaya sounded concerned. 'You looked terrified.'

'Nothing.' Maldwyn quickly answered. 'I just saw someone on the battlements.' Ailaya drew her brows together as she staggered down the steps. She wasn't convinced by his explanation. 'Then, there was a cold draught... I suppose I caught a chill.' He shrugged, hoping she would accept the answer.

'A chill?' She threw a sceptical expression his way. 'Mal, it really wasn't cold. Are you sure you're okay?'

He smiled in the most compelling way he could. 'I'm fine, honestly.' Maldwyn couldn't tell her that his magic had tried to tell him something. 'It's been a long day and it's getting late. I'm just going to turn in.'

'No matter Mal, I'll head off as well.' Ailaya, still not convinced, dropped the matter. 'I hope you feel better tomorrow.'

Stepping backwards, Ailaya turned and walked away. Maldwyn remained where he was for a while, wondering what had triggered his abilities to go on alert. He was glad he had contained his pulsating power. He rubbed his sandy eyes after the long day, the taste of ale still warmed his tongue. He turned down the hall and headed for his quarters.

* * * * *

The next day, Master Damyan requested Maldwyn assist the team of hunters with procuring meat for the royal dinner. Specifically, King Viktor wanted venison. Master Damyan had been concerned the standard hunting party might not be able to cover enough ground, and assigned a few extra servants to the team to lend a hand. Having grown up in a small village where Maldwyn and his mother needed to hunt for their dinner meat, he had been selected to help out.

The group gathered by the edge of the woods beyond the castle grounds and divided themselves into smaller hunting parties. Moss wrapped around the trees like fur coats and their wrinkled limbs reached toward the hunters as they entered the forest. The warm spring weather was barely noticeable in the dense wood, but there was a sweetness to the wet earthy smell that reminded Maldwyn of the warmth beyond the forest.

The quiver at Maldwyn's hip was heavy and full of arrows. He carried his bow in a slackened grip as he walked in silence with his cohort.

After a few hours, a muddy patch of ground revealed oval-shaped hoof prints headed in a north-western direction. 'Over here,' Maldwyn called.

'What have you got?' Erik was a rustic man with lank hair and a stubbled jaw. A scar ripped through his right eyebrow. He was a regular member of the hunting party.

'Some hoof prints. It looks as though the deer headed that way.'

'There's some droppings over here as well.' Greg, a tall, thin and ultimately gangly man, crouched a few metres away near a group of shrubs. 'Looks like we're close on its trail.'

Maldwyn nodded to Erik in agreeance.

'We'll press on.' Erik ordered, keeping his voice low. 'Make sure you're keeping a careful watch on any movement ahead and stay quiet.' Erik notched an arrow in his bow and led the way along the trail.

They fanned out, following the tracks. Every now and then they stopped to check they were still on the right trail. The trees were twisted into odd poses and the uneven ground kept them wary as they stalked through the woods like ghosts.

A short while later, Maldwyn caught sight of it in a small clearing in the distance. The deer roamed the jagged terrain with grace. Maldwyn stopped walking, notched an arrow and signalled to Erik and Greg that he had sighted the deer.

The others moved to Maldwyn's side. They beamed after hours spent searching the dense woods.

'You spotted it, Mal, you should take the shot.' Maldwyn felt a hand of encouragement rest on his shoulder. He looked at Erik's hand and, as the hand moved away, Maldwyn caught a glimpse of what appeared to be a birthmark on Erik's wrist. It was a strange birthmark made up of odd angles.

The familiar tingling of his magic began to dance within him as he considered the mark might have been a raven. His conversation with Ailaya about Princess Cassara, and her dreams about the thief with a raven mark, came to his mind. There had been many rumours that there might be a magical cause for the princess's nightmares. Some believed she was cursed by one of her father's enemies, while others thought she was a seer and could dream of the future. He took a deep breath to allow the surge of his power to subside.

'Come on Mal, take the shot before I do,' Greg pressed.

Maldwyn ignored what he had seen and let the thoughts about Princess Cassara's dreams go. Quiet as a mouse, he pulled on the taut bowstring and readied his shot. Taking a few more deep breaths, Maldwyn steadied his aim.

The deer stopped to snack on some leaves. The shrubs scrunched as the deer pulled at the foliage. He let out half a breath and then released his grip.

The deer screeched and whined as it stumbled and collapsed to the ground, falling into a heap. Maldwyn's near-perfect shot meant the deer died quickly and suffered as little as possible.

'Nice shot!' Greg gave Maldwyn a sharp slap on the back, pushing him forward. Erik started heading through the bushes towards the dying deer. 'You might want to consider joining the hunting party more often.'

Maldwyn snickered, tugging at the lobe of his ear. 'I'm not sure Master Damyan would allow that.'

'Who cares Mal? You have skill.'

Maldwyn stood up. Twigs crunched under his foot. There was no longer any need to remain silent, they had earned their prey. He and Greg made their way over to where Erik was assessing their kill.

'If the others manage to be this lucky, we will have enough meat to put on a royal feast. The kitchen staff will be very happy with this.'

Erik reached out with his hand to touch the deer, checking it was dead. His sleeve slid up his arm a little and, this time, Maldwyn saw the birthmark in full. It was a dark brownish colour that stood out on his pale skin. It was the mark of a raven.

Maldwyn contained a gasp. His power screamed at him. He thought about what the mark could mean, and about the warning which had come to Princess Cassara in the form of a nightmare.

'What's up with you?' Erik asked Maldwyn, who realised he was staring at the hunter's strange mark.

'Oh, um, I just noticed the mark on your wrist.'

'It's nothing, just a birthmark.' Erik pulled his hand back and covered up the raven mark with his sleeve. Maldwyn grinned and let the matter go, concealing his suspicion. He turned his focus to holding his magic in as he looked back to the dead deer on the ground, cradled in a bed of grassy shrubs. The arrow sticking out of the deer's chest had found its way to the heart and a pool of blood stained the deer's fur coat.

Greg's knee cracked as he crouched down beside the carcass. 'We'd better get this back to the castle.'

CHAPTER FOUR

Dreamer

PRINCESS CASSARA WAS SCREAMING when Maldwyn ran up the hallway. The radiant light from the torches flickered around the rough walls of the corridor. Guards rushed into the servant halls to the princess's room and banged on the sturdy door.

'You there, servant,' A burly guard with wide, bulging eyes yelled to Maldwyn. 'The main entrance to the princess's room is locked. Do you have a key to the servant door?'

'Of course,' Maldwyn answered as he pulled the heavy set of keys from his pocket, handing it to the impatient man.

The guard pushed his way past the others and the lock clicked as it turned over. Maldwyn stayed out of the way as the group overwhelmed the room. Except for the soldiers that stormed the room, the princess was alone, thrashing about in her sleep as she let out another shrill scream.

One of the guards gently woke Princess Cassara, while another shouted orders for a message to be sent to King Viktor, Prince Harlan and the court physicians. The room was busied with the band of soldiers checking every crevice of the princess's bed-chamber and others hurrying out to alert members of the court. Beads of sweat made the princess's forehead glimmer in the dim light.

The large man gave Maldwyn the key back. Princess Cassara whispered something inaudible through sobs to one of the soldiers sitting at her side. He was speaking to her in a soothing tone. Although she was distressed and drenched in sweat, the princess remained striking. She was a tall, athletic woman with jet-black hair and high-set cheekbones, giving her a classical, elf-like appearance.

'Perhaps you might bring the princess a drink, servant?'

'Yes, my lord.'

Maldwyn left the room and made his way down to the kitchen. He grabbed a tray and filled it with an assortment of fruits, a fine goblet—fit for royalty—and a jug of warming, red wine. Picking up the tray, Maldwyn headed back.

When Maldwyn returned, the physician was leaving through the servant corridors, the guards were all gone and King Viktor and Prince Harlan were in the princess's room. The prince leaned against a wall looking uninterested. King Viktor was sitting beside the princess, hanging on every word she spoke. Though she was not a child, Maldwyn noted that the king coddled her in a patronising fashion.

Prince Harlan looked up at Maldwyn when he knocked on the open door. Maldwyn clenched his jaw, bothered to be reminded of the angry bruise on the prince's face. For a moment, Maldwyn made eye contact with the prince and the feeling of familiarity returned to him. Quick as he could, he reminded himself of the present company and glanced down out of respect for his superiors. He waited to be given the proper permission to enter the room.

After a moment of waiting, King Viktor glanced back over his shoulder at Maldwyn. His face was marked with fear for his daughter's state, despite that she had significantly calmed since Maldwyn was here before.

'Enter,' the king called to Maldwyn, as he turned back to his daughter. 'It seems like there are some refreshments here for you. Harlan and I will leave you to rest now.'

King Viktor kissed Princess Cassara on the cheek in a tender, fatherly way. She suffered his affections, looking vexed by his condescending treatment of her. The king stood and glared at Prince Harlan a moment before exiting the room through the large grand doors that led out into the royal corridors.

Prince Harlan pushed himself away from the wall and followed his father out of the room. He stole a quick glance at Maldwyn as he departed.

Maldwyn closed the servant door behind him as he entered, giving the princess privacy. She stared at him as he placed the tray down on the bedside table, the nearby candle flickering. He saw that her sheets were drenched with sweat.

'Thank you,' the princess said.

It was rare for royalty to be gracious for the work of servants. Maldwyn bowed his head respectfully, then proceeded to fill the goblet with wine and offered it to the princess. She took the goblet and gulped down the drink. He felt bad for her. She was clearly quite bothered, both by her nightmares and by her overbearing father.

'May I offer you some fresh sheets, Your Grace?'

'Yes, thank you.' Her voice was cold with disdain. She tossed her hair back and stood, making her way over to the window. Maldwyn began pulling back the damp sheets. 'Do you ever have nightmares?'

Maldwyn paused and contemplated her peculiar question, carefully considering how privileged her life was that she might think herself the only sufferer of disturbing dreams. 'Sometimes, Your Grace. It's suffocating.'

Maldwyn pulled the pillow cases back and placed the sheets in a pile in the nearby basket that held the princess's worn garments. He opened the princess's stately closet to fetch some fresh linen. The closet doors had the symbol of the Helm of Awe carved into them. Eight spiked tridents radiated out from a single central point.

'Yes, it is. I have such awful dreams. They seem so real.' The princess crossed her arms and watched Maldwyn as he spread the fresh sheets across the bed. 'Tell me, have you ever met a man with a raven birthmark?'

Maldwyn thought about the raven mark he had seen on Erik's wrist, wondering what it could mean. If the princess had the gift of foresight, and Erik was the man in her dreams, then it was possible Erik was dangerous.

Maldwyn pushed the worrisome thought aside. Erik was a member of the staff who had worked in the castle for years.

If he had planned to harm the king, he would have done so long ago. More than that, Erik didn't strike Maldwyn as a cruel man. Perhaps a little secretive, but not a person who possessed malintent.

He mulled over the raven mark, and the way Erik offhandedly dismissed Maldwyn's comment about it. Having heard that some sorcerers bore such symbols, Maldwyn wondered whether this insignia might hold a deeper meaning, identifying Erik as a sorcerer and threatening his life in Dresden. That notion explained Erik's mysterious, guarded behaviour.

Maldwyn paused, the sheet folded back over his hand as he smoothed it out, and he wondered what might happen if he answered the princess truthfully. Bearing in mind that she might be a seer, and her own life could thus be in danger, Maldwyn figured it might help her to know that Erik had such a mark. Perhaps Erik could help the princess understand her gift in a way that Maldwyn could not. He decided to answer honestly.

'Yes. I have.'

'What?' The princess gasped in surprise, taken aback by the apparent possibility that her dreams were true. 'Who is he?' Princess Cassara brought her hands up to cup her cheeks, growing in distress, her breath quick and uneven with panic.

Maldwyn left the bedsheets partially laid out, and approached the princess. He respected the boundaries, keeping both his reach and his view away from her. 'Your Grace, might I suggest you calm yourself,' he said kindly.

She swallowed and focused on her breathing. The short, sharp breaths slowly subsided as she pulled her arms closer to her chest.

'Your Grace, I know it isn't my place to ask questions, but have you ever thought there might be more to your dreams?'

'Like what?' Her lip quivered as she began to sob softly.

'Like the power of the Norns? A seer's ability to dream?'

The princess stepped away from him. 'All magic is forbidden, both the power of divinity and seers' ability to dream. It is outlawed. Why would you say that?'

'Your Grace, it's okay. I won't tell anyone. They say seers are born with their own power that makes them able to dream visions of the past, present and future.'

Princess Cassara lowered her head in a curious way, as if assessing him closely. She neared him. 'Why wouldn't you tell anyone?'

'Because, Your Grace, I do not wish to see any harm come to you and I understand—as a servant—what it is to have to hide a piece of yourself from the rest of the world.'

The princess walked away and sat on an oversized, high-backed armchair near the cold fireplace. A draught swept down the chimney. Maldwyn shuddered.

'Do you think it's magic?'

'I don't know, Your Grace. I do know that there is a man with a raven mark in this castle and that you keep seeing him when you sleep.'

The princess rested her head in her hands. 'My father will kill me.'

'No, Your Grace. Perhaps you could convince him to see sorcery in a different light?'

'He hates magic. He would kill me.'

Maldwyn moved closer to where Princess Cassara was sitting. 'What is it about this man in your dream?'

She scratched her nose. 'It's different every time. The only consistent elements are the man with the mark and my mother's triple horn pendant being cursed. Each time, I am left with a feeling that someone's trying to hurt my father.' Confused she looked up at Maldwyn. 'What do you think it means?'

'Princess, I don't know anything about magic, or seers' dreams. I can't tell you anything that will help you. Maybe you should try talking to this man?'

'The man with the raven mark?'

'Do you have another idea, Your Grace?' She sniffed. Pitying herself, tears welled in her eyes and wet her cheeks. 'Maybe it will help you to understand what it all means?'

'I don't know.'

Maldwyn went and retrieved a handkerchief from Princess Cassara's set of drawers. 'Or, you could keep having the same dream and hope it goes away.' He knelt beside her and passed her the handkerchief. Princess Cassara used it to dry her eyes as Maldwyn poured her another goblet of wine.

She took the goblet and sipped at the wine instead of gulping it as she had before. 'Is he dangerous?'

Maldwyn let out a breath. He thought about how his magic had tried to warn him earlier, but then reasoned that it had reacted the same way to the princess the night before. His magic had never been under control and was often on the fritz. 'He is a member of the staff, Your Grace. I don't believe he would harm you.'

'Thank you, I'll think about it.'

Maldwyn returned to fixing the sheets, straightening all creases until they were perfectly flat and fit for a princess. When he was finished, he checked if there was anything further the princess required. She dismissed him, clearly eager to be alone with her thoughts. He took the dirty laundry and left Princess Cassara with her refreshments.

*   *   *   *   *

The following morning, Maldwyn knocked on Prince Harlan's door. He waited for no reply before entering the room. The room was dark, the curtains hadn't been drawn back, and the air was stuffy from the windows being closed throughout the night. He always took a moment to assess the state of the room before he started to work anywhere.

Prince Harlan's dirty laundry was tossed in a basket near the servant door, clothes draped over the side from the careless manner in which they had been thrown into the hamper. The bed sheets were strewn about in mountainous piles from the prince's restless sleep. There was a goblet beside an empty pewter jug sitting on the table.

Maldwyn started with the bed, stripping it bare and remaking it with fresh covers. To him, this was the most important step. The difference a fresh, tidy bed made to the appearance of a room was remarkable. He smiled after he plumped the pillows and placed them back on the bed. Maldwyn dusted the surfaces and neatened the cushions on the armchairs before the fireplace. He straightened the chairs around the dining table and took the goblet and jug back to the kitchen. When he returned to the room, he brought a tray with a clean goblet and a full jug of water with him.

Gently, he put the replacement tray on the low, heavy table near the plush, upholstered lounges. Maldwyn displayed it in such a way that the jug, the goblet and the small bowl of fruit formed a pyramid, pleasing to the eye. As his final task in the room, Maldwyn pulled the drapes back, keeping them in place with a simple, golden rope that he tied to a hook on the wall near the window frame. Once he opened the window, he paused and breathed in the clean morning air.

He looked out over the courtyard below and marvelled at the view. The skies above were mostly clear, but a few clouds floated in the air like huge misshapen orbs of fluff. The sun had not yet finished rising and hid its radiant beams, resting lazily behind the clouds as if it were pulling a blanket over its face so that it might get a little more respite.

Quiet footsteps sounded in the hall and, as they neared the door, Maldwyn remembered that where he stood, at the window staring at the world outside, was on the far side of the room from the servant door. It was his duty as a servant to complete his work unseen by members of the court. He could not be caught dawdling, nor working in the presence of his betters without the required permission.

He knew he would not be able to make a quick exit, yet still, in a feeble attempt, he darted across the room and grabbed the laundry hamper as he pulled on the servant door. Just as Maldwyn opened it wide enough to fit through, Prince Harlan entered his private chambers.

'Maldwyn... what are you doing here?'

The door banged shut behind the prince. Maldwyn let his hand fall from the door and halted. He had been caught. On the one hand, he was annoyed that his lingering had resulted in him failing to do his job well and, on the other hand, he was glad that it was Prince Harlan who had caught him. If anyone else had found him in their room, Maldwyn would be banished from the palace on the spot.

'Your Grace, I am sorry. I was over by the window pulling the curtains back and, um… well, I was just leaving.'

Prince Harlan, imposing as ever, stalked towards him. Arms folded across his broad chest. The red blotch on his jaw was just beginning to yellow around the edges. He was holding a large piece of rolled-up parchment in his left hand, which Maldwyn could see protruding out from behind his shoulder.

Maldwyn grew worried. Maybe he had been wrong. The prince had seemed to be in a bad mood the night before. Perhaps Maldwyn's presence was somehow offensive. Maldwyn fumbled the hamper, hunched ever so slightly and gazed to the floor to avoid eye contact.

'You weren't quick enough?'

'No, Your Grace,' he murmured.

The pause in remarks seemed to drag as Prince Harlan neared Maldwyn. Standing transfixed, holding the basket, Maldwyn felt his pulse hasten.

'No matter,' Prince Harlan replied, whacking Maldwyn in the shoulder in a mocking gesture. 'Maldwyn, it's fine. Relax, you look really worried.'

Maldwyn felt his forehead tighten, confused by the prince's reaction. Standing tall once more, Maldwyn readjusted his grip on the basket. 'In any case, sire, I apologise and assure you it won't happen again.'

The prince smiled at him, a little lopsided. His injured jaw prevented him from being able to offer a full grin. Maldwyn was troubled to see the wound affecting him. 'Come back inside and put the basket down. You can finish working. I don't mind.'

Maldwyn did as he was told, closing the door behind him. 'I was actually just about finished, Your Grace.'

Prince Harlan shrugged and took a seat on the lounge. He unrolled the parchment. Maldwyn could see it was a map of some kind. The forested regions were coloured in a deep, dark green and the ocean was painted in a dusky blue tint. The hills, mountains and trees were all marked in a variety of shapes, and the kingdoms across the realm were indicated by well-drawn castles. Smaller markings denoted the greater cities and villages of each kingdom. Dresden was located to the south of the map, with the beach on one side, and the Anhalt Mountains on the other. Prince Harlan ran his hand over the mountains, deep in thought.

'Are there troubles in that region again, sire?' Maldwyn asked, trying not to sound as if he were prying as he came up to the prince's side. He had heard something about these lands being disputed the day he delivered Ser Mikel's letter to Prince Harlan.

'Nothing you need to worry about,' the prince said, his intense stare fixed on him. 'You can sit down.'

Maldwyn gulped. He hesitated. He felt strange about sitting in the presence of royalty. The prince shifted over, making room for Maldwyn to take a seat beside him.

Unsure about the proper protocol in this situation, Maldwyn turned and sat on the sofa, sitting tall and perching himself on the edge as if he were uncomfortable. He fixed his gaze on the prince who was watching him closely. The prince's blue eyes seemed to see right through him.

Prince Harlan turned back to the map and leaned forward. Maldwyn felt the prince's weight shift on the seat beside him. He too turned his attention to the map and noted his home village, Alander, was on the northern border of Dresden.

He thought of how much he had hated life in Alander, and of all the things he had loved and lost. Just seeing the name written on the map filled Maldwyn with a mixture of longing and loathing. Two contradicting feelings that the past inspired.

'You seem troubled,' Prince Harlan noted, mumbling slightly from his wounded jaw.

Maldwyn realised his expression must have displayed his repugnance. He sat back a little and shook his head, offering the prince a contented look.

The prince squinted at him. 'You're a mystery.'

'How is your sister, sire?' Maldwyn changed the subject.

Prince Harlan smirked at him, clearly aware that he ignored the remark. 'She's hardly getting any sleep, but she assures my father that the physicians are doing everything they can. She thinks everything will be better soon.'

'That sounds positive, Your Grace.'

Nodding, Prince Harlan sat forward and filled his goblet with water from the jug. Ordinarily, when a member of the court, especially royalty, was in the presence of servants, the servant would fill the goblet and offer it to them. Instead, Maldwyn sat beside the Crown Prince of Dresden and watched as he poured his own drink. It was all very strange.

Prince Harlan drank the water and placed the goblet down with a hushed clunk. His plump lips moistened from his drink.

'I should go,' Maldwyn said. Prince Harlan drummed his fingers on the table and smiled, his eyes downcast.

The prince stood abruptly, and walked over toward his desk. Maldwyn wasn't sure if he was supposed to stay seated or whether he was meant to follow. The rules weren't exactly clear at the moment.

'I hope you could deliver this for me.' Prince Harlan brought over a letter that had been folded in thirds and closed with his royal wax seal, bearing the insignia of a rampant lynx. Maldwyn recalled what had happened the last time he had delivered a letter and tried to mask the concern on his face. 'Don't look so worried,' the prince admonished him.

Maldwyn stood and took the parchment. 'Of course, what could go wrong, sire?' Prince Harlan's face was hard to read. 'To whom shall I deliver the letter, Your Grace?'

'Your master, Maldwyn. To Master Damyan.'

Relieved that it wasn't intended for someone who might cause him harm, Maldwyn agreed and took the letter from the prince. In silence, Prince Harlan's coy expression said his goodbye as Maldwyn left the room.

* * * * *

Master Damyan was in the pantry when Maldwyn found him. The cook gestured to some freshly baked bread on the far counter. Maldwyn's mouth watered at the waft of another tray of steaming bread rolls being brought in from the kitchen. Master Damyan was agreeing with the cook about the menu when he spotted Maldwyn, who waited patiently for them to finalise the dinner list before approaching his master.

'Maldwyn.' Master Damyan glided over to Maldwyn. He was an older gentleman with impeccable posture, and, Maldwyn thought, a captivating presence. The silver streaks through his hair gleamed.

'Master Damyan.'

'What brings you here?'

'Prince Harlan sent me to deliver this letter to you.' Master Damyan took the letter and opened it. The paper rustled. His eyes moved from left to right as he read the words on the parchment. His face grew troubled. 'Is everything alright, master?'

'Hmm?' Master Damyan looked squarely at him, his face shrouded with concern. 'Yes... yes, it's nothing for you to worry about Maldwyn. Actually,' Master Damyan began folding the letter. 'Princess Cassara asked that you send her the raven. She told me that you would understand the message.'

'Yes, master.'

Master Damyan looked suspicious as he stared at Maldwyn, who offered a smile and proceeded to leave the pantry room, searching for Erik.

* * * * *

The fortified castle gatehouse rose from the land, ready to defy entrance to anyone at a moment's notice. Unapologetic it arched over the gravel path. Grass of the deepest green lay on either side of the trail and danced in the strong warm breeze. Erik was coming through the gatehouse, and the hunting team followed close behind him. Maldwyn's magic began prickling.

'Ah, Maldwyn. Come to join the hunting party again?' Erik, bow in hand, veered towards Maldwyn. Greg waved from the crew as they all continued up the path toward the castle. 'We could always use your skill after the other day.'

Maldwyn couldn't guess his own expression as he tried to hide any hint of his own pride. 'No, actually I am here for you.'

'Really? What can I do?'

Maldwyn lowered his voice. 'It's about your raven mark, Erik.'

His magic soared through him as he mentioned the mark. Maldwyn remembered that his power had reacted this way back in the woods, and then to the princess when he had seen her on the ramparts. He considered that it might be trying to tell him that there was magic nearby.

Erik pursed his lips. 'What about it?'

'Princess Cassara would like to meet with you. She's looking for information about your mark.'

'And, how did she find out about my mark?' Maldwyn broke eye contact. 'You told her, didn't you?'

'It's a sorcerer's mark, isn't it?' The bold manner in which he had asked the question made Erik step forward in an attempt to intimidate him. Maldwyn's power burned within.

'You haven't told anyone that, have you?'

Maldwyn swallowed. 'No, and your secret is safe with me.'

'I'll be the judge of that.'

'I only told the princess because she's dreaming about such a mark. It's been a recurring nightmare for her for the last few weeks. I think the dreams might be magical in origin. She's afraid that you mean her harm.'

'Dreaming you say?' Erik stepped back and softened his stance. 'Like a seer?'

'She doesn't know for sure yet where her visions come from. She wants to talk to you in hopes that it will ease her dreams.'

Erik scowled. 'Can I trust you?'

'Yes. I don't want anyone to get hurt, which will happen if her family work out what she is. It won't matter what the physicians give her if the dreams are magical.' Erik appeared to agree and rubbed his stubbled chin. He turned his bow over in his hand as he thought. 'I haven't told her about my suspicions that you're a sorcerer.'

Maldwyn waited for him to respond. He thought about telling Erik that he had a power of his own, but figured it best to protect himself.

Erik, clearly mulling the situation over in his mind, spoke in a reluctant voice as he stated, 'Okay, I'll do it.'

'Meet me inside, by the courtyard entrance to the servant halls. From there, I will take you to the princess.'

Erik agreed, swapped the hand in which he held his bow and began walking up the path. Maldwyn hung back for a moment, glad that everything had worked out. He stepped out of the way as a small contingent of mounted soldiers rode through the gatehouse to the kingdom beyond. The horses' trots clipped and clopped in perfect unison.

Maldwyn lingered as he made his way to the courtyard, giving Erik enough time to disarm and make himself presentable before taking him to the princess's private chambers. The flowers around the castle grounds were blossoming in the warmth of spring, hues of white, purple and blue decorated the deep green bushes. Insects ticked and birds tweeted from all around. Guards patrolled the streets, marching to a perfect near musical beat.

When Maldwyn made it to the rendezvous, he waited patiently for Erik to join him. Erik was wearing a fresh plain tunic and a clean pair of trousers that were no longer muddied from hunting in the woods. His weapons had been left behind. Erik held his hands out, showing off how well he had cleaned up.

'Well Maldwyn, how do I look?'

'Perfectly presentable.' Maldwyn kept a straight face for a moment before he laughed. Erik had outdone himself and looked better than an ordinary member of the staff. 'Come on, let's go.'

The princess's chambers were quite a walk through the narrow halls which were filled with servants at this time of day. Some walked in groups or pairs talking, and others rushed on alone, going about their work. People grinned and offered kind greetings to Maldwyn and Erik who chatted about the day's hunt and the weather, passing time as they pushed through the throngs of people. Maldwyn felt at home in these tight corridors. Here, he was a person; anywhere else in the castle, he was insignificant. He was the ghost that did the chores.

When they reached the princess's door, Maldwyn stepped forward and rapped three times. He waited for an answer.

'Come in,' the princess's indifferent voice called.

Maldwyn opened the door and stepped into the lavish room that had, only nights before, seemed like a crypt. His head was bowed and his hands were clasped before his torso.

'Your Grace, may I present to you, Erik Williamson.' Erik stepped in behind Maldwyn, his head bowed in a sloppy way and his hands hanging in a loose fashion compared to Maldwyn's proper stance. It was clear he was a hunter who spent little time within the castle, addressing noblemen and women of their various ranks.

'He's the one with the raven mark?'

'I am, Your Grace.'

Maldwyn didn't have the chance to answer the princess before Erik spoke. He flicked his eyes to Erik, who held his wrist out, his other hand pulling up his sleeve. Princess Cassara's shoes clicked on the floor as she came over and inspected the mark.

'What is this mark?'

'It is the mark of my people.'

'Your people?'

'Yes, Your Grace.' The princess pulled his hand closer and ran her fingers over the mark. 'Perhaps Maldwyn should leave.'

The princess let Erik's hand drop. 'No, I trust him. The servant stays.'

'Alright.' Erik's voice was firm. 'This is a sorcerer's mark. Not all sorcerers have them, but those whose people are devout worshippers of the gods and magic might bear such a mark. I was born into the Raven Clan, Your Grace.' Princess Cassara took in a deep breath as she listened to Erik's words. 'My people are a group of sorcerers who see themselves as dedicated caretakers of any and all information about magic: what it is, where the power comes from and how best to use it. My people may be considered as the librarians of magic, Your Grace.'

'The librarians of magic? That's quite a statement. Are your people dangerous?'

'My people are pacifists. We live by the oath that we will never use magic to harm, only to help or heal.'

Princess Cassara turned her back to them and walked a few paces away. 'And, what about you? Are you dangerous?'

Erik glowered at Maldwyn. 'No, Your Grace. I'm not.'

'He tells me I should trust you.'

'I swear to you, on my honour and my life, I mean you no harm.'

'And, what about my father?'

'The king, Your Grace?'

Princess Cassara stood tall, in an intimidating way. Her glossy, long, black hair formed loose curls, bouncing around her face. Erik's head was still dipped, and Maldwyn could see she was taller. He guessed they would be the same height if

Erik's head was held upright. She held a callous, stern gaze as she stared down at Erik.

'Yes, are you a danger to the king?'

'No, Your Grace. I am a member of the staff, nothing more.'

'Hmm, why are you a member of the staff? Why aren't you with your people?'

'When I was a child, my people were attacked. Slaughtered, really. Those of us who survived scattered throughout the lands and went into hiding.'

The princess stepped back, apologetic. 'I'm so sorry.' She relaxed her appearance. 'You say your people have a lot of knowledge about magic.'

Erik's bowed head nodded. 'They do.'

'Can you help me?'

'Your Grace? Help you how?'

'My nightmares are like visions. The people feel as real as you are standing before me now, but they're fragmented. In these dreams, I see a man with your mark. The dream changes every time, and I've never seen the man's face. The only consistent features are the faceless man with the raven mark, a feeling that someone is trying to hurt my father, and my mother's pendant—cursed.' Princess Cassara paused. Neither Maldwyn nor Erik spoke to fill the quiet. 'I've tried all sorts of remedies that have been prescribed to me by the court physicians and nothing has helped. If anything, they are getting worse. He thinks they might be magic,' Princess Cassara gestured towards Maldwyn, 'What do you think?'

Erik shifted his feet.

'Your Grace, I am afraid that I agree with Maldwyn here. I believe it is possible that you are a seer. That the power of the Norns is the source of your nightmares.'

Princess Cassara clicked her tongue. 'So, it's true. I am a monster and my father will have me killed.'

'You're not a monster.'

'If I am a seer, why are the dreams always different?'

'The dreams are always different because the future is always changing, and evolving, Your Grace. What we do today, affects what we do tomorrow. The present impacts the future. The only moments that are fated are fixed events in time. The future is malleable. Thus, your dreams change.' Erik picked at the skin around his nails, nervous to be giving information relating to magic over to the princess. 'Your ability to dream will guide you in understanding future possibilities. If you hone your skills, you will become better at understanding how to interpret the dreams. You may even come to control them. I believe that, as your gift was awakening, your dreams were telling you that there was a sorcerer in the castle who might be able to help you. That was me: the man with the raven mark. As for the threat against your father, that may still be out there, but I assure you the threat isn't me.'

Maldwyn had never learned anything about magic. He had been born with his abilities, unlike any other sorcerer in the world, and was fascinated to learn that the future wasn't completely mapped out. He was curious to know what moments were fated and wondered if there was someplace he could go to learn about destiny. Dispirited, he reminded himself that magic was forbidden. He had to keep it in check and pretend no power resided within him.

'Alright, I accept what you tell me.' The princess began pacing. Her shoes clip-clopping on the floorboards. 'Will you help me? To control it, I mean.'

Erik let out a breath that sounded filled with anxiety. 'Your Grace, you're asking me to break the law?'

'Yes, I am.'

Maldwyn watched Erik's mood struggle with the risk she was asking him to take. 'Yes. I will help you, Your Grace.'

The familiar pulsating of his magic grew. Maldwyn swallowed and clenched his grip over his rising power. He didn't understand why it sometimes rose up as if out of nowhere, tearing at his insides to try and escape.

'I will send for you when we can begin training. For now, you both need to return to work and not speak a word about what has been discussed here. Neither Erik, nor I, have anything to do with magic. Is that clear?'

'Yes, Your Grace,' both Maldwyn and Erik spoke in unison.

'You're both dismissed.'

They both bowed, unclasped their hands and returned to the servant halls. Neither spoke. They parted ways and went back to work.

CHAPTER FIVE

The Execution

MALDWYN HELD HIS BREATH and rolled his upper lip, trying to push the smell away from his nostrils. It didn't work. The air was thick with the scent of excrement. His shoes clacked on the stone floors, echoing off the heavy wooden doors keeping the prisoners caged.

Maldwyn hated tending to the dungeons.

The bowl of plain, mushy oatmeal was warm in his hands. A guard followed close behind him as Maldwyn made his way through the gaol, opening each cell Maldwyn reached as he delivered food to the convicts.

The final prison cell was at the far end of the cramped dark corridor. Maldwyn's power grew more active as he neared the door. He stopped and waited for the guard to open the cell. The lock sounded as the guard turned the key over.

Before pushing the door open, the guardsman turned to Maldwyn. 'When you enter this cell, I will close the door behind you.' His rough voice made Maldwyn uncomfortable. 'The prisoner in this cell is very dangerous. His hands are shackled behind his back, so you will have to stay and feed him by hand. When you are done feeding him, knock twice and I will come to let you out. While you're inside, I will be back at the end of the hall by the guards' station. Make sure you knock loud enough for me to hear you. Understood?'

Maldwyn knew better than to ask questions when tending to prisoners. These were criminals. Still, Maldwyn reasoned, they are people. Often, he had found that the prisoners in these cells were victims of terrible circumstances, leading them to make dark and dangerous choices in their lives, and ultimately bringing them to their miserable existence in the palace dungeons. Maldwyn couldn't help but wonder what it might take for him to follow a similar path in life. His magic made every day a risk. Even now, he felt it simmering.

Maldwyn nodded in response to the guard's instructions. 'Yes, sir,' he confirmed. The door whined as it pushed open.

The prisoner's eyes were sunken and his face was a roadmap of shadows. His grey hair looked unkempt and his beard was shaggy. The brown sack he wore was stained. The old man sat on the floor. His ankles were chained to the ground and his hands were shackled behind his back.

The door banged closed behind Maldwyn. Beaten, the elderly, frail man glanced up at the noise. His chains clinked as he shifted. Maldwyn moved closer to the prisoner.

'I've brought you some food.'

'What's the point?'

'You need to eat.'

'Why? My execution has been ordered. I only have a few days to live and I'm to spend them here, in this wretched cell.'

The four walls were cold, blank and covered in mildew. This was death's waiting room and it smelled that way.

'I'm sorry,' Maldwyn offered as he took another step closer to the old man. He kneeled beside him, noticing that the chains were engraved with runic lettering. Maldwyn held the bowl in a relaxed grip, and contemplated the rune markings, having never seen them on the chains of other prisoners. The man stared at the door, his expression sad and pained. 'Would you like to talk?'

'About what?'

'Anything. How about you tell me what brought you here?'

The man squinted as he thought. 'It was sorcery that brought me here... and—if it weren't for these enchanted chains—I would have used a spell to escape long ago.' The man peered up his nose at Maldwyn. 'Ironic, isn't it? The king wants to destroy magic, but to do so, he sometimes needs to use it himself... that which he hates so much.'

Maldwyn guessed this explained the runic inscriptions, and why the old man's hands were chained behind his back. If his hands were cuffed such that he could hardly move them, then he wouldn't be able to perform any larger, more ritualistic, spells that might free him from these hexed restraints.

'You were a sorcerer?' Maldwyn asked in a kind, soft voice as he scooped up some oatmeal on the bone spoon, offering it to the man. The man opened his mouth wide and dragged the oatmeal off with his teeth. He winced at the taste. Maldwyn had been told the meals for the prisoners were unpalatable.

'I was.'

'How did you end up here, in the dungeon?'

'I was betrayed by someone I thought I could trust.'

Maldwyn swallowed as the reality of his own dangers hit him. This man's fate could well be his own. This was the reason he never fostered his magic and why he needed to be so careful not to be caught when his power sometimes escaped his grasp.

'That's awful.'

'Yes, apparently my son believes in the king's war on magic.'

'Your son betrayed you?'

'Unfortunately.'

Maldwyn took up another spoonful of oatmeal. He scraped the back of the spoon on the bowl to stop anything from dropping as he offered it to the man.

'Had he grown up knowing that you were a sorcerer, or did he find out later in life—not long before he gave you up to the authorities?'

'He knew. He always knew. I guess that's why I didn't see it coming.'

The man accepted another mouthful and chewed the mushy oatmeal. He made a smacking sound with his lips as he pushed the food around his mouth.

'What changed?'

'Only the gods know the answer to that question.'

Maldwyn's magic once again flared. He took in a deep breath of the reek to ease his rising power and held back the desire to gag at the smell. The old man watched him close.

'What's wrong with you? Are you unwell?'

'Oh, no. I'm sorry, it's just—'

'This place,' the old man added before Maldwyn could finish. 'It's an acquired smell.'

Maldwyn agreed, relieved. The man had offered the lie Maldwyn needed to protect his power from being discovered, and he seized it.

'So, tell me what happened with your son?'

The man shrugged. 'He worked as a blacksmith and began spending more and more time with the king's guards, making their weapons and all sorts. They filled his head with all kinds of ideas about magic being evil. He began talking about the gods' gift as though it were a curse. He said that either everyone should have magic, or no one should.

'Of course, he knew that anyone can have magic, but it takes years and a dedication to the craft to learn to use it. You have to learn to tap into the power of the gods.' Maldwyn broke eye contact, hoping the man wouldn't sense his power. He hoped the spelled chains would keep him from being able to do that. 'Everyone wants the easy way, or no way at all. I ignored all the warning signs because I never believed he would truly betray me, his father. Eventually, he told the guards and they arrested me.'

Tears welled up in the man's eyes. He sniffed and wiped his dripping nose on his shoulder. Maldwyn wanted to offer the man something to comfort him, but there was nothing for him to give.

'You don't seem to condemn my use of magic, yet you work in the palace,' he muttered. His voice was breaking through his sobs.

'No?'

The man tilted his head to the side. 'You might want to be careful. Even magic sympathisers wind up in these cells... and executed.'

'Did I say I was a magic sympathiser?'

'I suppose not. So, you don't approve of magic?'

'It is against the law.'

The old man chuckled. 'You're a smart one, I'll give you that.'

Maldwyn held the spoon forward and the old, frail man again took another mouthful and grimaced at the taste. 'Tell me about what it was like being a sorcerer, before magic was forbidden.'

'Before?'

'Yes, you must have had some adventures.'

The man grinned and kicked out a leg. The chains dragged on the ground and the sound bounced off the walls.

'Oh, I did that.'

'Well?' Maldwyn pressed in the most excited tone he could muster.

The old man sighed. 'Well... it was a wondrous time. Magic was celebrated instead of being condemned. It was afforded the greatest respect because of the number of years spent learning and mastering the craft in servitude to the gods. Sorcerers even served and advised the king on magical matters.' His eyes sparked with anger, and the lines on his face laced together. 'Ah, it isn't the same anymore! After King Viktor's coronation, everything changed. The magical advisors were all removed from the palace and it slowly became more and more marginalised to practise the craft. Then, after his wife was found having an affair with a sorcerer, magic was forbidden and the queen was executed.'

Maldwyn's knees began to hurt from kneeling on the stone ground. He shifted just enough to relieve the pressure points and mused over what the man had said. He hadn't realised Queen Sonia had an affair with a sorcerer, or that her adultery was the crime she had committed leading to her execution.

'How many years did you study sorcery?' Maldwyn asked, trying to turn the man back to his more positive memories of magic.

'Fifteen years studying, twenty-seven spent in service before the king forbade its use,' he replied, bleakly.

'What was your favourite component to study?'

'Ooh, that's a hard question.' The man scrunched up his nose in thought. 'I guess—if I had to choose—it would be learning about prophecies foretold by seers.'

'Really? Why is that?'

'Well—you see—the future is malleable, ever-adapting to the choices we make. Although it is always changing, there are some moments that seers say are fixed. No matter how the future adjusts to the present, seers tell how these moments are prophesied and never change. They are destined… fated. As a sorcerer, I admire the gift seers have to dream of events in time.'

Maldwyn appreciated the way the old sorcerer described prophecies as moments. Erik had described it in the same way to Princess Cassara. It was both beautiful and haunting.

'Was there any particular prophecy that stayed with you?'

'There were a few. There's the Delarusian Prophecy, the Prophecy of the Birds, but my personal favourite was always the Quandiallan Prophecy, sometimes known as the Awakening of Firebird.'

Maldwyn's power rose and sent a shiver through him, sparking to life once more. He thought of the last prophecy the old man mentioned, curious as to why this might be his favourite telling of a fixed point in time. He speculated that this legend was important to sorcerers, judging by the way it was known by more than one title.

'Firebird? Why don't you tell it to me?'

The man's faraway gaze softened and he smiled. 'It's been a while, but I know it by heart. It goes like this:

'*When the Lynx suffers his greatest pain, Firebird will burn. His ashes will shroud the kingdom under the blackest sky and the tyrant king's reign will decline. Only in death will Firebird realise his power and thenceforth his magic will soar.*'

Defeated, the man's eyes saddened.

'That's beautiful. What does it mean?'

'No one really knows exactly. But Firebird is an important figure, appearing in several prophecies. The strange thing about this prophecy is that it is called the Awakening of Firebird, but it describes his death.' The old man gazed upward, considering the possible deeper meaning of the prophecy. 'Perhaps in death, he will evolve,' he supposed.

'Everyone evolves when we shed our physical form to join the gods,' Maldwyn argued, finding it difficult to accept the man's explanation.

'I don't believe his evolution is spiritual. I think it is something else. Perhaps in death, he will not only shed his physical form, but also the restrictions of his former life. Maybe in death, he will finally be free.'

Maldwyn didn't want to quarrel with the man about freedom, especially when he looked so full of wonder as he recalled the tale. Still, he harboured the thought that freedom was only an idea. Certain people had certain freedoms, but true freedom was something no one experienced.

'That's a lovely story.'

'What I would have given to see Firebird's evolution.' The old man's voice took on a dreamy tone.

'Maybe you're Firebird,' Maldwyn offered kindly with a sweet grin.

The old man let out a sad sort of laugh. The hollows of his aged face were shaded in the dimly lit cell. He drew his brows together, corrugating his forehead, as he took in another mouthful of oatmeal.

'I doubt that,' the old man said between chews.

Maldwyn smiled and offered another spoonful. The man held up his wrinkled hand to stop Maldwyn.

'Please, I couldn't possibly eat any more of that gruel.'

Maldwyn gently placed the spoon back in the bowl and stood to leave, not knowing what more he could say to the man with his execution looming. What glimmer of hope could he offer him? Maldwyn made his way across the room and knocked twice, as hard as he could, on the heavy wooden door.

'What's your name, boy?' the old man called to his back.

Maldwyn looked back over his shoulder. The decrepit man leaned against the wall. He gave Maldwyn a hopeful expression, despite that he happened to be a man without hope.

'Maldwyn.'

'Thank you, Maldwyn. You've reminded me that kindness still exists.'

The lock turned over and the guard opened the door. Maldwyn gave the old man a final sombre smile and then stepped out of the cell into the dark corridor. The walls seemed to be closer than they were before. The blackness was all-consuming. As he continued down the long hallway, his magic finally eased.

* * * * *

A few days later, the square filled with crowds of people that waited to watch the sorcerer burn. The stake had been erected with piles of wood around the base of the platform and guards paced around the public courtyard, keeping the hungry viewers back. The king stepped out onto a balcony that overlooked the square. Prince Harlan and Princess Cassara followed close behind.

Maldwyn didn't usually attend public executions, especially when the crime was sorcery, yet he had felt distressed since meeting the old man who had shared with him the tale of Firebird. Since Maldwyn had tended to the nameless man, he had thought a lot about the meaning behind this prophecy. It didn't make sense; all death was an evolution.

On the far side of the courtyard, people cheered as the sorcerer was brought forward. His chains rang like bells with each step.

The king waved a hand and gestured toward the old man. 'This man has been found guilty of practising magic. In line with the laws of the land, this sorcerer was sentenced to death and will burn for his crime.'

The guards tied the man to the stake and his head darted around as he took in the crowd. Maldwyn hated watching, yet he couldn't look away. It was as if he was looking at himself.

'Let the sorcerer burn!' The king shouted from the balcony. The guards carried flames to the base of the pyre and set the logs alight. The people roared with excitement.

'Firebird will burn one day! Your reign will end tyrant king,' the old man shouted defiantly, flames licking the sides of his legs. He shifted as if he could somehow escape the heat of the blaze.

Princess Cassara looked away. Prince Harlan, jaw fully healed and standing on display, looked over the square and rested his gaze on Maldwyn. Maldwyn turned his back and walked away. The old man's cries filled the square. Maldwyn's magic rose with his anger.

CHAPTER SIX

The Incident in the Night

MALDWYN MOPPED THE SMOOTH FLOOR of the long wide hall which was adorned with intricate oil paintings of faraway lands and portraits of past monarchs, finely woven tapestries of mythical scenes hung from the stone walls, and towering hall stands with intricate vases that had flowers pouring out the top lined the corridor. The arched ceiling was so high above him that even the sound of the swishing mop carried down the hallway. It was night. The only time that servants were permitted to enter the grand palace halls. Even then, servants were to be afforded permission by Master Damyan.

The mop squelched as he pushed it around the stone ground. The night was warm and quiet. Spring had ended and the summer heat had settled in the recent weeks. A bead of sweat formed on Maldwyn's forehead. He wiped it away with the back of his hand.

Maldwyn, still troubled by the execution he had witnessed several days ago, couldn't shake the worry that he had seen his own future through the death of the old nameless man. That somehow, he might one day be executed for sorcery and that flames would carry him into his next life. His fear of impending doom was interfering with his ability to sleep restfully since that day. Just thinking about it caused him to have difficulty swallowing the lump in his throat.

Right now, he needed to work to distract himself from his concerns.

Ser Theodor's footsteps clacked as they neared Maldwyn. He had been pacing up and down the hall while Maldwyn cleaned, sweeping the mop back and forth across the hall as he walked backwards. Ser Theodor was acting as his supervisor. Servants required a guard to escort them when working in the imperial areas of their betters. Maldwyn felt it was another way to shame the lower class.

'You've worked in this castle for a while now, right?'

Maldwyn paused for a moment, unsure if Ser Theodor had indeed addressed him or someone else. He noted that Ser Theodor stopped pacing and his feet were facing him. Maldwyn kept his head down.

'Yes, my lord. I've worked here for a number of months now.'

'Hmm, would you happen to know most of the servants by now?'

Maldwyn continued mopping. 'I would say so, my lord.'

'There's this woman on the staff. She has long red hair and dark, hazel eyes.' Maldwyn heard a hint of desire in Ser Theodor's tone.

The knight had a pure-looking, round face with a square jawline, prominent cheekbones and high-set brows, lending him a trusting appearance. He was tall and strong, wearing lightweight brown leather body armour and trousers. His sheathed ornate sword hung from his hip. Maldwyn held in a smile of his own as he noted the knight's hopeful manner.

'When she smiles, she has these charming dimples. I was hoping you might be able to tell me who she is?'

'It sounds like you might be talking about Ailaya, my lord.'

'Ailaya? That's a pretty name,' Ser Theodor said dreamily. Ailaya would be so pleased to know he was asking about her, and that he had a delighted expression on his face as he conjured up her image in his mind.

'She's a friend of mine,' Maldwyn offered, trying to keep the knight talking.

'Really?' An expectant Ser Theodor stepped forward. 'You know her well then?'

'Yes, she's my closest friend here in the palace... the city actually. I've known her since I first started working in the castle.'

'Is she being courted by anyone?'

Maldwyn tried hard not to laugh out loud. The lower class didn't worry about formal courtships.

'No, she isn't,' Maldwyn told him as he went back to pushing the mop around the floor. He wasn't supposed to ask questions, but figured he'd risk it given the topic of discussion. 'Is she of interest to you, Ser Theodor?'

'Tsk.' Ser Theodor rebuffed the question in a nonchalant manner, turning his back on Maldwyn and placing his hands on his hips. The sword swayed from his hip.

It didn't matter, Maldwyn let out a silent laugh to himself and looked straight up at the roof, knowing the knight was interested in Ailaya. She would love to hear about this conversation. Maldwyn imagined her reaction to the news in his mind. He pictured her beaming expression as her fantasy neared reality.

He supposed he shouldn't tell Ailaya about Ser Theodor's obvious affections, worrying that it might encourage her to pursue indulgent, yet dangerous, relations with Ser Theodor. Maldwyn didn't want to see harm brought to her for becoming enraptured with someone beyond her station.

A gust of wind swept up the hall causing the torches on the wall to flicker. The flames were almost snuffed out. The wind's howl sounded. There was a distinct scraping sound coming from the direction the wind originated. Maldwyn's magic came alive as he felt a presence watching them. He couldn't see anyone as he stared toward where he had heard the sound.

Ser Theodor whipped around to the eerie noises. 'What was that?'

'Probably nothing, my lord.'

'Hmm,' Ser Theodor seemed gladdened to have his answer to Maldwyn's prying interrupted. Once again, he paced. 'So, how about the execution of that sorcerer?'

'What about it, my lord?' The hairs on the back of Maldwyn's neck stood erect, as if telling him someone was watching them. The halls ahead remained empty. He shook away the feeling, trying to pay attention to his work.

'It was quite a spectacle, wasn't it?'

'The crowd certainly seemed to enjoy it.'

'You didn't?'

'I'm not really one to enjoy the suffering of others.' Maldwyn stood tall, rolling his shoulders back and sighed as he wiped his head on his forearm. 'Even if he used magic,' Maldwyn added, attempting to sound less like a person who sympathised with magic users.

Ser Theodor lifted his brows, surprised by Maldwyn's reaction to the execution. He looked up and down the hall, checking they were alone. He stepped closer to Maldwyn.

'Neither am I,' he whispered so that his voice wouldn't echo up the long hall. Maldwyn noted the slightly regretful tone in his voice, telling him Ser Theodor didn't condone the execution. Ser Theodor backed away, leaned against the stone wall and crossed his arms. His leather armour creaked as he moved.

Maldwyn parted his lips slightly, stunned by the knight's admission. 'You surprise me, sir. The prisoner was a sorcerer.'

'He was, but... sometimes I can't help myself from wondering, is that all it takes to make a man evil? Magic, I mean.' Ser Theodor was still speaking in a hushed voice. 'I was raised in this city, in Dresden, and I have watched first-hand countless people be brutalised, or lose their lives, over a power that was once revered. When I was a child—quite young really—the kingdom still ascribed to the belief that magic was a gift from the gods and it was viewed as a precious, sacred tool. It was the man using the power that was responsible for the outcome, good or bad, not the power itself.

'Then, for some reason or other, things changed… and now, magic is seen as a power that corrupts. A dangerous, insidious, influencing power that was never meant for mankind. Sometimes, I catch myself thinking about the way things were and the way they are now, and I wonder, what changed?'

Staggered by the knight's open-mindedness, Maldwyn ceased all movement. At times, he had caught himself thinking these very words. 'Did you ever work it out, my lord?'

'You mean, what changed?' Maldwyn nodded. Ser Theodor looked around, 'I have my theories, but they can never be spoken aloud. Even a man of my rank cannot mention certain thoughts.' Ser Theodor began toying with the hilt of his sword, running his fingertips over the intricate engravings.

Maldwyn sighed and returned to his work, assuming the conversation had ended. He heard the flames from one of the nearby torches pop.

'You tended to him before he died, didn't you?'

'I did.'

'Did he ever mention anything about a prophecy to you?'

Maldwyn's heart skipped. He contemplated how Ser Theodor could have suspected that the sorcerer spoke of prophecy to Maldwyn. He worried that the truth might paint him as more of a magic sympathiser than he already seemed. Further to that, Maldwyn felt the Firebird prophecy should not be shared, as if it might be dangerous for him to do so. Still, he was curious about why Ser Theodor would ask such a question.

'Only that he held an interest for them.'

'He never mentioned something called the Valuwan prophecy?'

Maldwyn cocked his head. He had heard of this prophecy somewhere before, but he couldn't quite remember where or from who he had heard about it. 'No, he didn't.'

Ser Theodor rubbed his chin in a thoughtful fashion. His brows knitted together as if concerned about something. Again, Maldwyn decided to risk questioning the knight.

'What is this prophecy, my lord?'

'I wish I knew, but it's nothing to worry about.'

Suddenly, as if out of nowhere, Maldwyn remembered where he had heard of the Valuwan prophecy. It had been mentioned to the king the night he witnessed the assault on Prince Harlan. As it turned out, the letter Maldwyn had delivered to the prince had led him to learn a lot of information in the last few weeks.

His mind wandered to Ser Mikel who had given Maldwyn the letter. The man had been a menace since Maldwyn started working in the palace, yet no one had seen him since that night. Moreover, he feared that he may have been the last person to see Ser Mikel. His chest felt tight and he pulled at his shirt, which clung to his damp chest as he took in a deep breath to calm himself. The heat in the hallway was heavy.

Maldwyn let out a breath and noted that he no longer felt the presence he thought watched them. The conversation ended and Maldwyn decided not to push Ser Theodor any further by asking about the disappearance of Ser Mikel.

Maldwyn returned to mopping as he thought of the Valuwan Prophecy. Mulling it over in his mind, he contemplated what this prophecy might be and why the king sought information about it.

* * * * *

Later, Maldwyn left the castle to clear his thoughts. He followed the trodden dirt path that meandered around the outside of the immense palace walls, leading toward the surrounding wood. Patches of moss grew on the fortifications like a fur coat. In the distance, he heard the waves crashing on the nearby shore and the air he breathed carried the salty ocean tang.

It didn't take him long to reach the sacred grove. A lone ash tree stood wide and tall, limbs reaching out in every direction, its rough surface rippled with age. The rest of the woods stayed back, encircling the sacred tree that linked this realm to that of the gods.

Maldwyn wondered about the gods as he gazed up at the imposing tree. His power surged within. He considered their infinite divine power and how sorcerers were able to tap into this magic. Looking down at his hands, he wondered how it was possible for him to have his own power.

There were times he wished he could use it. An ordinary man such as himself wasn't meant to have his own magic. It was as his mother always told him; he had been born wrong. He sighed and studied the wrinkled surface of the tree.

Tap. Tap. Tap.

Maldwyn spun around to the sound that came from behind him. A silhouette of a man leaning against one of the surrounding trees stepped forward. The dappled moonlight shaded the depressions in the face that neared Maldwyn. He knew this man.

'Ser Mikel?'

The man loomed over Maldwyn. His greasy smile made Maldwyn's skin crawl. 'Did you tell anyone about our conversation the last time I saw you?'

'No.'

'Good.' Ser Mikel shoved him backwards, as he grabbed Maldwyn's shirt. A knot tore through the body of the tree, like a scar. The rough, rippled surface of the bark jabbed Maldwyn hard in the lower back. 'There's something else I want from you.'

Maldwyn felt Ser Mikel's threatening hold on his shirt tighten. He couldn't stop himself from wincing.

'What might that be?'

'Information.'

'I am only a servant. I don't know anything important.'

Ser Mikel moved in closer and pulled out a knife, pressing the tip to his stomach. 'I doubt that. You might be unimportant, but, as a servant, you are the eyes and ears of the palace.'

His throat clogged and Maldwyn struggled to swallow. 'What do you want to know?'

'The princess… is she a seer?'

'Not that I know,' Maldwyn told him in an assertive tone, protecting the princess. He was good at lying.

'So, the rumours about her dreams were what?'

'Hearsay, nothing more. Last I heard, her nightmares have ended with treatment prescribed by the court physician.'

'That's a shame.' Ser Mikel seemed disappointed as he licked his lips. 'I could have used her help if she knew about magic. Ah well… she probably wouldn't have been trained in the proper way to use it anyway. I'll just have to find a sorcerer.' He seemed to be talking more to himself at the moment. His greasy smile turned back to Maldwyn as he stroked the knife along his gut. 'And, what about the prince and the king? How have they reacted to the news in my letter?'

Maldwyn stayed quiet. He didn't want to betray Prince Harlan. Ser Mikel pushed the knife into his stomach just hard enough to pierce Maldwyn's shirt and draw a drop of blood. The blinding sting of the blade made him recoil.

'They're at odds since I delivered the letter,' he informed the knight, pained.

Maldwyn breathed in deeply, relieved as Ser Mikel pulled the knife away. Then, a fist slammed into his gut. The world went black for a second. He collapsed to the forest floor. His magic tried to rush at Ser Mikel and Maldwyn just managed to contain his power.

'Perfect! That's just what the king deserves... his son's contempt.' Several of Ser Mikel's yellowed teeth were chipped. Maldwyn looked to the uneven ground on which he sat, crouched. 'I was hoping to exploit the princess as a seer, and to cause a rift between her and her father. Looks like I'll need to work on something else.'

'Why are you doing this?' Maldwyn mumbled.

'I've come to take retribution.'

'For what?'

'That's my business.' Ser Mikel stood, stomped on Maldwyn's hand and kicked his stomach. 'You've been more than helpful.' Ser Mikel's silhouette returned to the tree line. He stopped and looked back at Maldwyn. 'Not a word of this servant, or else you will lose your life.'

He disappeared into the woods. Sitting on the uneven ground, Maldwyn clutched his stomach, panicked and gasping for breath.

CHAPTER SEVEN

The Prince's New Clothes

THE SUN BURNED LIKE A BALL OF FIRE in the brilliant blue sky, rays searing the earth below while the bright light granted the world an incredible vibrancy. The market buzzed with slumping people, wilted like sun-damaged flowers from the heat. This hot weather was draining. Maldwyn sighed as he pushed his way through the throngs of rushing people.

He hated crowds and he hated summer.

Maldwyn found it to be an uncomfortable season. In winter, a person could warm themselves with extra layers of clothes and heat from a burning hearth. Yet, in summer, there weren't many ways to cool down, and the work of a servant never ceased.

As Maldwyn bored through the crowd of people a child knocked into him, hitting Maldwyn's injured stomach. A sharp pain fired through Maldwyn from colliding with the careless boy. He clutched his gut, bruised from his encounter with Ser Mikel, and suppressed a yelp. At least the wound from the knife wasn't too bad. It had punctured his flesh just enough to draw blood. Still, his stomach was quite injured from the combination of the knife and the subsequent forceful punching and kicking. It hurt.

In his bad mood, he scowled at the boy who continued on without so much as looking back, shoving through others as he passed. Maldwyn was relieved to leave the busy streets when he reached the tailor's shop. He had come all this way from the palace to collect a newly crafted tunic for the prince. Maldwyn was responsible for looking after the wardrobes in the royal chambers, ensuring the clothing hung in a neat and tidy manner to avoid the fabric creasing. He also handled dealings with the royal tailor, bringing new clothes from the tailor's shop to the wardrobe, and old clothes with rips and tears to the tailor for mending.

Maldwyn recomposed himself after having the boy knock into him. The tailor's shop was quaint: a timber structure that was reinforced with stucco walls, and it was covered with vines hanging like delicate curtains around the doorway. There were other tailors in Dresden of course, but this was the only one who crafted clothes for the royal family. When the pain subsided, Maldwyn reached for the handle and pushed the heavy door open.

A sweet-sounding bell dangled over the door and rang as it opened. Maldwyn noted that the shop smelled oddly of hazelnuts. The tailor, Alaric, an older man with short white hair wearing graceful blue and silver robes, made his way out from behind the counter. His shoulders were slightly hunched from his age.

'Ah, Maldwyn! It's you. Come to pick up Prince Harlan's tunic, I suppose?' He spoke with a gentle and quiet, yet husky voice.

'That's right,' Maldwyn told the tailor, who disappeared into a room behind the counter. Maldwyn assumed it was Alaric's workshop. He imagined the room being an organised mess of fabric swatches strewn across tabletops, barrels of colourful dyes, spools of a range of threads, wide, tall looms with some partially woven work hanging from the square frame, and a variety of needles in different sizes and thicknesses. 'Ric, how's business?' Maldwyn called.

'Great actually! Business is always best in summer.'

Alaric stepped out carrying a bundle of leather fabric in his arms as though it were precious. He laid it on the counter and unwrapped the bundle. Inside lay a bright green tunic embellished with an elaborate, fine, gold-threaded, leaf pattern. Maldwyn inspected the piece, running his hands over the tunic and flipping it over, confirming it was in perfect condition before being brought to the prince's wardrobe.

'Great news about the execution the other week! Another sorcerer has been cleansed from this world.'

Maldwyn's skin crawled. The tailor was brilliant at his work, the finest tailor in the entire kingdom, but, as a man, he was as eccentric as the king. Maldwyn fought hard to keep his bad mood concealed. He needed to tolerate this man as long as he worked at the castle.

Ignoring the remark Maldwyn folded the brown leather wrapping back over the tunic. 'Beautiful handicraft again,' Maldwyn offered.

'Maldwyn, you're too kind. That's why you're my favourite servant in the palace.'

Smirking at the irony of Alaric's statement, Maldwyn considered how different the tailor would feel if he knew Maldwyn had magic.

'I speak the truth,' Maldwyn told him, wrapping the tunic back up in its protective coverings. Sometimes stroking this man's ego worked well to remain in his favour. Ailaya had complained a lot about the way he treated people he didn't like, and Maldwyn always found it best to stay on his good side.

'Bad news about those skirmishes on the border, right?'

'Skirmishes?'

'Yes… you know,' Maldwyn shook his head, he didn't know, 'in those disputed areas. That mine was built by the blood and sweat of the people of Dresden. We have a right to claim it back.'

'The mine? I thought that was in the Anhalt Mountains, and that it was built by the Erendil?' Maldwyn asked, puzzled. He had never heard anything about the mine belonging to Dresden. Of course, it was coveted due to the precious metal inside, but, as far as he knew, it was never built by the citizens of Dresden.

'Then you thought wrong.' Alaric wagged a finger at him. 'The youth today! You know nothing about history.'

'My mistake,' Maldwyn lied, convinced Alaric was the one who was wrong. 'I had best get this back to the palace.'

'Shall I add this to the palace's account as usual?'

'Of course,' Maldwyn told him as he picked up the wrapped tunic and headed for the door. He too carried the encased article as though it were precious.

'Oh, before you go Maldwyn, I have a quick question.'

'Sure, go ahead,' Maldwyn said as he turned back to Alaric. The little man followed him toward the entrance.

'You wouldn't happen to know anything about a new belt for the king, would you?'

'New belt?'

'Yes, apparently the king is expecting to become the owner of a very special sword and he needs a new belt crafted to hold the sheath.' Alaric stroked his chin, deep in thought. 'Have you heard anything about this?'

Maldwyn shook his head. 'No, I haven't. Who told you the king wanted a new belt?'

'One of the knights came in a while back and mentioned something about it.'

'One of the knights?' Maldwyn gazed up to the roof, wondering which knight might have had any reason to interact with the royal tailor, and how this knight would know anything about the king expecting to acquire a new sword. 'I'm sorry, I haven't heard anything about a belt. I'll check with Master Damyan and let you know if there is an order to be placed.'

'Thank you, Maldwyn.' Alaric pushed his shoulders back, satisfied with Maldwyn's response. 'You have a good day.'

Alaric pulled the door open for Maldwyn, smiled and waved him through the door. Carrying the prized tunic,

Maldwyn was very careful not to knock anyone on his way back to the castle.

* * * * *

'Ooh, is that it?' Ailaya asked as she came up beside Maldwyn in the servant halls. Her simple, pale purple dress flowed gracefully as she walked, and her red locks hung loosely over her shoulder. There was a hint of a lavender perfume about her as a gentle breeze drifted their way. 'The prince's new tunic?'

'It is.'

'Well… aren't you going to let me have a look?' Ailaya reached for the leather wrappings. Her curious expression glowed with excitement. Servants were always keen to see Alaric's work. Most of them would never see, let alone own, such impressive and extravagant items of clothing.

'Not in the middle of the hallway.' Maldwyn scolded as he turned down a side hall, leading to the southern wing of the castle. This corridor was long, running for the entire length of this side of the castle, with spiral staircases tucked away into small, arched, nooks that connected this hall to the other levels, and linked the royal chambers to the rest of the palace. It was slightly wider when compared to the rest of the servant hallways, to compensate for the higher traffic that dashed up and down the area.

'Fair point.' Ailaya backed off and fell in step beside him. There was an extra beat in her step as she walked.

'You seem happy,' Maldwyn observed.

'I am.' Ailaya smirked at Maldwyn with a mischievous glint in her eye. He waited for her to speak and, after a short moment, the silence got to her. The corners of her mouth curled up into a proper smile. Dimples marked her cheeks.

Maldwyn shook his head at her and sidestepped to let another servant pass between them. 'What is it this time?'

'Nothing… I'm just in a good mood.'

Maldwyn admired her infectious ability to display every possible emotion with such intensity. When Ailaya felt happy, she was joyous, and when she was sad, she was sorrowful. He always found himself comforted by her near childlike sincerity. 'Does this have anything to do with Ser Theodor?'

'Believe it or not Mal,' Ailaya shook her finger at him, reproaching Maldwyn for his myopic remark, 'not everything that makes me happy has something to do with Ser Theodor.'

'So, it doesn't have something to do with him?' Ailaya's jaw dropped at the confirmation.

He grinned, knowing the comment would get under her skin. She shoved him, realising that he was being sarcastic. Maldwyn felt his stomach tighten and pull in reaction to her force. He grimaced, managing to hide that he was in any pain.

Ailaya's delighted grin grew further up her cheeks. 'It's actually because I've been given the night off from tending to the princess's chambers.'

Maldwyn paused as he considered what Ailaya had just told him, slowing his walking pace just a little. The thought occurred to him that the princess may have requested that the staff remain away from her chambers while she used the privacy to practice magic. Just a few days ago, Erik had confided in Maldwyn that the princess's training had begun and that he had planned an upcoming meeting with Princess Cassara to continue her learning. No matter the truth behind the princess's orders, as far as his friend was concerned, this was rare and thrilling news.

'That's great Ailaya.'

Maldwyn rapped on the servant entrance to the prince's bedroom, making sure the room was empty before opening the door. When he stepped inside, the room was as Maldwyn had left it earlier that morning. The prince must not have returned to his chambers all day. Opening the door nice and wide, Maldwyn waited for Ailaya to enter before closing it again.

She walked into the room, looking around at the various furnishings. It occurred to Maldwyn that she might not have actually been in the prince's room before. This wasn't one of the rooms she ever looked after.

Her cheeky expression confirmed his suspicions. She moved over to the sofa and sat down, crossing her legs, sitting tall and mocking the royal family's proper, formal behaviour.

'You're creasing the cushions,' he cautioned.

Ailaya scowled. 'So, you're telling me, you have never once sat on anything in these lavish, ridiculously, overly adorned rooms in this castle? Not once?'

Maldwyn had once, with the prince. He thought about how the prince's arms had brushed by him as he examined the well-detailed map that he had splayed out on the low table. Prince Harlan had seemed burdened by something that day, and his jaw was still swollen, having not yet healed. Maldwyn recalled being bothered by the sore.

Deciding not to indulge her, Maldwyn ignored her query, placing the tunic down on the dining table. Ailaya stood, fixed the couch, hiding any evidence that she had sat down on the upholstered sofa, and walked over to the table. Her silly grin lifted his sour mood. She gestured for him to show her the new tunic. He began unpacking the leather covers and revealed the beautiful tunic. In awe, Ailaya reached out, daring to stroke it.

'Oh, Mal. Alaric does stunning work with a needle and thread.'

'Yes, he does. Such a shame he's a wretched man.'

'Don't let anyone hear you say that,' Ailaya softly rebuked.

Maldwyn rolled his eyes. Ailaya had told him on many occasions of her own dislike for Alaric. According to her, he was extremely condescending and didn't like dealing with female servants. At least Maldwyn didn't have to worry about that.

'You know what I mean.'

She glowered at him, placing her hands on her hips. 'I do, but you're ruining my good mood.'

Maldwyn apologised and grabbed a hanger from the prince's wardrobe. He hung the tunic, flattening the fabric out to make sure it wouldn't crease inside the cupboard, and stowed it away where it would be safe and sound inside the closet.

'Shall we both head to the tavern later for some drinks if you're not working?' Ailaya clicked her fingers eagerly.

While Maldwyn closed the wardrobe doors, he turned towards Ailaya and twisted his torso in a way that pained his injured stomach. He winced, and immediately brought his hands to his gut to soothe his painful wound.

'Are you alright?'

Ailaya came up to Maldwyn's side and wrapped her arms around him, comforting and tending to him carefully. Again, he rolled his eyes.

'I'm fine!'

'I know you well enough to know that you're lying.' Ailaya said firmly, her worried expression making him feel guilty for snapping at her. 'What's wrong? Are you hurt?'

Maldwyn felt ambivalent. He trusted Ailaya, but he didn't want to place her in an unsafe situation by knowing it was Ser Mikel who had attacked him. Nevertheless, she was the only person in the castle he trusted at all.

'It's not that bad. One of the knights just took out some frustration on me.' Maldwyn held her hand and gave it a reassuring squeeze. 'It's fine… I'm fine.'

'Are you crazy? That's not okay Maldwyn.' Ailaya pulled her hand free from his grasp, moving gently to check how badly he had been wounded. Maldwyn swatted her hand away, preventing her from fussing over him. 'These knights can be real pigs sometimes, but don't brush it off. We are people.'

'What does it matter?' Maldwyn's frank voice sounded frustrated. 'It's not like it changes anything. If I get too angry about it, the only one it's bothering is myself.'

Ailaya conceded he had a point. She wrapped her arms around him and held him in a warming embrace. Footsteps sounded in the hallway beyond the main entrance to the room. Maldwyn figured it was the prince, and remembered that he had promised not to be caught dawdling in his chambers again. Not to mention, Ailaya was not even supposed to be in these rooms.

Maldwyn pulled back and let Ailaya go from the comforting embrace. The two of them filed out the servant door, and Maldwyn considered lingering long enough to catch a glimpse of the prince, but thought better of it. After reassuring Ailaya some more in the servant halls, he went back to his duties.

CHAPTER EIGHT

The Truth Hurts

SEVERAL DAYS LATER, Maldwyn's stomach was on the mend. The wound was more of a nuisance now, hardly hurting as he went about completing his chores. He hadn't seen Ser Mikel since the night in the sacred grove, nor heard anything further about Princess Cassara's lessons with Erik.

Maldwyn had seen Erik a couple of times in passing, but never got the chance to ask how the princess's training was going. There was no reason to believe things weren't going well. In truth, the more Maldwyn thought about the princess learning about sorcery, the more he noted that he was jealous, wishing he too could learn more about the gift of the gods. He felt it would help him to understand his own power.

Maldwyn had considered telling Erik about his abilities, that he possessed his own magic, but his fear of being caught held him back each time. He was terrified that even sorcerers like Erik might find him an abomination. People weren't supposed to have his power. He also contemplated confiding in Ailaya, his closest friend, yet every time he tried to tell her the truth about his magic, Maldwyn seemed to choke on his words and nothing that made sense came out.

'Maldwyn,' Master Damyan's mellow voice sounded behind him. Maldwyn stopped in his tracks and turned to his superior. Even in the dim light, the silver streaks in Master Damyan's hair shone. The wrinkles around the edges of his eyes reached out in jagged lines, like roads or rivers marked on a map, and were more noticeable in the dappled lighting of the halls.

'Yes, Master Damyan?'

Master Damyan's presence was as commanding as ever. There was an aura of authority about him that demanded attention.

'I need you to follow me to the council chambers.'

'Master?' Maldwyn stepped closer and folded his arms across his chest, a little baffled. 'That isn't an area I usually tend to.'

'Indeed,' Master Damyan agreed. His distant expression remained, giving Maldwyn no indication as to why he was required in the council chambers. 'However, there is a rather delicate matter at hand.'

'Of course, master. May I ask what this matter concerns?'

'I haven't the time to discuss everything at this moment. Follow me.' Master Damyan turned and began walking down the hall. 'I will explain everything to you shortly.'

Maldwyn acquiesced with his master, trailing his heels toward areas of the palace that were less familiar. Having never stepped foot inside the council chambers before, Maldwyn was looking forward to serving and attending this well-guarded area.

When they arrived in the servant zones near the chambers, Master Damyan spoke in a hushed tone with one of the guards, seeking admittance to see the king. These guards were the king's sentries and wore golden heavy armour. Their breastplates were smooth and polished, shining with even the faintest hint of light.

After a few back-and-forth remarks and a bit of probing, one of the guards muttered something out of Maldwyn's earshot, spinning around to guide them toward the council's meeting rooms. Twisting to face Maldwyn, Master Damyan gestured for him to follow the guard.

The door they were brought to was wider than most other doors in the servant halls. Master Damyan knocked on the smooth wooden surface. Voices could be heard talking inside the room. They waited for permission to be granted to enter the room, as was the proper protocol.

'Enter,' King Viktor called from inside the room.

Master Damyan pushed open the door and they walked into the council chambers. They were even grander than Maldwyn expected. The expansive space was filled with opulent furnishings. There was a long heavy timber table with eight bulky chairs around it, and an ornate desk with a single seat tucked away in a side room. Scrolls keeping the kingdom's secrets were rolled up and piled inside the shelves of a small stand that also held a tray of appetizers on the top. Tapestries hung from the walls and wax hung like icicles from the candelabras overhead. To the left of where they entered was an open archway that revealed an outdoor balcony. The sun's beams glowed through gaps in the ivy hanging over the archway, and vines swathed the stone balustrade. Maldwyn noted that there was a sort of haunting romance to these rooms.

The king and the prince sat at the long table, maps spread out in front of them as they were deep in discussion. The streak of black on the left side of the king's head was in clear view. The prince's flaxen hair was a stark contrast to his father's. There were no other council members present.

'Master Damyan,' the king exclaimed. His voice was slick as usual. 'I'll be with you in a moment.'

'Yes, Your Majesty.'

Unclear as to why he was here, Maldwyn stayed quiet behind Master Damyan, keeping his formal posture as faultless as possible.

'Make sure you approach from this route,' the king ran his finger along the map, indicating the path he was referring to. 'The Erendil can't know you're coming.'

'That's a very dangerous path father.' Checking first that Master Damyan couldn't see the direction of Maldwyn's gaze, he glanced over at Prince Harlan, noting that his clear, blue eyes looked sceptically at the king. His blonde hair was well-textured and parted to the side, giving him a neat gentlemanly appearance. His cherry red shirt accentuated his fair golden skin and brought out the natural undertones of his yellow hair. 'Those are disputed lands that have been having skirmishes along the borders for months.'

'There is no other path,' the king insisted. 'We don't know where their stronghold is exactly. This is the only area where they have been spotted, where you might be able to track them.'

The prince's thoughtful face examined the route. 'It won't be easy.' Prince Harlan, rested his head in his hand, leaning one arm on the table.

'Harlan, this is very important and I'm trusting you to get this done.'

Prince Harlan seemed perturbed, as if he was done with this conversation. The prince turned his gaze to where they stood waiting, and a hint of a smile touched the corners of his lips when his eyes caught sight of Maldwyn, as if he had only just noticed him standing there. Maldwyn immediately looked to the floor. The present company could not know that Maldwyn, a lower-class servant, had looked upon his better.

'They are dangerous, and who knows what they plan to do with the weapon. We need to protect the people from the perils of sorcery.'

'I understand father,' the prince sounded irritated, as though he had been lectured about the importance of this mission on several occasions.

King Viktor eyed his son closely. 'I hope you do. If it should fall into the wrong hands, then the consequences could be terrible.'

'I know how dangerous it is,' Prince Harlan rubbed his forehead, perhaps developing a headache from his father's berating. 'I know the reasons for protecting the realm from magic.'

A shiver ran down Maldwyn's spine as he listened to the king's prejudices. He thought of the way magic still existed in the heart of Dresden, hidden away like a dirty secret. Erik and Princess Cassara had been practising magic in the palace under the king's very nose for quite some time now. He feared what might happen to either of them if the king should ever learn the truth.

'I won't fail you.'

'We'll see. The Valuwan prophecy tells us how important this is. This weapon needs to be destroyed, at any cost. We need to avert the prophecies Harlan, and this is the only way to do it.'

'Yes, father.'

The room fell quiet as King Viktor and Prince Harlan exchanged powerful stares. The king shifted in his seat and broke away from the prince's glare.

'Master Damyan.'

'Yes, sire.'

'Is this your recommendation?'

'He is, Your Majesty.' Maldwyn wondered if they were talking about him and what he was being recommended to do. 'He seems strong enough.' The king stood, leaving the table and joining them by the servant's entrance. 'He isn't from the hunting party, are you sure you would recommend this servant over the others?'

King Viktor surveyed Maldwyn, circling and evaluating him. Maldwyn, although puzzled and unclear about what was going on, remained very still, as was his duty.

'Yes, sire. Maldwyn is a highly skilled servant. He is capable as a hunter, a cook, a cleaner, and a horse handler. I assure you—Your Majesty—he is a varied and seasoned servant who is loyal to the kingdom. He is my recommendation to accompany the prince and the small contingent on their journey.'

Maldwyn couldn't see the king's face to read his expression. Growing nervous, he recognised he was holding his breath and forced himself to let out some air.

'Alright, I shall trust your judgement.' The king turned around to face Prince Harlan, still seated at the table, examining the various detailed maps. 'I am needed to preside over some matters in the throne room, make sure he's briefed on what his duties will be.'

'I will, father.' The king strode out of the room and down the greater halls. Prince Harlan clicked his tongue. 'Nicely done.'

'This is the servant you requested, Your Grace?'

'It is.' The chair made a grinding noise on the floor as the prince rose from his seat. His towering height cast a shadow over the table. 'I trust him.'

'Then, I am glad to have served you, sire.' Master Damyan bowed to the prince. 'Shall I dismiss Maldwyn, Your Grace?'

Prince Harlan scraped his feet and moved gracefully toward them. Maldwyn fought the desire to look upon the prince and instead studied his fine, black leather boots. They were laced boots, that had rows of dress buckles up the side, hiding the laces. The polished, silver buckles glinted, reflecting the light of the sun pouring through the archway to the balcony.

'No, he may stay.'

Master Damyan faced Maldwyn. 'What we're about to discuss cannot leave this room. Understood?'

'Of course, master,' Maldwyn agreed, still confused about what was going on and what his purpose here was. 'You have my word.'

'Well, Prince Harlan, where do we begin?'

'I want to know everything about my mother's execution.'

A feeling of inquisitiveness awoke inside Maldwyn. As far as he was aware, the king told the prince that the servants had been sworn to never speak of Queen Sonia's execution with either Prince Harlan or Princess Cassara. For some reason, Master Damyan, who was the most loyal member of the staff, was willing to risk his life by telling the prince the truth about his mother's execution. To Maldwyn, it didn't make sense.

Moreover, besides that Ser Mikel's letter stated that the king had executed Queen Sonia, Maldwyn wasn't sure how detailed the letter had been. It didn't seem as though Prince Harlan knew that his mother had an affair with a sorcerer, nor that this was one of the reasons the king hated magic. For a moment, he considered that Master Damyan might censor the truth, telling Prince Harlan little more than the letter already had.

'Alright, I suppose I should start with the reason your mother was executed.' Master Damyan's frank tone was unsympathetic, and, Maldwyn believed, a little out of character. He was a poised man who was difficult to read, but Master Damyan was rarely callous. 'Sire, your mother's crime was adultery. She fell in love with one of your father's advisors.'

A warm summer breeze wafted in from the archway, carrying the fragrant smell of the ivy swaying in the wind. Disappointed, Prince Harlan withdrew. Maldwyn wanted to offer him some kind of support, but, with Master Damyan here, opted instead to stay silent.

'Who was it?'

'Are you sure about this, sire? I cannot take it back once you learn the truth.'

'I am sure. Go on.'

'His name was Kristian Sadler, Your Grace. He was one of the king's magical advisors before sorcery was forbidden. His being a sorcerer was one of the reasons your father removed all magical advisors from the palace.' Master Damyan wet his lips, finding the right words before continuing. 'His trust in those that practised the craft perished with your mother's crime. King Viktor believed that your mother had been enchanted, and that this was the reason for her betrayal, sire.'

The muscles on Prince Harlan's forehead tightened. He drew his brows together slightly and clenched his jaw. 'That wasn't the case though, was it?'

'No, Your Grace. Your father had Kristian executed, hoping to expose his magic by severing your mother's love for him.' Maldwyn guessed that such a spell was meant to end with the death of the spellcaster. 'But your mother mourned him, and continued to love him after he died.'

Prince Harlan's eyes were particularly blue in this light, like pure aquamarine gemstones, and they rushed with rage at his father. Just looking at his eyes, Maldwyn could swear he heard the tide of the distant ocean. 'And, for loving him still, my father executed her?'

'Yes, sire.'

Sneaking another glance at the prince, Maldwyn saw his expression shift to one of disgust. Prince Harlan must have been both disappointed in his mother's adultery, and abhorred at his father's response to her indiscretion.

'Is my mother's transgression also the reason that magic was forbidden in Dresden?'

'No, sire.' Master Damyan paused, giving Prince Harlan a moment to process the information. 'Your father had already headed down that path, placing restrictions over the use of magic, long before he learned of your mother's affair. If anything, Your Grace, it merely reinforced his beliefs.'

'Is there anything else I should know about her execution?'

Master Damyan straightened his perfect posture, unsettled by the conversation. 'Your father told the kingdom that your mother committed treason by plotting with her father, King Filip—the King of Mordiallok—to attempt to assassinate King Viktor. It's why your father went to war against Mordiallok when you were a child, and why you've never met any of your mother's family after the war ended. As you know, neither side was declared the winner of that war.' Master Damyan hesitated, as if unsure whether he should continue. He waited for the prince to indicate that he wanted to hear the rest of the story. 'The public doesn't know of her adultery, only the staff in the palace and a select few sorcerers that fled the castle once magic was outlawed know the truth and we were forbidden from mentioning it, sire. My life is on the line for this.'

The resentment in Master Damyan's voice was cutting. Maldwyn wondered why he had shared this information with the prince at all, especially since—as he had just stated—he was risking his life to do so. Master Damyan shrugged, as if that was all there was to tell.

'That's it,' Master Damyan said coldly. 'The end of their story.'

Prince Harlan's bottom lip displayed the hint of a quiver. Maldwyn thought he might cry, but no tears came. Instead, the prince blinked away any sign of a tear, and pushed aside all traces of his anger, returning to his poised, cold, regal veneer. Maldwyn hated that expression. In the last few months, he had come to see a different side to the prince, learning about his fragmented relationship with his father and seeing the pain of the loss he felt over his mother. Now, Maldwyn worried that this information would lead to Prince Harlan cutting himself off from the world around him, becoming more and more like a living corpse, existing for his duty to the crown.

'Thank you, Damyan. I'm sorry I used information against you to force your hand, but I needed the truth and my father was never going to tell me.'

Maldwyn hung onto these words, mulling over what information the prince had used to blackmail his master. What secrets did Master Damyan have that would make him turn on his king?

'I understand, sire,' Master Damyan said in a forgiving manner.

'You're both dismissed.'

Maldwyn and Master Damyan shared uneasy glances. Master Damyan bowed and headed for the servant halls. Maldwyn lingered a moment.

'Is there something you need Maldwyn,' an aloof Prince Harlan asked.

'Should I not be briefed on things, sire? Like the king said?'

'Not now, Maldwyn.' A touch of pain crossed the prince's face as Maldwyn looked him in the eye. Master Damyan was beyond the doorway by now and Maldwyn felt it was safe for him to resume certain comforts. 'Maybe later.'

Maldwyn nodded, bowed and also made his way back into the servant corridors, closing the door behind him as he left the council chambers. The romance of the rooms had been lost to the indecent nature of the conversation. He mused over the exchange of words, and thought about what it must have been like for Prince Harlan to learn the extent of his father's cruelty. He thought about going back, but the prince clearly wanted to be alone.

Disheartened at this notion, Maldwyn mulled over what might be the assignment he had been recommended to accompany Prince Harlan on. If it had anything to do with what the prince and the king had been discussing when he and Master Damyan entered the council chambers, then it had something to do with magic. Maldwyn's power flowed steadily. He thought about how careful he would need to be on such a journey, so as not to have his power discovered, and how dangerous this mission would be for him.

Maldwyn sighed, trying not to let his concerns consume him. He scratched his forehead and returned to his duties. Whatever the mission was, he would find out, in time.

CHAPTER NINE

Valiant

THE RIVER THAT RAN BEHIND the castle grounds and towards the forest, lapped at the bank. The sky was clear and the sun, although it had begun to set, was still shining high overhead. There was an open glade that was marked by a row of hedges that overlooked the water. Prince Harlan sat, brooding on a stone bench, staring at the water.

'You requested me, Your Grace?'

'I did.' Prince Harlan tossed a stone into the river. The surface rippled and swirled. 'I wanted to brief you on the upcoming journey.'

'Of course, sire.'

'My father received some news about a magical relic of sorts—one that could be dangerous—in the possession of the Erendil in the Anhalt Mountains. A few good knights and I are being sent to retrieve the item.' Prince Harlan gripped the back of the stone bench and leaned back, putting his weight on his hands. 'We're being sent to bring it back to Dresden, where it will be safe.'

'Is that wise, sire?' Prince Harlan shot Maldwyn a hostile look. 'Your Grace, I only mean to imply that, whatever this thing is, the Erendil seem to have kept it safe. They haven't used it. Might it not be safer to simply leave it with them?'

A moment in silence passed and a bird glided into the arms of a tree on the far side of the riverbank. The bird cawed and flapped its wings as it came in for its landing.

'My father fears it might fall into the wrong hands and that it would be best if it were brought to Dresden, where he can be sure that it is protected.' The prince cleared his throat. 'In any case, you will accompany us to perform the relevant servant duties. You will be doing the hunting, the cooking, the handling of the horses, and maintaining the equipment and supplies.'

Prince Harlan turned his attention back to the water, beating against the shore. The briny smell of the nearby ocean wafted their way.

'Might I ask, sire, why you requested my services?' Maldwyn had wanted to know the answer to this question since he had been recommended to the king. 'Why not get the help of a squire?'

Displaying a guilty countenance, Prince Harlan cocked his head to the side. 'I might have convinced my father to request that Master Damyan assess his staff and make a recommendation for the quest. I reminded my father that magic sympathisers can be anywhere, including in the palace. I told him that it was of the utmost importance that the servant accompanying us be, not only capable, but also able to keep the mission a secret.'

'Sire, you exploited your father's fear of magic?' Maldwyn couldn't help himself from sounding a little impressed by the prince's manipulation.

'Between you and me… yes, I did.'

'That doesn't answer my question though.' Prince Harlan looked up at him. Maldwyn was struck by his blue eyes. 'Why did you ask Master Damyan to recommend me?'

It was quiet and there was no one else around. Prince Harlan tapped the back of his heel on the gravel and took in a deep breath, closing his eyes for a fraction longer than a blink. The water stirred from the breeze and burbled quietly.

'Put it this way… the knights, the squires, the rest of the servants and everyone around the castle, really, works for my father… the king.' Maldwyn detected a touch of distrust in the prince's voice. 'But, you're newer to the castle and I trust you. That's more important to me. I need someone watching my back out there.'

Biting his lower lip, Maldwyn nodded. He understood. After everything the prince had learned about his father, he had every reason to doubt him.

'When do we leave, Your Grace?'

'First thing tomorrow morning.'

Maldwyn looked out over the river, just as a small honeybee hummed along its erratic flight path. The sharp bite of the sun burned down on them. Maldwyn moistened his lips when Prince Harlan looked elsewhere.

'I need to get back to the castle.' The way the prince said his name roused an odd sense of pride within Maldwyn. The prince stood tall. 'Will you be heading back also?'

'Yes, sire.'

The gravel on the path crunched underfoot as they walked towards the palace. The sea was on the far side of the greater city, but the waves could just be heard pulsating softly as they crashed against the shore.

The rest of the way, Prince Harlan remained quiet, as if thinking over something troublesome. Maldwyn guessed it was related to the news of his mother's execution. When they reached the palace, Prince Harlan ignored the soldiers guarding the door, entering the castle without a thought to Maldwyn, who could not follow.

Maldwyn paused and watched the prince disappear into the open parlour beyond. Smiling to the guards, Maldwyn walked along the outside of the tall foreboding castle walls, headed for the servant entrance, which led to the rabbit warren of tunnels.

* * * * *

Early the next morning, Maldwyn said his goodbyes. Master Damyan had given Maldwyn a formal briefing regarding his duties on the mission ahead, whilst keeping a close watchful eye on him and seething with suspicion. He clearly questioned Maldwyn's selection for the assignment. Maldwyn didn't know what to do to assuage his concerns. Thus, he kept his head down as he worked, staying out of the master's way.

Unlike his master, Erik, who had freshly shaved the lengthy stubble on his face, was in good spirits and pleased to see Maldwyn had been awarded the opportunity to work outside the castle. He told Maldwyn that he was wasted working in the palace and deserved the opportunity to spread his wings.

Unsure when they would next see each other, Erik also took the time to thank Maldwyn for keeping his secret, and for encouraging him to teach Princess Cassara in the ways of magic. Apparently, training the princess had helped Erik to feel reconnected with people, as if the constant hiding had left him completely alone in the world even though he was surrounded by people in the palace.

Although Erik shared the princess's trepidation about her father learning the truth about her being a seer, he also expressed his concern that the princess's paranoia about her father might somehow endanger them. Maldwyn understood her fears. Lying about having magic was exhausting and—as Erik pointed out—isolating. Even though Erik didn't know it, Maldwyn had experienced this firsthand, and, nevertheless, was confident that Erik could help to keep her calm.

When Maldwyn moved on from Erik in the servant halls, he had gone searching for Ailaya. He couldn't leave without saying goodbye to her. When he found her, Maldwyn told Ailaya that he would be leaving and didn't know when he would be back.

Ailaya was terrified that Maldwyn would be in danger, especially after he had already been assaulted by one of the knights, and begged him not to go with the prince. There was no point though, it was his duty. She knew this was the case. Being the closest thing that Maldwyn had to family in the city, he reassured Ailaya and held her close before departing, knowing that he would miss her most of all.

The courtyard in front of the palace was lined with the beautiful steeds Maldwyn and the stableman had prepared for their journey. There were five knights that would be accompanying Prince Harlan, and Maldwyn was the only servant that would be in attendance to the company. The knights all wore lightweight brown and blue leather armour, perfect for travelling in the woods and not drawing too much attention to the group.

Prince Harlan's armour was more ornate and bore the mark of his family's crest, a rampant lynx. A sword hung in a finely crafted scabbard from his hip and a knife was sheathed beside it.

Maldwyn knew he looked plain in comparison to the rest of the group. His white shirt tucked into his tan trousers and his chocolate jacket, all felt very underwhelming in their prestige assembly. But this was the typical attire for his station.

It wasn't yet mid-morning and the sun scorched the open courtyard. Heat raged from the stone, cobbled ground and the rough granite walls of the palace. King Viktor watched them from the castle steps as they all mounted the horses. A few formal words were exchanged between the prince and the king, and then, with a wave of his hand, the king dispatched them to commence their expedition.

Prince Harlan turned his horse and led the way through the square to the greater city below. Peasants watched as they rode by, none the wiser as to what they were doing, where they were going, or when they might return. One final time, Maldwyn took in the mixed aromas of the city: the burning coal, the nearby ocean, the scent of the spices, fish and meat in the markets, and the still-blooming flowers.

When they entered the dark woods beyond Dresden, the warmth of summer seemed to be left behind. Birds squawked as if warning them to leave. The noise of the city died, and the sun hid above the forest canopy overhead.

Over the next few weeks, the group moved swiftly, trekking across the difficult terrain with minimal speaking. Maldwyn, very much the errand boy, jumped to meet the demands of the nobles. Surrounded by his betters, Maldwyn felt more than ever as though he were less than a person.

Even Prince Harlan ignored him. Of course, given his station, Maldwyn hadn't expected the prince to address him directly, yet he was inexplicably irritated that Prince Harlan hadn't so much as acknowledged his presence, not once. Before leaving the city, he had come to find comfort in their stolen glances.

While tending to the horses, Maldwyn wished he was back in Dresden with Ailaya. She always treated him as a man and would understand his weariness of nobles. He missed her company. In the past, whenever Maldwyn felt insignificant, Ailaya had been the person who lifted his spirits.

An owl hooted from somewhere close by, and Maldwyn caught the hint of pine wood carried on the wind. The trees swayed in the breeze and the crickets' persistent chirping filled the night air. The thick vegetation hid the campsite from where Maldwyn was alone with the horses.

Soothed by the moment to himself, Maldwyn breathed in the cooler night air. He was glad to escape the heat of the day.

Maldwyn took off the saddles. He grabbed a brush and began grooming the stallions when he heard a rustling in the scrubs behind him. He turned to the sound.

Prince Harlan stepped through the thickets. Assuming the correct posture, Maldwyn bowed to the prince. Looking at the forest floor littered with dried crunching leaves, twigs and fallen branches, Maldwyn pondered why the prince had left the camp.

'It's alright Maldwyn. There's no need for that. It's just me.'

Relaxing his stance, Maldwyn resumed brushing the horses. He didn't bother trying to sneak a glimpse of the prince. He wasn't sure how that would be received.

The horse whined and shook its head. Maldwyn was gentle as he pulled the brush through the horse's coarse hair.

'Is there something you require, Your Grace?'

'Require?' Prince Harlan sounded unsure. He probably wasn't used to being overlooked in return. 'No, I just came to clear my mind and to have a few moments alone.'

'Shall I leave, sire?' Maldwyn asked, trying not to sound too annoyed. The prince had said he wanted to be alone.

'Only if you want to. I can be alone with you here.'

Maldwyn was a little offended, though he supposed the prince didn't intend the remark the way it sounded. Keeping his back to Prince Harlan, Maldwyn closed his eyes and recomposed himself, letting his frustration subside. The horse neighed. The owl reminded them of its presence.

'Are you angry with me?'

'Angry, Your Grace? Why would I be angry?'

'I don't know.'

Prince Harlan placed his hand on the grey horse's muzzle. The horse nuzzled into him. The prince seemed dispirited. Maldwyn finally gave in to the urge to peek at the prince, his face was melancholic.

'Is everything alright, sire?'

He seemed gladdened to see Maldwyn acknowledging him. The edges of his mouth curled up a fraction as if a smile might appear at any moment. His blue eyes were darkened under the evening's dim light, yet still shone like the glimmering stars.

'I just have a busy mind is all.'

'Can I help to quiet your mind, sire?'

A crow cawed at the hooting owl. The wind whipped through the waving trees. The waxy leaves clapped in the draught.

'You already are, Maldwyn.'

Smirking to himself, Maldwyn chewed his lower lip. Prince Harlan went quiet. Considering that it might be the mission that was bothering the prince, Maldwyn wanted to know more about where they were going.

'When do we reach the Anhalt Mountains?'

'We have. We've been in the Erendil's territories for about a day now.'

He assumed that was what worried Prince Harlan. Maldwyn didn't know much about the Erendil, but had heard that their rangers were among the greatest marksmen, and that they were not particularly welcoming of outsiders. This was especially the case with trespassers. From here, they would need to be very stealthy to ensure they weren't attacked.

Prince Harlan stroked the horse's mane as Maldwyn brushed further down its back. Even though Maldwyn had been annoyed with Prince Harlan's distance, he felt strange to be quiet in his company.

'Have we much further to travel?' Maldwyn forgot to add the formality of properly addressing his royal title and wondered if he should tack it on before the prince spoke.

Prince Harlan didn't seem to notice, so Maldwyn let it go, pretending he hadn't noticed either.

'A few days.'

'What do we do when we get there, sire? The Erendil won't just hand over whatever it is we are after.'

'No, they won't. But, don't worry, it will all work out.'

Maldwyn didn't like being kept in the dark about their plans, but he knew his station and understood that there was no reason for Prince Harlan to tell him anything about the quest. Still, it was frustrating.

Having thought a lot about the prince's state of mind, especially since Master Damyan shared the truth of the queen's execution, Maldwyn wanted to ask how he was dealing with the knowledge of her infidelity. As Prince Harlan's tranquil gaze moved to the sound of trickling water from the nearby stream, Maldwyn felt close to him once more, and decided to risk a more personal query.

'Sire, how are you coping with the news of your mother?'

For a moment, Maldwyn thought Prince Harlan might leave. He had traded his serene glow for a more forlorn guise. Sadness crept into his eyes. Maldwyn immediately regretted asking.

'I'm sorry, I had no place to ask that, Your Grace.' Maldwyn backed away. He bowed and said, 'I will leave you to your thoughts, sire.'

'No, Maldwyn... wait.' Prince Harlan grabbed him by the arm as he turned to leave, dismissing himself. 'I don't mean for you to go. I'm just not used to people asking me things like that, much less meaning it when they do ask.'

Maldwyn swallowed. The prince pulled his hand away as if he had somehow invaded Maldwyn's space. Prince Harlan moved back a pace or two.

'Okay,' Maldwyn uttered.

Prince Harlan let out a frustrated breath. 'I try not to think about it too much. If I do, then I'm angry and hurt that my father could lie about something like this for such a long time. To go to war over it and never tell the truth, not once. And now, I must lie to my sister, to preserve her memory and her faith in our father.'

Maldwyn mulled over how wrong he was. Princess Cassara had given up on believing in their father. Her trust in him had ended, and it wasn't because the king killed their mother, it was because he might kill her too.

Maldwyn stepped forward, wondering if he should tell the prince the truth about his sister, though it wasn't his place.

A scream roared from the camp. Metal clashes made the horses jump. Letting go of the bridle he had been holding, Prince Harlan leapt into action, vaulting the enormous tree roots and fallen branches. Afraid, Maldwyn trailed after the prince through the verdant scrubs.

Smoke billowed from the campsite. Two of the knights lay on the ground, arrows sticking out of their necks. Shadowed forms slunk out from the darkness of nearby trees. Bloodcurdling shrieks filled the night air.

The hooded figures swept through their camp as if they were ghosts summoned forth to kill. They did not fight like soldiers.

The campsite that had been so calm and quiet had become pandemonium. Knights battling spectres and arrows flying everywhere.

Prince Harlan drew his sword free from its scabbard by his hip. A distinctive ring of steel screeched. An arrow shot past Maldwyn's head.

Magic rising, Maldwyn felt himself losing control. The prince dashed forward to help his men. His blade severed one of the attacker's raised arms and exploded through another's chest. Blood and bone sprayed about the camp.

The prince ran into the heart of the danger. Missiles soaring everywhere, Maldwyn didn't know what to do.

He was no fighter.

An arrow headed for the prince. Maldwyn's magic erupted. Everything stopped.

The crying birds overhead hovered still in the sky, the wind stopped, the horses were silent, the arrows were motionless, and the battling people halted in their tracks. Not knowing what he had done or how long it would last, Maldwyn ran for the prince. He had to save him from that arrow.

The world slowly began moving with him. Maldwyn needed to make it to stop the arrow from killing the prince. Sensing he was losing time as the world caught up with him, Maldwyn did the only thing he could think to do, he jumped in front of Prince Harlan. The arrow fired into his chest.

Crippled by the force and the pain, Maldwyn fell. The battle resumed, and the world went blank. He thought he heard the prince shout something, but believed it was only in his mind. This wasn't how he had thought things would turn out.

CHAPTER TEN

Lethal Arrow

MALDWYN JERKED AS HE WOKE UP. All around was quiet. Only the chirping crickets and the howling wind could be heard. He didn't recognise the area.

The entire region was thick with enormous trees: leaning alder that had serrated leaves of a deep, rich green; birch trees stood thin and tall like giant twigs; oaks held their limbs low, in a lazy fashion; and pine trees with huge bulbous roots that were bursting from the ground. Rough bark wrinkled the trees, marking them with deep crevasses like valleys between mountains which gave them a flaky, leathery appearance. Lush bushes filled the undergrowth. Prince Harlan was kneeling behind the cover of a wide oak tree, his back facing Maldwyn.

Maldwyn's left shoulder ached. He looked down at the pain. An arrow was sticking out of his chest, blood gushing from the wound. Groaning he tried to move. A twig cracked under his foot as he pushed himself up, lifting himself into a better-seated position.

Prince Harlan whisked around, and gently pressed Maldwyn back against the tree which kept him upright. His hand was warm, and his touch was soothing. In the dim evening glow, the prince's eyes were a steel blue, glinting in the moonlight. Prince Harlan didn't look as if he was injured.

'Don't move. You're hurt.'

Exhausted, Maldwyn let his head drop back against the tree. His arm throbbed and his hand felt numb.

'Sire, where are we,' Maldwyn murmured. 'How did we escape?'

Prince Harlan placed a comforting hand on Maldwyn's shoulder as he looked around, checking that there weren't any Erendil in the vicinity.

'When you took the arrow meant for me, I saw you fall.' Maldwyn recalled the moment he stood in between Prince Harlan and the arrow, choosing to save his life. He remembered that he had used magic to make it there in time, and noted that the prince didn't appear to have noticed his use of sorcery. Somehow, Maldwyn had gotten away with it. 'We couldn't fight them… they took us by surprise. I called for the others to run into the trees. We had to scatter to get away. I carried you with me to get you out of there. I don't know if any of the others made it out alive.'

'You should have left me there, Your Grace.' It hurt to talk. The slightest movement pained him. 'You should have saved yourself and headed back for Dresden.'

'And leave you to die?' Prince Harlan mocked and smiled, clearly trying to cheer him up. Maldwyn offered the prince a grin in return. Turning more serious, Prince Harlan lowered his voice. 'I'm the reason you're here… the reason you're hurt. I couldn't leave you to die back there.'

Maldwyn gulped. In the time that Maldwyn had come to better know the prince, he had learned that Prince Harlan was honourable and loyal to a fault. He even extended this loyalty to someone like Maldwyn, a lower-class servant.

'Sire—'

'Maldwyn, please don't argue with me.' Prince Harlan sounded firm. 'We're not safe here. They're still out there and I need to get you somewhere sheltered to treat your wound.'

Maldwyn nodded. He wasn't going to change Prince Harlan's mind. It was best not to fight him on his decision.

'Do you think you can walk?'

Maldwyn considered the question a moment. He had just returned to consciousness and hadn't tried to stand, so much as walk. There was no pain in his legs, only his shoulder. He felt drained, as if he might pass out again with hardly any notice.

'Yes, sire… I think so.'

'Good.'

The prince wrapped Maldwyn's good arm around his neck and helped pull him up to stand. The world spun, and feeling quite lightheaded Maldwyn believed he was slipping. He forced himself to keep his eyes open as Prince Harlan supported him for a moment.

'Are you alright?'

'Mmm.' Maldwyn couldn't get any words out. The blinding pain made his stomach churn. Inhaling deeply, Maldwyn collected himself.

'Hang in there Maldwyn.'

'I'm okay, sire,' Maldwyn confirmed, though that wasn't exactly true. 'Let's go.'

It was rough terrain and they moved slowly, trying to keep as quiet as possible. It was hard for Maldwyn to lift his feet. He kept drifting in and out of complete consciousness. He knew they had made their way down a mountain and into the valley below, but hadn't taken much notice of anything else.

Massive moss-covered boulders concealed the entrance to a cave close by a rapidly flowing stream. The sun was beginning to rise and orange hues streamed through the leafy canopy. The damp rocks were slippery. Prince Harlan was strong, and had held Maldwyn up most of the way, almost taking his complete weight as they entered the cave.

Helping to lower him to a seated position on the cold, hard, rocky ground, Prince Harlan was careful of the bolt that still stuck out of Maldwyn's shoulder. Looking at his own hands, Maldwyn saw that they were deathly pale.

Seeming lost, the prince shook his head as he assessed the injury. 'I'm not a physician.'

'It's alright, sire. I can help to walk you through removing the arrow and treating the wound.' Maldwyn was not a physician either, but, having grown up in a small village, he had a basic understanding of dressing such an injury. 'You'll need to start a fire to cauterise the wound once the arrow is removed. Don't do anything until you have a fire going.'

Prince Harlan did as Maldwyn instructed, leaving the cave in search of decent firewood. When he came back, he had brought a bundle of dried branches that would be perfect for lighting a campfire. He knelt down, constructing the base of the fire and Maldwyn noted the straight, unbending line of his back.

It was clear to Maldwyn that the prince hadn't needed to light many fires in his life, especially without any supplies to assist him. Everything they were carrying had been left behind, and the horses had, Maldwyn assumed, run off into the wilderness. Watching Prince Harlan struggle lifted Maldwyn's low mood.

While the prince was distracted, trying to start the fire, Maldwyn summoned his magic, hoping to help the prince. He focused all his attention on channelling his power into one single thought: burn.

A flame sparked.

Prince Harlan looked pleased with himself. Maldwyn smiled too. This was the third time he had used magic in front of the prince and gotten away with it. More than that, this was the first time he had actually controlled his magic.

'Now what?' The prince asked, waiting for Maldwyn to instruct him further. He rubbed his hands together.

'Well, sire, you'll need to cut back the clothes and widen the wound around the arrowhead with your knife. Then, pull out the shaft.' The prince looked doubtful and shifted by the fire, readying himself to follow Maldwyn's directions. Maldwyn held up a hand to halt him while he finished explaining. 'Make sure you get the arrowhead out. Then, heat the blade in the flames and use the flat side of the knife to burn the wound. This will cauterise it and stop the bleeding.' The prince's apprehensive expression showed his reluctance. 'Sire, I will probably pass out from the pain, so if there is anything you aren't sure about, you should ask me now?'

Full of thought, Prince Harlan bent down beside Maldwyn, checking the wound again. The prince didn't try to hide his worried face, clearly doubting his ability to give Maldwyn the aid he required. He ran his fingers around the sensitive site, careful not to apply any pressure. Maldwyn's skin, beneath his clothes, tingled at the prince's touch. Prince Harlan's fingers gently pinched together a piece of Maldwyn's white shirt. It was stained with his deep, red blood.

'What about dressing the wound once it's cauterised? I don't have any supplies or cloth to wrap around your shoulder.'

Considering his question for a moment, Maldwyn looked at his own ruined shirt. This was probably the best thing either one of them had to use as a bandage. 'You should clean around the gash. You can cut some cloth from my shirt and wet it in the stream.' Maldwyn indicated the direction of the stream beyond the cave with his head. 'Then, using another piece, bandage the area.'

Prince Harlan pulled out the knife from his belt. He held it at the ready. He hesitated. Maldwyn looked into his worried eyes. They were so pure and blue.

'You can do this, sire,' Maldwyn encouraged.

Prince Harlan offered an apologetic expression.

Maldwyn winced and clenched his teeth as the blade dug into the site, loosening the clothes and widening the wound for the arrowhead to be removed. He tried not to cry out in pain as the bolt was cleared from his chest, but couldn't contain all sound from escaping.

Focusing on the trickling water, Maldwyn tried to soothe himself while the prince warmed the blade in the fire. Warm blood gushed from the site, pouring down what was left of his shirt. The prince apologised again and pressed the blade into the blood-soaked gouge.

As Maldwyn expected, the pain was too much. Blackness crept into his periphery and the world sailed away into nothingness.

*   *   *   *   *

Over the next couple of days, Maldwyn continued to worsen. His mind flowed in and out of awareness. Burning hot, he was sweating all over. Maldwyn supposed it was a fever.

His mouth was dry. His head pounded. Eventually, he lost all sensation in his left arm, unable to so much as move it. His chest was heavy, as though a weight pressed down on him.

Vision blurred, he squinted at the brightly burning fire. The daylight beyond the cave's entrance pained his eyes. Thankfully, judging by the colour of the light, the sun was beginning to set.

The water continued to trickle from beyond the rocky walls, but the stream sounded to have slowed its rushing. The place reeked of algae and mildew. Grit roughened the smooth, rocky surfaces.

Falling back to sleep, Maldwyn battled to keep his heavy eyelids from closing. His breath slowed. Maldwyn knew what his symptoms meant, and he wanted to be awake when Prince Harlan returned from hunting.

Breathing in and out with slow measured breaths, he heard an awful rattling sound as phlegm bubbled in his lungs. He was not going to get better.

When Prince Harlan returned, the sun had set and the fire was dying. His tall, muscular form filled the cave entrance.

Maldwyn didn't need to squint so much now that the brightness of the day had diminished.

The prince was carrying something. Maldwyn assumed it was a rabbit from the size of the animal. At least he would be eating tonight. Placing it down by the fire, Prince Harlan saw that Maldwyn was awake.

He came to Maldwyn's side. His helpless, sad eyes took in his condition. He placed a kind-hearted hand near the blood-soaked dressing.

'I don't understand why you're not getting any better,' the prince mumbled.

Maldwyn tried to reach for his hand, but couldn't. Fighting to speak through his struggling breaths, Maldwyn was able to shift his head, to better see the prince.

'It's not your fault, sire.' There was no easy way to tell the prince what was wrong. Maldwyn didn't want Prince Harlan blaming himself for his condition. 'It's poison. The arrow must have been poisoned.'

'Poisoned?' The prince's voice cracked. 'But then, there must be an antidote.' Prince Harlan was hopeful to the last. Maldwyn admired that.

'There's no use, Your Grace. We don't know what poison the Erendil use on their arrows. There's no way to know what the cure is, and there's no time.' Prince Harlan's expression sank. 'Sire, you need to leave. Please, save yourself.'

'Please don't talk like that.' The prince was evidently upset with Maldwyn's request. 'As long as you're alive, there's still time.'

Maldwyn needed to reason with the prince. It was obvious that he wasn't thinking rationally right now. He wished he understood why the prince cared so much if Maldwyn lived or died. Prince Harlan should have abandoned Maldwyn after the attack. Anyone else in his station would have. That's what he was supposed to do.

Maldwyn was beneath him.

'Sire, I don't want you to lose hope that I might somehow—against all odds—live. I just want you to save yourself.' Prince Harlan hunched forward. His gaze was downcast. 'You will be the king of Dresden one day. You need to think about saving yourself.'

'What if I don't want to be king?'

Maldwyn had never considered that the prince might wish to abdicate the throne. Prince Harlan would make a far kinder king than his father. He wondered how he could convince the prince that he was the best person to lead his people.

'And then what, sire?' The fire popped. Maldwyn coughed, bloody spittle spraying from his mouth. He struggled and, lifting his good hand with great difficulty, Maldwyn wiped the drop of blood that landed on his lower lip with the back of his hand. 'What happens to Dresden then?'

Prince Harlan scowled at Maldwyn. 'My sister can have the throne.'

'Your sister hasn't been raised as heir to the throne. She hasn't been taught a lot about politics or tactics. Not to mention, what if she doesn't want it?'

The prince shrugged his shoulders. He rubbed along his forehead, following the line of his eyebrows.

'So, I'm just supposed to do my duty, regardless of what I want?'

'Yes. It's precisely the reason you deserve the title, Your Grace.' Maldwyn clenched his jaw, trying to think of the right words. 'You might try to hide it, but I know that you care about the people you would rule. That's important.' Maldwyn coughed again. Phlegm rattled deep in his chest. He wheezed. 'It's too late for me.'

'I don't accept defeat!' The prince's face sparked with frustration. 'There are always possibilities.'

'I know that I'm going to die.' Maldwyn caught Prince Harlan's gaze, and tried to offer a comforting smile, as if it might somehow help him to let go. 'I accept that.' Maldwyn's voice was firm. 'And, so should you.'

Defeated, the prince clicked his tongue, wanting to argue. Prince Harlan looked Maldwyn up and down, seeing that he was nearing his end, and hesitated.

'I can't just leave you here, Mal.' The prince tilted his head to the side. His mournful face was racked with guilt. 'You're dying because of me. That arrow was meant for me.' The prince reached out and stroked Maldwyn's cheek with the back of his hand. It was a kind and caring gesture. 'I should be the one dying in your place.'

The embers cracked in the background. Maldwyn tried again to lift his good arm, but didn't have the strength. All he could manage to do was to dip his head closer to the prince, sapped of all energy.

'I am proud to have served you, sire. You treat me like a man and I am honoured to die in your stead.' Prince Harlan wasn't convinced to leave him by the sorrowful look on his face. 'Please, sire… go. Otherwise, my death will mean nothing.'

The prince's crystal blue eyes welled with tears, but none streamed. As ever, he remained poised. Despite his despair, Maldwyn thought he looked very regal and handsome.

'Alright, but I'm going to stay with you for a while,' Prince Harlan told him. 'At least until you fall asleep.'

Maldwyn felt tears in his own eyes. He managed a nod. The prince made himself comfortable beside Maldwyn, watching over the dying flames.

He never bothered to feed the fire or to skin his kill to cook his dinner. Maldwyn guessed his worsening condition had put the prince off eating. Sinking back into the smooth, cold, rock wall, Maldwyn once again felt himself falling into dreamland.

In his delirium, Maldwyn was neither awake, nor asleep. His eyes were closed and he wasn't sure what was real. He thought he felt something brush his lips.

It was warm and tender. He imagined it was a gentle kiss, but told himself it was all in his mind. Then, weightless, he was floating through the air.

This was the end.

PART TWO

CHAPTER ELEVEN

Halls of Healing

'HOW'S HE DOING?' An unfamiliar voice asked bluntly. He had a faint accent that Maldwyn didn't recognise, pronouncing every word with perfect diction.

'Much better.' Answered another voice. This man had no distinguishable accent, but his voice was deep and booming, resounding off the walls all around. 'He should wake up soon.'

Maldwyn lay still, his eyes were closed. Head aching, he felt foggy. The painful throbbing in his left shoulder pounded, as though someone was hammering into his chest.

'Good. He may prove to be useful.' The man with an accent said flatly. His speech was both beautiful and melodious, bouncing with rising intonations as he spoke.

'Useful?' The booming voice asked. 'Against the prince?'

Maldwyn grew worried and contemplated where he was and how he was alive as the voices spoke around him. He wanted to peel back the lids of his eyes as he awoke, but instead decided to continue listening in on the conversation. He reasoned that they were discussing Prince Harlan and wondered what they might mean by using Maldwyn against him.

'Yes. The prince cares if he lives or dies.'

'It's strange, isn't it?' The baritone-voiced man sounded to have lowered his speech as he posed the question. The soft rumble as he spoke had a soothing effect. 'Why would the prince surrender himself to save a servant's life?'

'I don't know,' the other, accented voice answered. 'But the sovereign wants to know when he wakes.'

'What will he do?'

'Interrogate him, I imagine. He might be able to shed some light on a few things.'

'Like what?'

One of the men scuffed their feet on what sounded like a stone floor. Maldwyn turned his head ever so slightly to relieve the pressure at the base of his skull. He had clearly been lying here in this position for some time. The plump cushions were soft and warm but provided little support. The men didn't seem to notice his minute movement.

'Hopefully, he can tell us more about Mikel.' Maldwyn admired this man's voice, it was like listening to a harmonious, lyrical song. 'He said he had big plans for Dresden... and we know he was there before he went missing. Servants know everything going on in a castle. I wouldn't mind betting that he knows something about our old friend.'

Maldwyn's interest was piqued. What did they want with Ser Mikel? He kept his breath slow and deep as if he were sleeping.

'He's trouble. Are you sure you want to find him?'

'I don't.' Maldwyn imagined the accented man shrugging at the remark. 'The sovereign does. He has ordered us to find Mikel to stop him from using the stone he stole from us.'

The deep voice never replied. Silence filled the room. Maldwyn stayed very still. He wished he could open his eyes to read the expressions on their faces but repressed the desire. He might learn more if he continued eavesdropping.

'In any case, let me know when he wakes. When we're done questioning him, we'll use him against the prince.'

'Of course,' replied the deep, calming voice.

Footsteps echoed. A door creaked open and clicked shut. The other pair of steps paced around Maldwyn. He tinkered with what sounded like glass vials and pottery bowls. Maldwyn almost flinched when the man inspected his wound, pulling back the bandages that had glued to his seeping wound.

Water splashed beside Maldwyn. He heard the man wringing out some sort of cloth. Again, Maldwyn nearly jumped as the cold damp cloth slid around the gouge, mopping up the oozing blood.

As the man added a little pressure, rubbing at the dried splotches that stuck to his sensitive skin, Maldwyn gritted his teeth, trying not to grimace. The man was more focused on Maldwyn's injury than his face, not noticing the minor changes in the nuances of his blank expression as he feigned unconsciousness.

After a while, the wound was cleaned and dressed. Banging things around, the man tidied the mess he had made. Maldwyn lay still with his pulsating wound. Eyes closed, he moved his fingers on his left hand, testing whether he had regained any feeling since he was in the cave with Prince Harlan.

Maldwyn felt the smooth, satiny sheet laying over him with the tips of his fingers. His rough, work hands scratched the smooth bed linen. Maldwyn hadn't been able to move his hands the last time he was conscious. Before now, his whole arm had been paralysed, deadened by poison.

For some reason, these people had treated Maldwyn's wound. Since he was awake and, in general, feeling better, Maldwyn presumed he had been given the antidote to the poison that had been killing him.

He figured he was with the Erendil. It was their poison. They would have the cure in their possession.

The man's footsteps moved across the room. Once again, the door opened and closed. Maldwyn waited to be sure there was no one else in the room.

Peeling back his heavy eyelids, Maldwyn's view was assaulted by the variety of colours around him. Sheer orange and red draperies hung from the roof. Gaudy patterned silk cushions were piled like mountains along a stone bench on the far wall. Glazed pottery bowls marked with busy swirling designs had been stacked in an orderly fashion on a wooden countertop. Vials of colourful tinctures stored in a timber stand shimmered. The teal amphorae were painted with shining, gold, geometric motifs.

Maldwyn groaned as he pulled himself up to a seated position. His head pounded. A rush of pain swept over him like a crashing wave, making Maldwyn think he might faint again.

He didn't.

Maldwyn knew he was the picture of death from the way he felt. As he took a moment to gather himself, he wondered where he was as he gazed around the foreign-looking room. He pondered where the prince was being held. There was no sign of him.

Scratching his head from the confusion he had awoken with, Maldwyn contemplated the conversation he had overheard. What had they meant about the prince surrendering himself? The last thing Maldwyn could remember, Prince Harlan had agreed to save his own life. Maldwyn had been prepared to die. What had happened? Why was he alive?

Maldwyn swallowed. His mouth was dry. He turned his thoughts to the mention of Ser Mikel. Maldwyn contemplated what their business with the missing knight might be. What was this stone he had stolen from these people?

Right now, nothing made sense.

There was one thing for sure that Maldwyn did know: he needed to get out of here, wherever here was. He couldn't risk being used to extort the prince.

He hauled himself up to stand. Weak, he stumbled and pushed through the pain, making his way across the room toward the door, shifting the loose, floating draperies out of his way. Left arm hanging limp by his side, Maldwyn reached for the door with his good hand.

He hesitated, unsure where the door led. Shaking off his concern, Maldwyn yanked the door open and slipped through the gap.

The space beyond was lavish, to say the least. There were no windows, but the golden walls glowed from the orange torchlight with such a warmth that no sunlight was necessary. The polished mosaic floors were a collage of glimmering colours. Drapes still hung delicately from the roof. A hint of sandalwood caught his attention.

Turning to the smell, Maldwyn saw chips of wood burning as incense. The smoke from the incense danced, swaying from side to side. He had never seen a place as opulent as this. The palace of Dresden had a certain romance, but this place had something else, something more. This was luxurious.

The room was empty of people. Maldwyn pressed on, searching for a way out.

On the other side of the room, through the fabric, Maldwyn spied an arched doorway. He walked across the room and, when he went to step through the arch, a massive man with dark tanned skin, wearing plain black pants and a gold-coloured shirt, filled the doorway.

'Well, well… look who's finally awake.' Maldwyn recognised the familiar deep voice from the conversation he had overheard. The man's intimidating pose unnerved Maldwyn. He took a step back, afraid of what his captor might unleash on him for trying to escape.

'Where am I?'

'In the Halls of Healing.' The man stalked toward Maldwyn. He thought about running but had no idea where to run.

'Halls of Healing?' The man's eyes peered deeply at Maldwyn. His crooked nose didn't match his chiselled features. 'And, where might that be? Who are you?'

'You're in the Anhalt Mountains.' The man held a hand to his chest. 'I am Anton, the healer.'

'Are you people the Erendil?'

Anton pursed his lips and crossed his arms over his chest. 'The people here are, but I am not.'

Maldwyn cocked his head, still stepping backwards from his intimidating captor. Reaching for his power, Maldwyn felt nothing answer his call. He was too weak.

'You shouldn't be up.' Anton was a seemingly towering man, who was actually not much taller than Maldwyn. 'You were poisoned.'

'Where is Prince Harlan?' Maldwyn asked as he backed himself into the cold walls. Anton lifted his leg and rested it on a stone bench, which was covered in piles of cushions. This bench was larger and more like a couch than the one in the room in which he had awoken. Anton rested his forearm on his knee and leaned forward.

'You'll see him soon enough.'

Anton grabbed at Maldwyn's shoulder in a swift motion. He pressed into the gouge. Blinded by pain, Maldwyn collapsed to the floor. His eyes welled from the searing pain.

'What are you going to do with me?' Maldwyn muttered. His vision blurred and Anton became nothing more than an unclear form standing over him.

Anton ignored Maldwyn's question and crouched down beside him in his weak state. 'What do you know of Mikel Tanzer?'

Maldwyn looked down at the colourfully tiled floor. He thought about any information relating to Ser Mikel that might help him in the current situation as his captor loomed nearer.

'I only know that he is a knight for the lordship of Karana Downs. I heard he came to Dresden as the new liaison.'

Mikel had been in Dresden longer than Maldwyn. There wasn't much information he could offer, especially without taking the time to consider things more carefully.

'I think the previous representative had been called back to Karana Downs for some reason, and Ser Mikel was his replacement.' Maldwyn brought his good hand up to soothe his injury. It ached. 'Some healer you are.'

Anton sneered. His gritted, slightly yellowed teeth bared. 'Hmm, do you know why the previous representative was retracted?'

'How could I,' Maldwyn snapped. 'Ser Mikel's been in the castle longer than I have?'

Disappointed, Anton shot his gaze away. 'That's a shame. We had hoped you would be useful.'

Wanting to know more, and not knowing what they would do to him if they truly thought him useless, Maldwyn supposed he had to offer something to keep the conversation flowing. He racked his brain for everything that had happened since Ser Mikel had been missing from the court. He recalled the letter the knight had addressed to the prince and the mention of needing a sorcerer in the sacred grove. He loathed Ser Mikel and didn't mind giving Anton anything that might help them to locate the missing knight. His only real concern was what they wanted with the prince.

'What do you want with Ser Mikel?'

'The Erendil only want to retrieve something he stole from them.' Maldwyn knew this already. At least he knew Anton was not lying.

'He took something?'

'He did.'

Maldwyn could tell that the thread of conversation he was trying to maintain was ending. He needed to redirect things so that he could gain some answers.

'He's very interested in the royal family,' Maldwyn told Anton, who was assessing the damage he'd done to Maldwyn's shoulder.

'Oh?'

'Yes. He's very interested in all kinds of rumours about the family in the castle.'

Maldwyn wondered if he should keep the knowledge of the letter about Queen Sonia's execution a secret. Figuring that there were already a select few people that may have spread rumours of the truth of the queen's execution after fleeing the kingdom's capital, and that Prince Harlan already knew the true reason for her sentence, Maldwyn chose to risk telling Anton more.

'He sent a letter to the prince telling him of the queen's execution.'

'Figures he would do that.' When Anton finished pulling the bandages back, the wound gushed with blood, dripping down Maldwyn's chest and arm. 'I'm going to have to redress this.'

Anton helped pull Maldwyn up to stand and directed him back toward the room where he had awoken. Wound still throbbing, Maldwyn was happy to comply with Anton's direction. He needed treatment.

'I never much liked Ser Mikel,' Maldwyn admitted, trying to keep the discussion alive.

'Ser Mikel!' Anton scoffed, shaking his head. He had a brisk, erect walk as he herded Maldwyn toward the treatment room. 'He's not a real knight, you know?'

'What?' Maldwyn's jaw dropped as he slowed his pace. Anton guided him onwards. 'What do you mean he's not a knight?'

'He's a plant… a spy. He works for the King of Mordiallok.'

Maldwyn pushed orange chiffon out of the way as he headed toward the bed he had been lying on when he awoke. Still standing, Maldwyn leaned against the overly cushioned, high-standing bed. The frame dug into his lower back. Anton was rifling through his supplies on the countertop, opening drawers and pulling out bandages.

'A spy? That can't be possible.'

'I promise you it's true.' Anton unravelled fresh wadding and pressed it into the gushing sore. Maldwyn winced. Anton wasn't being gentle as he sopped up the bleeding. 'He's one of King Filip's grandchildren. He's the son of Duke Kasper, Queen Sonia's youngest brother. You know him as Ser Mikel Tanzer, Knight of Karana Downs. His true name is Mikel Wolff, Prince of Mordiallok.'

If this information was true, then this made Mikel a member of the royal family in Mordiallok. Even so, he would be quite removed from being in line to inherit the throne. Be that as it may, this also made Mikel Prince Harlan's first cousin.

Maldwyn thought about that for a moment. 'Are you sure?'

'Yes, I am certain. He told me himself.'

When the bleeding finally slowed, Anton began wrapping bandages around his shoulder. Maldwyn's headache reminded him it was there, banging inside his head.

'How did you meet Mikel?'

Anton stared at him with his steely eyes. 'He came through here a while back and boasted about being on a mission to avenge the queen's execution. He said he was sent by King Filip himself.'

'So, you knew he planned to cause havoc in Dresden?' Maldwyn asked, sounding shocked. 'Why didn't you warn anyone, or try to get a message to King Viktor?'

'We all have our reasons to hate that king.' Maldwyn picked up on a trace of anger in Anton's deep, booming voice. Anton's angered eyes betrayed his cold expression.

'What's your reason? You said you aren't one of the Erendil.'

Anton smirked in a slimy way. 'Very good.'

Pulling back his sleeve, Anton revealed a familiar mark: a raven. Its head dipped inquisitively. This man was a sorcerer, belonging to the raven clan. He was Erik's kin.

'You're a sorcerer?'

'I am.'

'The raven?' Maldwyn feigned ignorance.

'It's the mark of my clan.' Anton's expression was saddened. 'They were a peaceful people, and King Viktor destroyed them. My people resided near the border of the Anhalt Mountains and were among the first to be cleansed from the world.'

Maldwyn had heard the king refer to such cleansing before. Over the years, King Viktor had sent soldiers into towns that were known to harbour sorcerers and ordered them to eradicate any trace of magic. The ambiguity of their orders and the confusion regarding which persons were sorcerers had, in most cases, led to a slaughter where the town was burned to the ground and wiped off the maps of the greater kingdom completely.

'Only a handful of my people remain scattered about the lands, fleeing for their lives. I have my reasons for not caring for the king.'

Maldwyn understood. He didn't want to confide in Anton about his power, and thus give his captor any information that could be used to harm Maldwyn, but he understood the man's reasons for hating King Viktor. At times, Maldwyn had felt this same loathing and resentment for the king, which usually quickly turned on himself as his mother's words echoed in his mind.

Maldwyn thought about the prince, growing curiouser about his views regarding magic. He wondered if Prince Harlan was as fanatical about the destruction of the gods' power, as was his father. Looking at Anton, Maldwyn considered what Anton's opinions about the prince were and whether he felt the same contempt for Prince Harlan.

'And the prince?'

'What about him?'

'Mikel's meddling has harmed Prince Harlan more than it has the king thus far. Do you think the prince deserves to face the consequences of his father's actions?'

Anton considered Maldwyn's question a moment as he tied off the bandage. 'Perhaps not, but he has been raised by his father. He has not shown any love or kindness to the people his father condemns.'

Maldwyn had never spoken to the prince about magic and had no knowledge of his true feelings about the matter. He couldn't be sure of what Prince Harlan's views were. Maldwyn hoped Anton was wrong.

'You can't be sure about that.'

'Maybe not, but I am fairly confident.'

Maldwyn didn't like the way the conversation had turned off-topic. He turned his thoughts back to Mikel and considered what he might have taken from the Erendil.

'I don't suppose you'll tell me what Mikel took?'

Anton was tidying the countertop, reorganising the mess he had made redressing Maldwyn's wound. Blood-covered wrappings were strewn into balls. Anton discarded them into a bucket to be burned.

'No, I won't.' Anton walked over toward the door. 'I would get some rest if I were you. You need to heal.' He slithered through the door and locked it closed behind him.

The gaudy room had become Maldwyn's prison. Maldwyn wanted to tell the prince what he'd learned but didn't know where to begin searching for him. He didn't even know how he might escape this room without his power.

Laying back on the bed, head still in agony, Maldwyn mulled over the new information about Mikel and his connection to the royal family in Dresden. Though it explained a lot, Maldwyn still had so many questions. There were still pieces to this puzzle that Maldwyn was missing.

CHAPTER TWELVE

The Interrogation

'HE SHOULD HEAL WELL,' Anton said to the tall man that entered the healing room. The man was sacerdotal and heavily robed in pastel shades of blue. A silver and white sash wrapped around his waist. A ring hung from a long chain around the man's neck. Maldwyn could not make out much beyond the shadows of his face beneath his low hood.

'Good,' the man ignored Maldwyn, who was seated on the healing bed, and unhooked a pair of metal shackles from his waist belt. Maldwyn recognised the accented voice from the conversation he had listened to when he awoke from his coma. 'I have passed on the news of his waking, and of what he told you of Mikel, to the sovereign. He will be interrogating the prince soon and wants the servant to be brought to the Imperial Hall.'

Anton nodded and grabbed the shackles. The orange, red and maroon-coloured chiffon drapes swayed as he walked across the lavish room.

'It won't be good for you if you try to resist.' Maldwyn could get the meaning behind Anton's words.

One way or another, they would get the restraints on him. Holding his hands out, Maldwyn's shoulder screamed in pain. For now, as Maldwyn's power was expended, he figured it would be best to go along with what these people wanted.

The cold metal gave Maldwyn a shiver as Anton closed the cuffs around his wrists. Anton grasped Maldwyn's arm and pulled him off the bed, helping him to stand. Maldwyn staggered a little, just managing to stay on his feet. Anton turned him over to the heavily robed man. Maldwyn noted this man's slight effeminate frame. Wearing several golden rings on his fingers, each with different shining gemstones and designs, Maldwyn supposed this man was some sort of priest.

Looking out the door, Maldwyn saw four other hooded men waiting, each armed with bows, arrows and a variety of knives. Their robes were dark brown with a dash of red silk appearing beneath the leather belts that wrapped around their waists.

Although they were skillfully crafted, they were far simpler robes than those of the man talking with Anton. These were Erendil rangers, like the men who had attacked their camp when Maldwyn was injured. They were infamous for their stealth and expertise as archers.

Pushed forward by the heavily robed man, Maldwyn tripped over his feet, catching himself before he toppled to the ground. He was quickly encircled by the rangers. Like cats, they were agile and moved with dexterous grace.

'Come,' said the priestly man, leading the way out of the Halls of Healing. The group of men escorting Maldwyn trailed close behind. Anton did not follow, instead, he turned back and remained in the empty halls.

Like the draperies hanging from the ceiling, the ranger's robes flowed in a ghostly fashion. If he weren't their prisoner, Maldwyn would have thought these people were beautiful.

Through each room they led Maldwyn, there were no windows, but the colourful floors, walls, rugs, and drapes compensated for the lack of natural light. All around him, there was no surface left untouched; finely detailed swirling designs marked every facet. The architecture was excessive, Maldwyn thought, yet it was one of the most magnificent places he had ever set eyes upon.

All passers-by wore robes in a range of colours and with ornate detailing, hoods kept low and covering their faces. Maldwyn didn't see a man or woman who wasn't robed in the elegant attire of the Erendil.

A massive set of carved oak doors loomed at the far end of the corridor. Thrusting the enormous doors wide open, the rangers grabbed Maldwyn and pushed him into the great room beyond. Inside was the Imperial Hall.

The ostentatious tiled ceiling was domed and met by white walls that were bespattered with blue and gold paint. On the far side of the hall was the throne. It was exceedingly cushioned, like a couch, and sat proudly at the top of a set of steps. A painted timber structure with sheer fabric pinned back on all sides sheltered the extravagant throne.

A relaxed figure wearing the finest robes of all leaned back, his leg dangling over the arm of the great chair. This man was twisting a knife over in his hands, as if inspecting the blade. As he was paraded up the hall, each of Maldwyn's escorts bowed respectfully.

'Sovereign, I have brought the servant to you as requested.'

'Thank you, Tolamin.' He spoke with a beautiful, songlike, lilting accent. 'Please, come and stand by my side, the prince will be here shortly.'

The man Maldwyn now knew to be Tolamin gestured for Maldwyn and his escorts to move off to the side of the steps. Tolamin glided up the stairs, standing next to the sovereign's throne.

The room fell silent as they waited. Maldwyn's tender shoulder bothered him after all the pushing from the rangers that had guided him here. His head throbbed.

Maldwyn wondered what the prince's condition might be. As a member of the royal family in Dresden, he considered that Prince Harlan might be a treasured prisoner, treated more like a guest than a captive. Perhaps he was being held in a sumptuous room with views of the outside world. He hoped this was the case. Maldwyn would find out soon enough.

The doors burst open, making a low resonant sound. Under heavy guard, and with hands tightly bound together, Prince Harlan was shoved into the Imperial Hall. The prince looked incensed and Maldwyn noted that his outer leather armour had been removed, leaving him in only his travelling pants and lightweight undershirt, which had become tattered from captivity. Red welts blotched the prince's wrists where he had fought hard against his restraints. His blue eyes raged at the guards as he stumbled. The prince's height and strong build were in contrast with the elegant grace of the Erendil.

'Prince Harlan… welcome.' The sovereign sat up in his seat, no longer dangling over the throne in a nonchalant fashion. Tolamin tilted his head a little as he scrutinised the prince, reading the situation. 'I trust you are enjoying your stay?'

Clicking his fingers and flicking his hand towards the guards standing in front of Maldwyn, blocking him from Prince Harlan's view, the sovereign smiled. The rangers stepped aside. A boot jabbed into the back of Maldwyn's knees. Forced to the ground, he was prevented from rising when one of the rangers placed an inhibiting grip on his injured shoulder and held a sharp, cold blade to Maldwyn's throat. The pain of the grip on him was brutal.

Prince Harlan's fiery gaze softened at the sight of Maldwyn. A pleading expression flashed across the prince's face as he turned to the leader of the Erendil. The prince swallowed and replaced his pained countenance with his usual poised façade.

'Well, sovereign… I'm not convinced being held captive in a dungeon equates to a welcoming visit.'

A knot formed in the pit of Maldwyn's stomach. To learn that the prince had not been looked after as an important hostage angered Maldwyn. He considered what sort of people the Erendil were.

They had taken them both as prisoners, bound and, presumably, tortured the prince, keeping him locked away in a dungeon. Furthermore, they had healed Maldwyn with the intention of using him to taunt the prince. A cruel manipulation to try and force Prince Harlan to share his kingdom's secrets.

It would not work. The prince would not divulge any confidential information to protect someone like Maldwyn. Someone who was inferior to him.

The sovereign scowled. He and Tolamin shared a glance. 'Well, trespassers aren't welcome in our lands, Your Grace.'

'Trespassers? Please… we were just passing through.' The prince's tone gave away that he was mocking the sovereign.

Snapping his fingers, the sovereign signalled to Maldwyn's guards. A ranger stepped forward. A fist drove into Maldwyn's gut, forcing the air from his lungs. Tears welled in Maldwyn's eyes. Coughing, he gasped for a breath.

Prince Harlan wrestled with his bindings in a bid to get to Maldwyn. It was no use. They were too tight. A blow to the prince's stomach stopped him from pulling at the ropes.

'Please,' the prince implored. 'He doesn't know anything! He's innocent!'

'I know, Your Grace. It's you that will be answering my questions. But, each time you lie, or you avoid answering, your servant will suffer the consequences.' The sovereign's voice was melodic and its sweet rhythm almost lulled Maldwyn despite the horror of the current situation. 'Do you understand?'

Prince Harlan looked at Maldwyn, his eyes were like jewels that gleamed with despair. Maldwyn wasn't sure if he was supposed to divert his gaze. They weren't in Dresden anymore, and Maldwyn had a feeling the prying eyes of the Erendil noticed such things. Chances were, they had already noticed. He didn't bother to look away.

'I understand. What do you want to know?'

'I want to know why you are here. You've come a long way.' The sovereign stood from his seat, descending from his dais to face the prince, and holding the knife handle firm in his fist. 'Well, Prince Harlan, why are you here?'

'I was sent here by my father.'

Tolamin shifted forward on the steps. The sovereign held a hand up to halt him. Tolamin obeyed.

'The king? And what would the king want from us?'

Prince Harlan didn't answer. Maldwyn understood. The prince couldn't betray the secrets of his crown so easily.

Another gesture from the sovereign and a blow from one of the rangers landed upon Maldwyn's face, cracking his nose. He contorted his face from the agony. Blood immediately ran down his lips. The metallic taste filled his mouth.

Prince Harlan moved forward. The guards pulled on his arms. It took three men to hold him back from reaching the sovereign. The blade at Maldwyn's throat had nicked him when his head jerked back. He felt it pressing into his skin, stinging where he had been cut.

'Well, prince?'

Prince Harlan gnashed his teeth. He was clearly struggling to reconcile his silence against the torture of a defenceless Maldwyn. He rolled his eyes back, shaking his head at the state of affairs.

'The Valuwan prophecy.'

This was not the first time Maldwyn had heard of this prophecy and he was still no closer to understanding what it meant. He wished he had thought to ask the sorcerer in Dresden about it before he was executed.

'What about it?' Prince Harlan hesitated to answer the sovereign's question. 'Do you want me to hurt him again?'

'My father believes the prophecies have been set in motion,' the prince confessed. 'I was sent here because of the sword, Iluvitar.'

'Iluvitar? The sword forged by Wayland, the smithy god?' Maldwyn realised that this was what Alaric, the tailor, had been talking about back in Dresden. That this was the sword King Viktor expected to own. 'Why would King Viktor send you here for it?'

'For some reason, he thinks it is in your possession.'

'What for?'

'I don't know.'

The knife dug deeper into Maldwyn's neck. This time, on purpose. It stung and Maldwyn gulped as he struggled for a breath.

'I don't know!'

The sovereign signalled to the guard to stop. Maldwyn's head drooped from the pain. His breath wheezed from the pressure on his throat.

'Here's the thing, Your Grace. I don't believe you. There must be something... anything?'

'All I was told was that my father received information telling him that the Erendil were protecting a coveted relic of the gods. It was said to be something precious, something divine that would help my father change the Valuwan prophecy. For some reason, my father believed this thing to be Iluvitar.'

The sovereign wheeled around, facing Maldwyn. From this angle, Maldwyn could finally see his dark unreadable eyes and his long black hair. 'What about the Valuwan prophecy?'

The prince shook his head. 'I don't understand.'

'Why does your father believe the prophecies have been set in motion?'

Prince Harlan's eyes apologised for the hurt Maldwyn was experiencing. The sovereign grinned at Tolamin then took the knife he had been assessing on his throne and slid it along Maldwyn's right cheek. It wasn't deep enough to leave a scar, but it was enough to bother him from the sharp hurt, causing Maldwyn to wrench his head back.

The prince writhed against his captors.

'Because Firebird is alive!' His arms were thrust forward, holding his hands as open as he could, trying to convince the sovereign that he was speaking the truth.

The sovereign whipped around. Despite the pain that left Maldwyn weak and limp in the grip of the rangers, his interest grew. The elderly sorcerer back in Dresden had spoken of what he called the Quandiallan prophecy, or the Awakening of Firebird. Maldwyn had thought it a pretty story, but nothing more.

'Firebird? Alive?'

'So I am told.'

'Hmm, interesting.' The sovereign walked back up the steps, stroking his chin in deep thought. He slumped back into his plush throne. 'I assume your father knows what is written in these prophecies.' Nodding, the prince appeared confused. 'Forgive me, Your Grace, I am puzzled. Firebird is told to be a very powerful man. His use of magic would be unmatched by any sorcerer. Tell me this—your father hates magic—if Firebird were alive, why does your father want Iluvitar?'

'My father sees magic as a corrupting and dangerous power.' Maldwyn's heart jumped into his throat. He wondered if the prince agreed with King Viktor's assessment. He hoped that the prince was merely voicing his father's beliefs. 'My father wants to destroy the sword. He believes that this would prevent the prophecies from coming true. That Firebird will never find his true power and will die as an ordinary man. Until he can destroy it, he would keep it for himself, and safe from falling into the wrong hands.'

'It is a very powerful divine weapon, but your father was wrong. It isn't here.' Tolamin leaned over and whispered something into the sovereign's ear. Maldwyn wished he could hear what he was saying. 'Your father must have quite the ego.'

The sovereign paused and scratched his chin. Prince Harlan gulped. Maldwyn wanted to know more, but he didn't want another injury in exchange for the prince's words.

'Tell me, prince, have you heard of the Quandiallan prophecy?'

'The Quandiallan prophecy says that Firebird will die and that this will signal the end of the tyrant king's reign.' Prince Harlan pulled his arm to loosen the grip of the guards clutching his biceps.

The sovereign sat silently mulling over the prince's words. Tolamin stood still by his side, assessing everything with his watchful gaze. Maldwyn licked the blood from his lips, which ran from his nose into his mouth. He wished his hands were free so he could tend to the mess they had made of his face.

Once again, he grasped for his power, which remained dormant, as if out of reach. It was probably for the best. Prince Harlan likely felt the same about magic as his father and would condemn Maldwyn for his abilities.

'Prince Harlan, you can't be as narrowminded as your father. What do you think the prophecies mean? If Firebird is alive, who do you consider is the tyrant king?'

'My father believes the tyrant is the King of Mordiallok… my grandfather, King Filip. It is not for me to question my king.'

'But you do have an opinion?'

'I do.'

'And?'

Prince Harlan lowered his gaze to the floor, giving nothing away. 'Destiny is for the gods to decide. I believe the prophecies will reveal themselves to us in time.'

Maldwyn got the feeling that his worries had been misplaced. Perhaps the prince did not truly condemn magic as did his father. What the prince wasn't saying spoke louder than his words. Still, Maldwyn couldn't be sure.

'How very diplomatic of you, Your Grace.' The sovereign waved his hand. 'Take him away.'

Prince Harlan fought the Erendil hauling him backwards. His muscles fired with every jolt he made against his captors. 'How long do you plan on keeping me prisoner?'

'As long as I want,' the sovereign answered as he was dragged out of the hall. The prince's loud protests boomed from the corridors outside.

Maldwyn ached. He imagined his battered and bruised face. In his mind, it was a hideous sight, bloodied beyond recognition.

'This is Mikel's doing,' Tolamin told the sovereign. 'No doubt. He lied to the king about the sword to get the prince out of the way.'

'I agree Tolamin, but what I don't understand is why? I would have thought he would have killed Viktor by now.' The sovereign rubbed his forehead. 'He must be planning something else. What is our old friend playing at?'

Tolamin made his way down the steps, shoes clicking on the tiles. 'I wish I could help. But I am afraid I am as puzzled as you are, sovereign.'

'We aren't any closer to working out where Mikel is, are we?' Tolamin shook his head, face still hidden beneath his hood. 'We need to get back what he stole from us. Chances are, he plans to use it in Dresden.'

'I know, sovereign. We will find him.'

Tolamin gestured to Maldwyn's guards and began heading out of the hall. 'One other thing, Tolamin.' The sovereign held up his index finger, as if he had been struck by a thought. 'Make sure the prince doesn't learn the truth. He can't know about the book we have. I don't trust what he would do with the information, and we must keep it safe for Firebird. If he is alive, perhaps he will come for it sooner than we expected. We cannot become complacent. Our role is important in his story.'

'Of course.'

Shaky and hurting all over, Maldwyn went with the guards willingly, paying attention to every turn he took, trying to get his bearings. Anton was waiting for him in the healing room. He treated Maldwyn's wounds and left him locked alone in the room.

Maldwyn rubbed his temple, his hands still cuffed. His head pounded. Everywhere ached. His clothes were now more covered in blood than ever. Maldwyn collapsed back on the bed, thinking about everything he had learned.

He didn't understand why the prince had answered the sovereign's questions to protect Maldwyn. Nor did he understand why Prince Harlan was rumoured to have brought him here. Maldwyn was frustrated. He had so many questions about the prophecies and after everything that had been mentioned in the prince's interrogation, Maldwyn found himself with more questions than ever.

Maldwyn recalled the way the prince had looked when they pulled him into the hall. His clothes were tattered, and he fought the grip of the Erendil. His restrained wrists had bled. The prince seethed with anger at the sovereign. Everything in him wrestled against being their captive, that was, until he had seen Maldwyn. Prince Harlan had then surrendered to his role as a prisoner, and gave up his kingdom's secrets, to protect Maldwyn.

He thought about that for a short time. He remembered the prince's blue eyes. Even angered, they were like comets.

CHAPTER THIRTEEN

The Banquet

MALDWYN EXHALED. He was growing tired of staring at the same four walls, no matter how luxurious the healing room appeared. He hated being cooped up all the time, alone with no answers as to where the prince was being held prisoner. Anton was Maldwyn's only link to the outside world, but he only came to dress wounds, bring food, and offered little conversation. Every time Maldwyn asked about Prince Harlan, Anton would find a way to dodge the question.

Lying on the bed, Maldwyn stared at the smooth golden stone ceiling. He considered trying to escape with his power which had returned, but put the thought out of his mind. Maldwyn figured he would not get very far before being recaptured and, once the Erendil knew about his abilities, he would likely never see the light of day again. Anton was a well-accomplished sorcerer that had sided with the Erendil and would not allow Maldwyn, as their prisoner, to get far, even if he had magic.

In fact, the longer Maldwyn spent in their captivity, the more he felt Anton's watchful gaze, as if he was becoming suspicious about something. Maldwyn had worked hard to suppress his magic since it had returned, especially when Anton was around. Maldwyn didn't want the sorcerer learning anything that he could use against Maldwyn or the prince.

Maldwyn rubbed his sandy eyes. Without any natural light, there was no way for Maldwyn to be sure of how long he had been locked in this little extravagant healing room. It had been quite a while. His broken nose had healed, his bruises were gone, the cut on his cheek had closed over and, as expected, left no scar, and the gaping hole in his shoulder was no longer a seeping wound that needed daily washing and dressing. Overall, Maldwyn felt good, and almost back to full form.

Frustrated, he got up and started pacing. The shackles were itching his wrists. Maldwyn tugged at the cuffs. He didn't expect them to come off, but he pulled at them regardless in a feeble attempt to placate his annoyance.

Maldwyn guessed Anton would be bringing his dinner soon. Having spent so long in these walls, Maldwyn had learned the routine and knew when to anticipate Anton. With the mood he was in, Maldwyn contemplated throwing his dinner at the healer.

He continued pacing and rubbed his nose with the back of his hand. Maldwyn burned with irritation toward the Erendil. Even the tiniest things were becoming bothersome to him. The draperies hanging in his way, the obsessively ordered countertop of healing tinctures and implements, the lairy walls, the plump cushions, all of it, scratching at his consciousness.

Finally, the door creaked. Anton stepped inside the confined space, empty-handed and seemingly in good spirits.

'You can't keep me here like this!' Maldwyn shouted in his frustration and pointed accusingly at Anton, holding his cuffed hands up in his rage. 'You people have no reason to be keeping me prisoner!'

Anton held up a hand to hush Maldwyn's ranting. 'You were captured for trespassing. They have every reason to hold you as their prisoner.'

'Why do I get the feeling that isn't the reason I'm being held?' Maldwyn snapped. 'If I am being held for a crime, then why have I not been sentenced for anything, and why am I not being held in a dungeon? Why am I still here?'

'I understand that you're angry.' Maldwyn hated being patronised. 'I have spoken to the sovereign about your situation and I am to take you to be prepared.'

'Prepared for what?'

'Tonight.'

'What's happening tonight?'

'The prince will be brought to a banquet tonight with all the Erendil dignitaries. You are to attend the feast to allay your concerns.'

Maldwyn calmed himself and swallowed his pride. 'How is the prince?' He neared Anton, interested in the answer. This was the first time Anton had mentioned Prince Harlan, despite all of Maldwyn's enquiring.

'You will see for yourself soon enough.' Anton's crooked nose shadowed his cheek in the dappled light. 'Please, come with me.'

'Where are you taking me?'

'Somewhere to be cleaned up before the feast.'

Maldwyn looked down at his torn, bloodstained clothes. His rough, grimy hands had dirt that had built up under his fingernails. There were patches of dried blood from wounds that had healed which still marked the surface of his skin. He moistened his lips, feeling the prickly stubble on his upper lip. Anton hadn't given him anything to shave with for a few days.

'Alright,' Maldwyn agreed.

Anton guided Maldwyn beyond the Halls of Healing and through the maze of winding corridors. To Maldwyn's surprise, there were no rangers escorting them. Their steps echoed, reverberating off the tiled floors. The high ceilings were arched and formed from glazed, brightly coloured tiles.

When they reached a wide, solid timber door, Anton grabbed the large iron knocker, shaped like the head of an aggressive, fiery dragon, and banged hard. As the door swung open, they were greeted by a voluptuous woman with long, dark chestnut-coloured hair and greyish-blue eyes. Her curled locks were pinned back behind her ears, exposing her long slender neck. She wore a black corset that accentuated her slight waist. Her sheer pants hung loosely from her wide hips. Heavily made up, she was adorned with a variety of jewels.

'Ah, Tiana,' Anton greeted. 'This is Maldwyn. Ensure that he is prepared for tonight's banquet.'

'Of course.' Tiana's tempestuous voice sounded deeper than expected, likely from the smoking pipe she casually held in her hand. 'My girls and I will make sure he is well prepared.'

Anton shunted Maldwyn over the threshold. Inside, the room was fashioned out of white marble. Gold and turquoise glazed tiles cut through the blankness of the marble and were stuck on the walls in a symmetrical leafy pattern, outlined by geometric motifs. The wet floors terminated at the edge of a pool, glistening from glassy, teal mosaics that gave the water a purifying impression. Smiling women bobbed in the bath, each of them giggling at him like water sprites teasing their prey.

Maldwyn turned back to the grinning Anton. 'What is this?'

'The sovereign's concubines. They will prepare you for tonight.'

Anton closed the door as Tiana pulled Maldwyn by his cuffed hands. He jerked against his restraints, which remained tightly in place, locked around his wrists. Out of the corner of his vision, Maldwyn spotted a bunch of neat towels and satin pillows that were immaculately arranged on a bench.

Tiana stopped Maldwyn at the water's edge. The pool was perfumed with a gentle, pleasing floral scent. The women continued to laugh sweetly. Maldwyn swallowed, nervous to endure this humiliation. He pondered whether the sovereign somehow knew how uncomfortable this would make Maldwyn.

Sucking in a breath through the smouldering pipe, Tiana smirked. She blew the smoke in Maldwyn's face. He caught the grassy aroma. She offered him the chance to take in a breath of the substance. Maldwyn refused. Tiana kneeled beside the pool and passed the smoking pipe to one of the bobbing concubines.

Pulling out a fine sharp knife, she cut at his garments, swiftly undressing Maldwyn. The warm, moist air clung to his bare skin. Fury at being stripped like an animal being skinned for its meat surged through him.

Shackled, naked and humiliated, Maldwyn stood still and quiet, facing away from the pool. Tiana placed a careful hand on Maldwyn's chest, and pushed him backwards with such a sudden force that he fell into the pool. The water splashed loudly and the girls dove out of the way.

Tiana stood tall and placed her hands on her hips, clearly pleased with herself. The women circled around Maldwyn in a tight formation.

'He's very pretty! Can we keep him?'

'And his muscles—he's so strong from all that hard work!'

Their saccharine voices taunted all around him. Maldwyn held his breath, very uncomfortable with his situation. The water lapped at his body as the women swam about him.

'The prince will be very happy to see him when we're done with him.'

'The prince?' Maldwyn's gaze darted from woman to woman. 'You mean Prince Harlan?'

'Ladies—look—he speaks,' Tiana teased as she loomed over them. The women all chuckled in unison.

Maldwyn glared at her. One of the other concubines began soaping and rinsing his skin, taking care not to aggravate the slow-healing gouge in his shoulder. They washed his back with meticulous strokes.

'Why are you doing this?'

'Well, you want to see the prince, don't you? The sovereign merely wants to ensure that you are presentable to be in the company of his officials.' Tiana crouched beside the bath and ran her index finger along his jawline. Her smooth brow arched. 'He's been very worried about you.'

'What are you getting at?'

'Why... nothing Maldwyn.' The women continued wiping the slippery soap up and down his torso and arms. He tried to pull away from their touch. Tiana smiled, amused at his discomfort. 'You know... I wish you could have seen it.'

'Seen what?'

The women tittered. With gentle and deliberate movements, they ran their hands over his skin.

'When the prince brought you here for healing.'

Maldwyn swallowed. He still couldn't work out why the prince had chosen to save his life instead of escaping the rangers in the woods.

'You were there?'

'We all were!' One of the other concubines chimed in, her voice livelier than Tiana's. 'You really should have seen the way he carried you... refusing to let you die, and surrendering his freedom.'

'Some might say it was... caring,' Tiana agreed.

Maldwyn remembered having imagined that the prince had kissed him in the forest cave as he lay there, dying. He considered that it hadn't been in his mind.

Tiana leaned closer and flicked water at Maldwyn. He jerked away. The concubines began washing his thick hair. Using beautifully crafted water scoops, they ran the water over his head and soaped his hair as though they were bathing a dog.

'The prince left us all questioning: why would he risk his life to save his servant?'

A lump formed in Maldwyn's throat. He thought of the prince, and the way Prince Harlan had answered all the sovereign's queries to keep Maldwyn from further harm. His chest pounded.

'Why all this pomp and pageantry? Why not present me as the prisoner I am?'

Tiana signalled something with her hand. The women slipped out of the water and headed to the towels. Their strokes were painstakingly fastidious as they dried their soaking bodies. Tiana strode over to the bench, grabbed something small, and returned to the bath, throwing a cloth at his face.

'I think you can wash the rest of yourself, don't you?'

After Tiana walked away, seeming to glide through the room with ease, Maldwyn took the soapy washer and cleaned his groin, legs and feet. Although he struggled to wash with the restraints keeping his hands together, Maldwyn took his time bathing, eager to keep his distance and regain some privacy from the concubines.

Tiana brought Maldwyn a towel, waiting as he climbed up the slippery steps. She appraised him a moment and patted the velvety towel over his skin.

Uncomfortable, he tensed at her touch. Tiana turned and picked up a small, sharp blade that had been lying on a bench behind her. Carefully, she began shaving his face. When she was finished, Maldwyn stroked his jaw with the back of his hand, feeling the return of his smooth skin.

Tiana clicked her fingers to her ladies. Wrapped in their towels, the women strutted towards him, lathering their hands in a strong, woody-scented oil. They applied the oil all over him, working it deep into his pores. Maldwyn cringed.

The women drew a pair of sleek, black-fitted trousers over his legs. Tiana gave Maldwyn a warning glare, and unlocked his handcuffs. The women took his free arms and pulled a fine white and gold tunic over his upper body. Tiana held up a new ornate pair of shackles. Maldwyn noted that, although these were restraints, they were more like jewellery. Trinkets for his presentation.

The women left him standing there as they finished dressing. They helped each other to put on their costumes, and adorned themselves in layers of makeup, heavily outlining their eyes with a kind of black paint. They donned a range of jewels and gemstones.

Eventually, Tiana stalked towards him, carrying her smoking pipe again. The women formed a perimeter around Maldwyn and cornered him against the dripping tiles. Tiana inhaled and passed the smoking apparatus to the other concubines, each of them taking in a few deep breaths. The pipe passed to Maldwyn.

'Your turn,' Tiana told him.

The grassy smoke from the other women had already made him begin to feel groggy and hazy. Tiana took his hands that held the pipe and guided them up to his mouth. He placed the long shaft in his mouth and breathed in deeply. Smoke filling his lungs, he coughed.

Maldwyn felt his awareness become vaguer and the room grew overly bright. He felt relaxed, yet quiet and reflective too. He wasn't sure if he felt good or bad. In fact, he wasn't sure of anything now.

'What now?' Maldwyn thought his own voice sounded far away.

Holding his cuffs, Tiana led Maldwyn by his trinket shackles. The other women fell in step behind them.

'Now, we head to the banquet. We're to be tonight's entertainment.'

Ordinarily, Maldwyn would have been angry and might have fought this kind of humiliation, but his mind had been placed in a sort of trance that kept him from caring. Led by the chains, Maldwyn followed the giggling, spritely group. He felt as though he watched himself wind through the halls from a great distance.

*   *   *   *   *

They waited at a door until they heard the steady, provocative beat of an unfamiliar song. The concubines chuckled. The doors flung open, and Maldwyn obediently followed the dancing women into the massive dining hall.

His senses were overwhelmed by the brilliant colours of smooth, gently, flowing fabrics spread over the table which was piled high with a range of platters. There was a zesty aroma coming from the array of food filling the long, oak table. Sheer teal draperies hung delicately from the roof. Plush silky cushions were heaped along a low couch.

The dignitaries cheered as the concubines entered the grand dining hall. People crowded everywhere around the room. Maldwyn didn't recognise most of the people seated at the table. He did however recognise the sovereign, seated at the far end; Tolamin, seated to the sovereign's right; and Anton, who sat beside Tolamin.

Tiana pulled the trinket chains on Maldwyn's wrist. The rest of the women danced and swirled around him. They waved flowing black chiffon fabric through the air as they pirouetted.

In his daze, Maldwyn searched the room for the prince. Pulled onward by Tiana, he moved far enough into the room that he spied Prince Harlan seated on the other side of the sovereign. His pulse quickened.

Tiana ran her hand along his forearm as she guided him through the room. The other women were all spinning, moving from seat to seat, batting their lashes, swirling their chiffon and tempting the Erendil officials. She halted Maldwyn in between the seated prince and sovereign. Prince Harlan looked away, irritated. The hooded and heavily robed sovereign gazed upward.

The prince's hands were tightly bound and bleeding. His clothes were tattered and his demeanour was defeated. Unlike Maldwyn, the prince had been given no such comforts.

Tiana whispered something in Prince Harlan's ear. She lifted his chin and directed the prince's gaze toward Maldwyn, who shifted his weight on his feet. The prince's eyes were sad. In Maldwyn's daze, the world fell away and all that existed was the prince.

Tiana laughed, in a mischievous way, turned and continued parading Maldwyn through the room. The music buzzed. The concubines twisted and twirled.

After what must have been a while, the music hushed and the women finished their tantalising dance. Maldwyn was guided over to sit on the low, overly cushioned couch. The conversations resumed. Maldwyn felt the world spin a little, and, having lost all sense of control, he accepted the range of fruits being fed to him by the concubines.

Tiana and the sovereign shared facetious expressions. The sovereign muttered something to the prince. Maldwyn pushed the women seated all around him back, and sat bolt upright.

He tried to hear what the sovereign was saying, but couldn't make out any words.

Under the effects of the smoke offered to him by Tiana, Maldwyn didn't care that he was in a room surrounded by people. He reached for his magic. It heeded his call. Anton shot a look at Maldwyn. He focused his power on wanting to hear their words, and, as if Maldwyn sat at the table among them, he listened to their chatter.

'You see… I told you he was being looked after,' the sovereign said quietly to Prince Harlan. The sovereign's low hood shaded his dark eyes.

'I'd say he's been treated with a great amount of care,' Tolamin added, his silvery-blue robes shining in the overwhelming brightness of the room.

The sovereign reclined in his chair, taking a sip from his goblet. Anton did not look pleased with their taunts, firing an annoyed glare at the sovereign.

'Tell us more about your father believing Firebird is alive,' the sovereign ordered, giving in to Anton's stare.

'What do you want to know?'

'Since your father believes the prophecies are upon us, does he have any inkling as to who is Firebird?' The cunning expression on the sovereign's face could not be masked by his low hood.

Prince Harlan sucked on his lower lip. 'No.' The prince waved a hand at the sovereign, ignoring the juicy, meaty dish on his plate to answer the question. 'Many of the sorcerers my father has executed in the last few years have spoken of sensing a growing power. Ser Mikel had already come from Karana Downs with news of rumours relating to Iluvitar being in the Anhalt Mountains. My father guessed that the magic the sorcerers have felt could be Firebird... but none of those that have been interrogated and executed have given any hint as to where this power has been felt.'

'This... Ser Mikel, couldn't have known whether the sword was here.' The sovereign made a supposing gesture as he feigned ignorance of the identity of the knight. 'Why did King Viktor believe this story?'

Tiana was talking loudly to the other women behind Maldwyn as Prince Harlan made two fists with his restrained hands and held them together under his chin.

'Ser Mikel was sent from the Lord of Karana Downs with this news. My father knows Lord Darius well and trusted his reference.'

'So, your father is a fool,' Anton interjected as he leaned his body over the table, knocking his plate loudly. It spun for a moment before settling. 'That doesn't surprise me.'

Tolamin pulled Anton back. 'Calm down Anton.' Anton settled back in his seat. His face was fuelled with contempt. 'Prince Harlan is not his father.' Anton took in a deep breath to soothe himself and drank from his cup.

'Forgive my friend, he has suffered greatly at your father's hands,' The sovereign said as he bit the tip of his thumb. It looked to Maldwyn that he was picking food out of his teeth. 'Your father killed his people. Only the gods know why your father hates their power so much.' Tolamin avoided the prince's gaze and stared at the food on his plate. The sovereign watched his priest as he spun the ring on his long chain. 'Speaking of the gods... tell me, Your Grace, what do you know of the god Uller?' The sovereign's voice lilted in its usual melodic fashion.

Tolamin grabbed the ring hanging from a long, fine chain around his neck, and uttered a discreet oath. The priest pressed the ring to his lips.

'He's the God of Winter and the Hunt,' Prince Harlan answered.

'Yes... but, what do you really know of him? I mean Uller the man, not his role in divinity. What drives him?'

Tiana lit another pipe, hanging her supple body over Maldwyn's shoulder. With a gentle hand, she pulled his head around and blew the pungent smoke in his face. Maldwyn's head whirled as he yanked it back.

Prince Harlan didn't offer a reply to the sovereign's question. Frustrated, he rested back in his seat and banged his bound hands on the tabletop. His blood was kept on display.

'I'll tell you, sire.' The sovereign leaned forward, lowering his voice. Maldwyn struggled to focus his power on the conversation through his sickening trance from Tiana's pipe. 'He's driven by desire. By his passions. Uller loves the winter, because he can skate recklessly over the ice and snow, and he relishes the thrill of a hunt. For him, because of his passions, life is… intoxicating. Life is a drug, a rush, when you live it to its fullest. You,' the sovereign pointed at Prince Harlan, 'could learn a lot from him and live your life more for yourself.'

Temptation sparked upon the prince's face. He smirked at the mere thought of what he might do. Maldwyn wondered what desires Prince Harlan harboured.

'Why might I do that?'

Disappointed, the sovereign licked food from his fingers. 'Perhaps you're meant for more than being the King of Dresden, Your Grace.'

'What more is there? It is my destiny, my duty in life to be the king after my father. There are no other options for me.'

'You're right, of course.' The sovereign stroked his chin. 'It is your duty and destiny to eventually be king, but that is only one facet of your future. Let me put it to you this way... who is Harlan? Who are you other than the future king?'

Tiana shoved more food into Maldwyn's mouth. The concubines talked among themselves, taking turns smoking from the pipe. Prince Harlan looked over to Maldwyn. The prince's warm azure eyes charmed his hazy mind. The sovereign bent forward, close to the prince, who stared across the room to Maldwyn.

'You know what you're missing out on, Your Grace: Life.' The sovereign tapped the tip of his index finger three times on the table and offered a wry smile. He gulped down more of his wine. 'Besides...who knows,' the sovereign shrugged, 'maybe the sooner you learn to live your life beyond your father's rule, as opposed to just existing, the sooner the prophecies will reveal themselves.'

Prince Harlan drew his brows together. 'What does that mean?'

'Maybe nothing.' The sovereign reclined back in his chair, sipping from his goblet. 'Or, maybe something.'

The sovereign reached for some flatbread, tore off a piece and used it to scoop up the spiced, citrus-flavoured pulled meat on his plate. Prince Harlan continued to ignore his food while the other dignitaries picked at the range of dishes that splayed the length of the table.

'I must admit, I expected better from your father.' The sovereign wagged his finger at the prince.

'How so?'

Looking at Tolamin, the sovereign frowned. The shade from his hood accentuated the downward curvature of his mouth, emphasising his disapproving expression. 'When I first took you captive, I sent word to your father in an attempt to negotiate a treaty for the disputed lands, in particular, the mine.'

Prince Harlan lifted his head, interested in what the sovereign was about to say. Tiana burst out laughing beside Maldwyn at something one of the other women had said. She clapped her hands at the comment. Doubling his effort to listen to the conversation as the noise around him increased, Maldwyn shuffled forward to the edge of the couch and turned one ear toward the conversation.

'He refused to meet with me.' The sovereign's songlike accent somehow made the words seem less cruel. 'The Crown Prince of Dresden gets captured by the enemy, and the king doesn't want to discuss any terms that might secure you your freedom.' Prince Harlan's sullen face searched the room.

'I wish I could say it surprised me,' the prince admitted.

Maldwyn wanted to walk across the room and take the prince's hand in his, offering him the comfort he desperately needed. Tolamin rested his elbows on the table, clasped his hands together and propped his chin on his grasp. Anton cast a glance in Maldwyn's direction.

'Hmm, his response said something to the effect of not negotiating with his enemies. It puts me in a bit of an awkward position.' The sovereign pulled on the lobe of his ear. 'Deciding what to do with you, I mean.' Indicating to Maldwyn with his head, the sovereign continued. 'Your servant doesn't deserve to be treated like the enemy, he would have just been following your orders, as you followed your father's. Since you have begun to wear out your usefulness to me, I had your servant brought here tonight so that you could see for yourself that we have treated his wounds and are taking fine care of him while we decide what to do with you.'

The prince pulled on his restraints. They were clearly bothering him. 'What do you intend to do with me?'

Waving his hand, the sovereign beckoned to a small group of rangers that Maldwyn's hazy mind hadn't noticed until now. 'I thought about ransoming you, but your father wouldn't pay that either. So, I intend to keep you prisoner for now.'

The rangers pulled the prince up from his seat and led him out of the hall. Looking back over his shoulder, Prince Harlan stole one last glance at Maldwyn as he exited.

'Don't you think that was a bit much?' Anton waited for the doors to close and for the prince to be well and truly out of earshot before he posited the question. 'Not to mention, someone's been listening.'

From beneath his low hood, the sovereign's dark eyes looked up at Maldwyn. 'Are you sure he can hear us?'

Tolamin wrapped his hand around the ring at his chest. The concubines laughed at something behind him again. Tiana stroked Maldwyn's jawline. He tilted away from her. She rolled her eyes.

'I am certain. I can feel the disturbance from his power in the air all around us.' Anton held his hands out as though he could touch the air. 'He's listening.'

The sovereign, in a subtle gesture, waved at Maldwyn. Immediately, Maldwyn ceased using his power to eavesdrop. Their voices quieted until all he could hear was the spritely laughter of the concubines. His heart raced. They knew that he was listening, that he was using magic. How was that possible?

CHAPTER FOURTEEN

A Royal Prisoner

'WHAT WAS THAT BACK THERE?' Maldwyn spun on Anton when they were alone in the corridors, heading back to the Halls of Healing, Maldwyn's prison. This was his chance to appeal to the sorcerer, searching for answers. 'You know I have magic?'

The bump on Anton's nose protruded from his profile. 'Of course, I know! I am a sorcerer. It took me a while to realise there was a spark of magic inside you, but once I sensed it, there was no mistaking the power you have.'

Panicked, Maldwyn worried that they had told Prince Harlan about his abilities. His heart raced at the mere thought of it. Knowing King Viktor's harsh views on magic, Maldwyn reminded himself that he had no way to be sure of the prince's views.

Maldwyn didn't want his secret to put Prince Harlan in a position where he might need to compromise his beliefs, choosing between the servant whose life he had saved, and upholding his father's laws, sealing Maldwyn's fate. Besides, would the prince really wish Maldwyn to be executed like his father would? Maldwyn stroked his chin, perhaps the prince did not condemn magic. Perhaps he would not despise the power Maldwyn possessed.

Dizzied from worry, and the drugs that were still in his system, Maldwyn steadied himself with his hand against the warm, hard walls. His sweating palm slipped just a little.

'Maldwyn?' Anton tried to comfort him, placing a hand on his shoulder to help to support him. Maldwyn pushed Anton away. Angry and confused, Maldwyn tried to regulate his shortening breaths.

'Did you tell the prince?'

'About your power?'

'Yes.' Maldwyn's tongue glued to the roof of his dry mouth. He struggled to swallow. 'Did you tell him?'

'No.'

Relieved, Maldwyn closed his eyes. He breathed deep, until his mind calmed and his racing pulse eased. 'You told me I would see the prince.'

'You did see him.'

'I thought I was going to be able to speak with him!' Maldwyn heard that his own voice was thick with resentment.

Anton's regretful expression told Maldwyn he didn't agree with the torment. 'I am sorry, but the sovereign had other plans for the banquet. Once I told him you had magic, he chose to test you.'

'This was all a test?'

'Yes,' Anton hissed, looking frustrated. His deep voice bellowed all around Maldwyn. 'It was a test, and you both confirmed a few suspicions. You with your magic and the prince with his father. You both acted in exactly the way we expected.'

'Why is the sovereign doing this?'

Maldwyn pushed himself off the wall and stretched his neck. The world spun. Blackness crept into the edges of his vision. Resisting the urge to collapse, Maldwyn tensed the muscles in his thighs to keep himself upright.

'Everything the sovereign does has a purpose. I don't always agree with his methods, but his intentions are good.'

Maldwyn didn't know whether to believe Anton. So far, he hadn't given Maldwyn many reasons to trust him. Moreover, he knew he did not trust the sovereign, or Tolamin for that matter. There was only one way to know the value of Anton's words, and that was to speak to the prince.

If Maldwyn could talk with Prince Harlan, then he would know if the Erendil had shared the knowledge of his power. He would know whether Anton had lied to him about this matter. Plus, Maldwyn figured he would be able to find out where the prince was being kept. He would know what they had done to the prince in captivity. He would learn exactly what they had told the prince about why they were being held here. More than all of this, he would find out if the rumours of the prince saving his life were true.

'I want to speak with the prince.'

'I'm afraid I can't let you do that Maldwyn,' Anton told him flatly. 'Please, you can trust me. We need to get you back to the healing room.'

'Where you'll lock me away again?' Maldwyn stepped back as if he might attempt an escape. They knew he had magic. There was nothing stopping him from using it now, except his lack of control over his powers, and his want to keep this knowledge from Prince Harlan. 'If you really want me to trust you, then you need to take me to him. Unfortunately, your word isn't good enough for me.'

Ambivalent, Anton rubbed his forehead, considering the point Maldwyn had made. Maldwyn took another step back, ready to run at any moment. 'Will you return to the healing room with me willingly if I take you to see Prince Harlan?'

'Yes,' Maldwyn blurted. His trinket chains rattled as he moved closer to Anton, showing his willingness to cooperate.

'Alright... fine. I will take you to him.'

'And, I can speak with him?'

Anton pursed his lips and nodded. 'Come on, follow me.'

Maldwyn's pulse quickened. He hadn't spoken to the prince for weeks. For some reason he was nervous.

Weaving through the bright halls, they descended through the city into darkness, moving through cramped corridors that smelled of wet earth. These walls were rough and unfinished, carved from clay. The further they walked, the more Maldwyn realised this place was a network of tunnels that burrowed into the heart of a mountain.

He considered that realisation and noted that he had seen no windows since being in this place. The deposits of burning incense around the refined, higher traffic areas must have been used to defeat the damp, dirt smell. The heavy tiling and decorative surfaces kept the city pristine, and the air perfectly clear.

Unlike everywhere else Maldwyn had been in this extravagant city, these tunnels were simple and narrow. The walls were blank canvasses, and the torches that lit the way were spaced further and further apart.

Along the way, they passed several rangers that took little notice of them. Their earthy-hued robes were as graceful as ever.

Stopping at a rough, beaten table, manned by a lone ranger, Anton cleared his throat. The man peered up from beneath his dark, chestnut-coloured hood. His brown eyes gleamed with amber tones from the torchlight. Holding a large, flamboyant feather quill, the ranger brushed dust from the thick record book on the desk in front of him.

'Anton! How are you, friend?'

'Good, Jaecen. You?'

'Great!' The man glowed, ecstatic about something he was wanting to share. 'I found out my wife is pregnant.' His cheerful smile grew, extending up into his cheeks. 'Seems I'm going to be a father.'

'Congratulations! That's wonderful news!' Maldwyn scuffed his foot on the gritty ground, already tired of their pleasantries. Anton glared at his impatience. 'Anyway, I was hoping you might be able to sign us in to visit the prince's cell.'

Jaecen crossed his arms. The dense air made Maldwyn's head spin. He felt sick from whatever he had been forced to smoke. He was so close now and needed to hold on long enough to see the prince.

'Does the sovereign know he's here?'

'No,' Anton answered honestly. Maldwyn glared at Anton, who seemed to be sabotaging Maldwyn's chance to speak with Prince Harlan. 'But... I think it will be in everyone's best interest to grant us access.'

'Oh?'

'You must know that I have the sovereign's trust when it comes to our prisoners?'

'I do... and I will grant you access, but I will also tell the sovereign you've brought him here.'

'Understandable.'

The ranger shifted in his seat, the chair creaking below his weight. Jaecen uncrossed his arms. He dipped his quill into a small pot of ink and inscribed their names into his record book with smooth cursive, runic lines. Handing Anton a small iron key, Jaecen waved them through.

'You know his cell Anton. You may go.'

Thanking the ranger, Anton offered a final compliment for the news of his unborn child, and guided Maldwyn passed the desk. The confined hall was dark and poorly sculpted from hard clay. Still, it was much cleaner than the dungeons in Dresden.

Maldwyn's throat tightened when Anton halted at a door and placed the key in the lock. His anxiety grew at the thought of the prince being in the cell beyond the door. The lock clicked.

'I will wait for you here.' The depth of Anton's voice was so low it might have been a whisper. 'The sovereign won't be happy about this, so I recommend keeping it brief. Agreed?'

Maldwyn consented to Anton's suggestion. The door groaned as Maldwyn pushed it inward. Inside the cell, the floors were crafted from rough bricks of golden sandstone.

The walls were uneven with deep pits that created shadowy blotches from the dim light. A small bed, with sheets of poor quality that were bundled messily on top, was pushed into the corner against the back wall. A petite bedside table, with no doors or drawers, had several candles upon it. Wax piled at the base of each stem, running down the edges of the stand, like icicles collecting into slippery spears. The flames burned steadily from each candlestick.

Prince Harlan was sitting on the floor with his knees at his chest, and his head resting in his hands. Defeated, the prince ignored the open door and his visitor.

'Your Grace?'

Prince Harlan's head jerked up, his eyes gazing at Maldwyn. His chiselled features were more defined in the dim light. His strong arms fell to the sides of his legs, and he pushed himself up to stand. Rapt in disbelief, Prince Harlan stood quietly for a moment, filling Maldwyn with exuberance. The prince stepped forward in the dappled light.

'Maldwyn?'

'In the flesh,' Maldwyn answered. His mind felt far away. 'Are you alright, Your Grace?'

'I'm fine.' The prince, now standing close, studied Maldwyn with his intense stare. 'You? You're the one that keeps getting hurt.'

Maldwyn let out a breath that was like a laugh and offered the prince a grin. 'I'm okay, sire. I'm all healed up.'

Prince Harlan brought his tied hands up to the neck of Maldwyn's fancy tunic, assuming a comfortable familiarity, pulling back the fabric and exposing the dried, slow-healing gouge on his shoulder. Prince Harlan's hands were soft and warm, inspecting the sore. It was more itchy than painful now anyway.

'I'm okay,' Maldwyn reassured.

The prince let his shirt go. Maldwyn held his breath. The room whirled around him and, in his daze, Maldwyn felt he might finally collapse. Unsteady, he shifted, trying to fight the darkness consuming his sight.

Prince Harlan's hands seized his tunic, holding him up and guiding him to sit on the rock, hard bed. The mattress was a little spikey from the stuffing that filled it. The prince crouched in front of Maldwyn and checked his eyes. He looked worried.

'What's wrong with you?'

Maldwyn threw his head back against the dirt wall and let out a spontaneous laugh. He wasn't sure why he did that.

'They drugged me,' he admitted, rubbing his forehead. His mind was loud and confused. He thought he should offer the prince more conversation. 'You were supposed to leave me to die,' Maldwyn announced. He hated that he said that, it must have sounded so ungrateful.

'Sorry about that.' The prince's voice was sarcastic in tone. Considering their circumstances, Maldwyn supposed there may have been some truth to his remark.

'I didn't mean for that to sound—'

'Don't worry about it.'

The prince rested his bound hands on Maldwyn's bent knees. It was comfortable and tender. It reminded Maldwyn of Will, his touch had always felt calming and considerate. The memory of Will filled Maldwyn with a surge of grief that brought tears to his eyes, leaving him paralysed from the ache of his memory.

Maldwyn sniffed, and let the feeling go. Striving to settle himself, Maldwyn sat tall and reminded himself why he was here. It was clear the prince didn't know about his power. Prince Harlan would have said something by now if he had known. Still, there was more Maldwyn wanted to talk to the prince about, such as what he had learned of Mikel.

'Sire, I've heard things since being here… things I think you should know.'

'Okay?'

Maldwyn pinched the bridge of his nose and clenched his jaw, trying to think of the right words. 'Ser Mikel, sire… he's not a knight. He's your cousin: one of the grandsons of the King of Mordiallok. He's your mother's nephew.'

Prince Harlan shook his head in disbelief. Maldwyn leaned forward and reached for the prince's hands, catching his own piquant, woody perfume.

'It's true, sire.'

'Why?' the prince stammered.

Maldwyn remarked how soft and smooth the prince's unblemished hands were to touch. His shackles jangled, like bells warning him from being too close to the prince. Prince Harlan didn't seem to mind his caress.

'He's a spy.'

'What's he after?'

'The Erendil don't know. They thought he was meant to kill your father, but he hasn't. Instead, he told you about your mother's execution and he's stirring up trouble with rumours in Dresden.'

Maldwyn's eyelids grew heavy and he lost track of where his words were going. Looking at Prince Harlan's tightly bound hands, Maldwyn finally saw how badly the ropes had dug into his wrists. They were reddened from blisters and bruises, and Maldwyn felt guilty he hadn't noticed sooner.

'Your hands.' The words escaped his lips in a hushed mumble. Prince Harlan broke his stare, pulling his hands away.

Grabbing his thick, coarse bindings, Maldwyn brought the prince's hands closer and began loosening the restraints. Unravelling the wrappings, the cord gathered into a pile on the floor.

The prince gulped. 'You're probably going to get into trouble for that.' Maldwyn turned his hands over, assessing his red blotches. 'Thank you,' the prince murmured. With his free hands, the prince ran his fingers over Maldwyn's golden trinket handcuffs. 'If only I could break metal to return the favour.'

Maldwyn chuckled. The prince had no idea Maldwyn could likely use his power and remove the shackles at any moment, especially now he knew the Erendil were aware of his abilities.

Prince Harlan got off his knees and sat on the bed beside Maldwyn. His arms brushed against Maldwyn's, pulling at his silky tunic. Even sleepy from the drugs, Maldwyn's heart skipped.

Trying to focus, Maldwyn recalled what he had been talking about. He remembered it had something to do with Mikel. Then, Maldwyn realised that he had not mentioned that Mikel had stolen something from the Erendil.

'There's more, Your Grace. Mikel stole something from these people… something powerful. The Erendil want it back. Sire, if news about Iluvitar came from Mikel, then he lied. He had already taken what the Erendil had.'

'I guessed he had been wrong about the sword when the sovereign told us Iluvitar wasn't here. I figured, wherever Mikel had gotten his information was unreliable, or something. It hadn't crossed my mind that Mikel had lied.'

'You didn't think the sovereign lied about Iluvitar?'

Prince Harlan looked down. His thoughtful expression seemed a little troubled as he considered the sovereign for a moment.

'No, there's no vanity in it. The sovereign, well... he's all about showmanship. I would expect a man like that to boast about such a weapon, especially when his enemy—me— already believed it to be in their possession. More to the point, I am their prisoner. There's no reason for him to lie about it.' Prince Harlan scratched his head. 'The sovereign is a lot of things, but I get the feeling a liar isn't one of them. He's very careful with his words.'

Given that the prince didn't specifically mistrust the sovereign, Maldwyn considered that Anton had been right. Perhaps the sovereign's intentions were good, no matter how absurd his actions appeared.

'Do you think we can trust him?'

'I'm not sure I would go that far. I'm not clear about what he's after, especially since my father won't negotiate with him.' The prince half-smiled. 'Everything the sovereign does has a deeper meaning. I just wish I knew what he wanted, so I could get us out of this.'

Prince Harlan sat forward, gripping the edge of the bed. His knuckles whitened. The prince's jaw was clenched from his frustration, and his stare was fixed on the cell door.

Maldwyn studied his jawline. It was smooth, square and slightly angled downward from the way the prince held his head. The light from the bedside candles shaded the part where Prince Harlan's jaw met his strong, tall neck.

The way the prince struggled to work out what the sovereign wanted reminded Maldwyn to stop dwelling on his affections. Maldwyn concentrated his thinking on the Erendil. He pondered the sovereign's interest in the prophecies and Firebird. Maldwyn knew so little about both things.

'Sire, what is the Valuwan Prophecy?'

Prince Harlan looked back at Maldwyn, brows furrowed. 'It's, um… not exactly something that makes sense, and I don't know the proper wording. It has something to do with uniting the realm and bringing about a time of peace.'

Prince Harlan rubbed his sore wrists. The movement of his arms reminded Maldwyn of how close he was sitting. Maldwyn held in a shiver.

'And, Firebird?'

'A myth… probably. He's supposed to be very powerful.'

'Like a sorcerer?'

The prince turned his head to the side and clicked his tongue. 'Not exactly. He's supposed to be more powerful than that.'

Maldwyn wiped his gritty eyes. Head reeling, Maldwyn sunk into the jagged, earthen wall. He could feel his consciousness slipping.

'How did you get Master Damyan to tell you about your mother?'

Prince Harlan was taken aback. The question appeared to have struck the prince as suddenly as it had Maldwyn. He seemed as if he were considering telling Maldwyn the answer to his query.

'I suppose I can trust you to keep a secret.' Maldwyn nodded, feeling very tired. 'That sorcerer who was executed— not long before we left Dresden—told me that Master

Damyan, and another who he didn't know, used to hide sorcerers and other people that could be linked to magic in the castle, helping them to escape the king.' Bearing a guilty expression, Prince Harlan bit his cheek. 'That letter I had you deliver to him... it was a letter blackmailing Master Damyan.'

'You didn't tell your father?'

'No. It was more useful for me to keep the information to myself for the time being.'

Maldwyn's eyes grew weary and he felt sluggish. 'Have you learned who the accomplice was?'

'No.' Prince Harlan scratched behind his ear. 'I didn't think he'd answer that question no matter what I blackmailed him with. Besides, there are other ways to learn that sort of information.'

The blank, bleak walls loomed out of the blackness. Maldwyn took note of how awful and wrong it was that Prince Harlan had been left to rot in this dank prison chamber, unfit to host royalty. It was made worse when Maldwyn fathomed that he, a worthless servant, was being held in the extravagant Halls of Healing.

At some point, the prince had leaned against the wall too. His head rested right next to Maldwyn's.

'I should be here instead of you.' Prince Harlan faced Maldwyn and sighed. Maldwyn felt his warm breath brush his neck and he wondered what the prince was thinking. 'Why did you save me?'

Hesitant to speak, Prince Harlan's enchanting blue eyes were fierce with magnetism. The prince took in a deep breath.

'What do you mean?'

'When I was dying in the cave, you promised to leave me and save yourself. You were meant to make it back to Dresden. The Erendil told me you brought me here. Why?'

'Well, you, um… fell asleep. I had planned on leaving you. I was just going to wait with you until it was all over… so you wouldn't be alone.' Prince Harlan scratched his nose. 'While you slept, you were deteriorating and your breaths sounded, um… well, they kind of rattled. You were struggling so hard to breathe, and it was really difficult to listen to. I couldn't ignore it, and I just couldn't let you die.' The prince's crystal eyes shone in the dappled light, like shimmering stars. 'I figured that—since it was poison killing you—the Erendil would have the cure. They would be fools to poison arrows without keeping an antidote around. So, I brought you here… for healing.'

Prince Harlan's scent was leathery and carried overtones of his sweat from weeks spent in captivity. Maldwyn noted how soft the prince's lips appeared. He thought of the fiction he had created in his mind: the one where the prince had kissed him in the damp cave. Maldwyn felt overcome. He tore his eyes away, reminding himself of his station.

'Thank you,' Maldwyn mumbled. His distant mind grew ashamed of his desires and Maldwyn wanted to flee, hiding from the prince as though he might read his thoughts.

Maldwyn sat in silence, growing more and more distant and reflective. The prince's strong, cosy hands grasped around Maldwyn's. His cuffs jingled. Prince Harlan offered Maldwyn a soothing squeeze.

Tired, Maldwyn moved his head on the wall. Its bumpy surface scratched his scalp. Gently, the prince ran his hand along Maldwyn's forearm, making him tremble. Prince Harlan's caress ceased when his hand reached Maldwyn's bicep, coaxing him closer, until Maldwyn's head lay on the prince's shoulder. Prince Harlan sniffed and rested his head on Maldwyn's.

'I'm sorry I got us into this mess.' The prince's voice was low and smooth.

'You're not responsible for their actions.'

Comfortable and tired, Maldwyn thought he might drift off in the prince's embrace. His drugged, hazy mind was soothed by the prince's touch.

Prince Harlan slipped his hand along the small of Maldwyn's lower back, resting his hold on Maldwyn's waist. Nestling his jaw on the top of Maldwyn's head, Prince Harlan gripped Maldwyn's palm with his free hand.

'Rest now. You'll feel better when you've rested.'

Maldwyn let himself be at ease. His sandy eyes scratched the back of his eyelids. The prince's even breaths tickled Maldwyn's hair. He closed his eyes, letting himself rest, forgetting that Anton was waiting for him outside the prison cell. Eventually, in the quiet comfort, Maldwyn fell into the dreamworld. For the first time in quite a while, Maldwyn's dreams were calm and auspicious.

CHAPTER FIFTEEN

A Meeting with Sovereignty

EVERY NOW AND AGAIN, Maldwyn shifted beneath the prince's comfortable hold. He was very aware of the places where their bodies met. Prince Harlan's warm breath tickled the nape of his neck, sensitive to the slightest brush.

At some point, while Maldwyn slept, he had fallen from the prince's broad, cosy shoulder and laid down on the small, hard bed. The rough sheets were pulled up over Maldwyn's body, and his arms hugged his chest. The candles on the bedside table smelled buttery, and had burned down considerably, puddles of wax set into a solid rippled pool.

Prince Harlan had tucked himself in behind Maldwyn, laying on top of the sheets. His arm was draped over Maldwyn's side. The gentle weight of the prince's arm had him tense all over. The rise and fall of his chest against Maldwyn's back was a tormenting reminder of the prince's closeness.

Secure in Prince Harlan's embrace, Maldwyn wanted to stay in this moment and dwell. The prince wriggled in tighter behind Maldwyn, legs pushing into the back of his knees. The prurient sensation of the prince's hips pressing into him had Maldwyn's heart hammering in his chest. Prince Harlan's hand twitched.

Maldwyn bit his lower lip. He needed to put some distance between them. Slipping his fingers over the prince's smooth knuckles, shackles rattling just a little, Maldwyn carefully lifted the prince's arm, slipped back the sheets and slid out from beneath him.

Prince Harlan didn't wake.

Maldwyn stood and gazed at the sleeping prince. He neared the bed, crouching beside Prince Harlan, and studied his restful face. His features were flawless and his long, dark lashes curled out from his closed eyelids. Mouth slightly parted, Maldwyn listened to the prince's idle breaths.

He reached out to stroke the prince's perfect face with the back of his hand, never actually making contact. His cuffed hands floated in the air above Prince Harlan, feeling the humming of the space between them. He was fastidious not to wake the prince.

The prince was very handsome, in an effortless kind of way. Will had always been like that. Maldwyn thought of Will, and how much the pain of losing him hurt. Though he thought of Will less and less over time, the intensity of his loss never diminished.

Maldwyn swallowed.

Since being captive, his thoughts had centred around Prince Harlan. Where he was being held by the Erendil, how they were treating him, when Maldwyn might be able to see him, or why the prince had rescued Maldwyn from the brink of death. Maldwyn had also thought a lot about their imagined kiss. The way the prince's soft lips pressed against his in a tender fashion felt like both a promise of something more, and a bittersweet goodbye as he journeyed to the afterlife.

But, of course, that had been his imagination, and this was reality. This was becoming his never. A fiction that would live in his head.

Outside, Maldwyn heard distant murmurs. He remembered Anton was waiting, and that he had promised to have a brief meeting with the prince. Maldwyn hadn't expected coming down from his high to have made him so tired and confused. Nor had he expected the prince's strong shoulders to have been quite so warm as Prince Harlan caressed Maldwyn into a world of peaceful dreams.

Maldwyn replayed the moment in his head. The prince's hand on his lower back had felt soothing, and his other hand wrapped around Maldwyn's, heated him to his core. *Rest now. You'll feel better when you've rested.* Prince Harlan's voice had been low and calming, like a berceuse. Maldwyn smiled at the memory.

The door whined open. Maldwyn abruptly backed away from the bed, noting that the prince still didn't wake. The sovereign leaned on the door frame, his arms crossed and cloak flowing elegantly as usual. He lowered his hooded head in a judgemental fashion, glancing at the sleeping prince.

'You need to come with me,' the sovereign whispered.

Prince Harlan stirred. Maldwyn felt torn. He had promised Anton he would leave willingly, but he wanted to stay, unsure of when they would allow him to see the prince again.

'What if I don't go with you?' Maldwyn asked, keeping his voice as quiet as possible. He reached for his power and felt it brimming, ready to defend him if unleashed.

'I wouldn't.' The sovereign warned, unfolding his arms. 'Let me level with you… you have magic, but you have very little control over it. Anton has spent his life studying sorcery. You're not ready to take him on.'

Gulping, Maldwyn knew the sovereign was right. There was no way he was a match for Anton.

Taking one final look at the prince, Maldwyn made a mental note of how he would savour this memory, not knowing when he might see him next. Maldwyn considered waking Prince Harlan, so that he would know Maldwyn was leaving, but he didn't want to disturb him. He looked so calm.

Stepping forward, Maldwyn followed the sovereign out of the prince's cell, the door quietly clicking shut behind him. Anton waited in the hall.

'I hope you and the prince caught up on everything.' Anton eyeballed Maldwyn, before shooting a bothered expression at the sovereign.

They were obviously at odds about something. Maldwyn mulled over what they might have been talking about in the hall, prior to opening the door to the prince's cell. Whatever it was, they weren't seeing eye to eye.

'Maldwyn, follow me. We have a lot to talk about,' the sovereign told him. Anton's disapproving glare made Maldwyn uneasy.

The sovereign led the way out of the dungeon. Together, the three of them left the oppressive prison, returning to the bright, untainted, impressive halls, filled with elaborate baroque embellishments, teeming with the elegantly robed Erendil.

* * * * *

The sovereign took Maldwyn to a wide office room with saffron golden-coloured walls. The ivory-tinted tiling was bordered around the edges of the room with marigold-shaded mosaics in a geometric pattern. Sandalwood incense burned from a theatrical stand. Piles of paper were spread out over the tabletop in a disorderly state. The chair behind the desk was ornate, carved with perfection from oak beams, and its high back reached toward the domed roof. Another two short-backed, simpler chairs with cushions that were less plump than the seat behind the desk, were tucked away in front of the table.

The sovereign glided into the room, finally formally introducing himself to Maldwyn as Jerrik Taramae, and sat behind the desk. He indicated for Maldwyn and Anton to take the other two seats. The cushion was soft and moulded to Maldwyn's form under his weight.

'How long have you known I have magic?' Maldwyn looked from Anton to the sovereign, and back again.

Anton gestured for Jerrik to reply.

'Only for a few days.' The sovereign's melodic accent was soothing as usual. He stroked his clean, shaven chin. His eyes were dark and shaded beneath his hood. 'When Anton sensed you using your power at the banquet, our suspicions were confirmed.'

'Suspicions?'

'Maybe you should explain it to him,' the sovereign said to Anton, who looked troubled. 'Anton, doesn't think we should give you answers. He's worried that it will prevent things from unfolding as they are supposed to. I have reminded him, that prophecies cannot be averted.'

Anton sighed. 'Maldwyn, I believe… we believe—since the prince told us he was alive—that you are Firebird.'

Maldwyn pulled back. He raised his eyebrows, incredulous at the ridiculous notion.

'Me? Firebird? That's ridiculous!'

'Yes, Maldwyn,' Anton replied emphatically, leaning over the arm of his chair. 'Your power is unlike anything I've ever known before. Your magic is pure.'

If it weren't for the serious expressions on both of their faces that told Maldwyn they were being sincere, Maldwyn would have thought he was in the middle of some sort of cruel joke. The sovereign shifted some papers and pulled out a thick, leather-bound book, holding it as if it were precious.

'This is for you.' Jerrik slid the book across the table, over to where Maldwyn sat.

Picking up the book, his shackles sounded as he inspected the hardcover. There were unusual markings inscribed on the front. The designs of the cursive language were not familiar. He guessed it was not written in the common tongue.

'What is this?'

'This is an ancient text written by the god Kvasir.' Anton spoke in a loud voice that boomed, proud to share his knowledge of magic and the gods. 'This book outlines the origins of the gods' power, and—we feel—that it might help you to understand your power.'

'How could a book about the gods help me understand my power?'

'Your power is your own, much like the gods.' Anton chewed on his lower lip. 'The rest of us who practice sorcery, tap into their divine power. The magic comes from them, it is not our own.'

Maldwyn scratched his head, still clinging to the notion that his being Firebird was ridiculous. 'What language is this?' Maldwyn asked as he placed the book in his lap, figuring it would be of no help since he wasn't able to read it.

'This is the language of the gods,' the sovereign told him, pointing at the words on the cover. 'It says: The Power of Divinity. Very few people can read this. The book was translated into the common tongue and—after someone used the knowledge of the book to mess with the natural order of the world—the original was destroyed. This is the translated copy of the book and was given to we Erendil to protect. Beneath the cover, the words are in the common tongue. I am giving it to you.'

'Why are you giving it to me?'

Anton glared at Jerrik. Maldwyn figured he didn't agree with the sovereign's choice to give Maldwyn the book. Jerrik placed his elbows on the desk.

'I believe the book will be safe with you,' the sovereign said, more for Anton's sake than for Maldwyn's. 'Plus, I believe it may give you some answers.'

Maldwyn considered rejecting the offer, but he guessed from the expression on Jerrik's face that the sovereign would not have taken the book back. A part of him doubted the sovereign's actions but, since speaking with Prince Harlan, he pushed the feeling aside, considering that he might have good intentions.

'What about the prince and me?' Maldwyn leaned forward and felt the smoothness of the lacquered tabletop. His shackles caught on the edge of the desk. The sandalwood burning in the background seized Maldwyn's attention.

Anton scratched his chin and turned his gaze away. He signalled for the sovereign to answer Maldwyn's question.

'I am willing to give you both your freedom, if you help me with something.' Jerrik clasped his hands, interlocking his long fingers. His nails were trimmed and well-kept.

'What must I do?' Maldwyn asked, a little tentative about the answer to come. He looked at Anton, who was still giving no indication as to what the sovereign wanted from him.

'Anton tells me you overheard that something was stolen from us.' The sovereign slumped back in his seat, but his eyes were inquisitive. 'Mikel has come to you for information about the royal family before, has he not?'

Worried, Maldwyn felt his facial muscles tighten. He was nervous about what the sovereign wanted him to do to buy their freedom. Maldwyn thought of the memory of the prince's sleeping face, calm and flawless, and decided he couldn't leave Prince Harlan alone, rotting in that awful cell. It was up to Maldwyn to bargain for the prince's freedom.

'He has.' Maldwyn picked the skin around his fingernails and fixed his gaze on the sovereign, trying to keep what little control he had over his anxiety. 'What did he steal?'

Anton crossed his arms and turned back to face Maldwyn. 'The mine in the Anhalt Mountains has been a disputed territory between the Erendil and the king in Dresden for some time. As you are aware, the mine is currently under the Erendil's control.' The sovereign remained quiet. 'A while back, they found something other than iron ore in that mine.'

Maldwyn turned on his seat to better face Anton, interested in the information they were about to share. 'What did they find?'

'A gemstone called draconite.' The bump on Anton's nose was quite subtle from this angle and his tanned skin was more bronzed in the golden room. 'This stone has certain magical properties.' Anton waved his hand.

'What can it do?'

Jerrik sat tall again. 'We're not completely sure.'

Anton shot a glance at the sovereign. He had intended to answer, but the sovereign interrupted him.

'We were only able to identify what the stone was right before Mikel stole it. Anton hasn't found any information telling us what it can do. All we know is that it is a sort of gemstone which forms from the scales of a deceased dragon. It's incredibly rare to find—'

'Which is why there is so little information about it,' Anton finished the sovereign's sentence for him, seeming a bit annoyed that he had stolen his thunder. 'I think—from the information that I have managed to locate—that the stone is a potent magical ingredient in spells, specifically curses.'

'Since finding this stone,' Jerrik chimed in, waving a hand for Anton to stop rambling. 'We are protecting the mine more than ever.'

Maldwyn remembered hearing that the disputes along the border had increased in frequency when he was still in Dresden. 'Do you think there are more stones in the mine?'

'Yes,' Anton quickly replied. 'Where there is one, we think there might be more. A dragon must have died in that cave centuries ago, and—since we know the conditions are perfect for creating draconite—there likely is more than one of these gemstones in that mine.'

'So, Mikel has this stone. What do you want from me?'

The sovereign's hellish grin curled up the sides of his cheeks. 'I want you to stop Mikel from using the stone and to make sure he doesn't share this information with King Viktor. If the King of Dresden learns about the draconite in the mine, he will start an all-out war for control over the region, which we could never win.'

'How did Mikel know what the stone was? He's not a sorcerer.' Maldwyn watched Anton's regretful expression. 'Why was he here in the mountains with you?'

Reluctant, Anton turned away again, scratching at the nape of his neck. 'I'm afraid that was my fault. Mikel came to us from Mordiallok, claiming he had been sent by King Filip to improve relations in the region. He was here for quite a few months, and over time he confessed that he had been tasked with spying on Dresden and developing a plan to avenge the death of Queen Sonia. As King Viktor is responsible for murdering a great many sorcerers and anyone who is so much as believed to be a magic sympathiser, no one moved to stop Mikel.'

Jerrik let out a breath. 'In fact, we might have helped him by finding the draconite.'

'He was here when we found the draconite,' Anton explained, motioning his hands in unison with his words. 'When I figured out what the gemstone was, Mikel was there and I left the stone with him, unattended.'

The sovereign held his hands out, palms open and facing upward. 'It was when Anton returned with me to tell me what he had learned, that we realised Mikel had fled, and taken the piece of draconite with him.'

Maldwyn considered the draconite being a magical ingredient, which was in Mikel's possession. He noted that it explained why Mikel had been hoping Princess Cassara was a seer that may have also studied sorcery in secret. It also gave meaning to why Mikel mentioned needing a sorcerer. He wanted someone to use the draconite for him.

'So, what happened when he left here?' Maldwyn asked, hoping for more answers that might fill the gaps in time between when Mikel had fled the Anhalt Mountains and appeared in Dresden.

'He went to Karana Downs,' the sovereign answered. 'By the time we learned he had been there, he had already moved on to Dresden. We sent someone after him, but he quickly disappeared.'

Maldwyn recalled how edgy Mikel had been in the servant halls the day he delivered the letter to Prince Harlan. This had been the last night he had been seen by anyone other than Maldwyn.

Jerrik pushed some papers around the table and clasped his hands. 'We don't know what he did to buy his entrance into Karana Downs, or what was agreed upon between him and the lord of that region, to have him placed in Dresden as the liaison officer for Karana Downs. That's something we still have no answer to.'

Maldwyn locked his ankles together under his seat. 'Why do you think I might be able to stop Mikel? He may have already told the king of the stones, or by now he could have cursed him.'

'The king would have invaded the mountains if he suspected there was more to the mine than the iron ore. Plus, Mikel came to you once, chances are, he will come again,' the sovereign answered in a hushed speculating tone. 'If the king has been cursed, then there is nothing that can be done. I am more concerned about ensuring the knowledge is kept from the court in Dresden. We cannot win if war breaks out, and we cannot rely on anyone in the region to aid us against the king. Everyone would want a piece of the mine.'

'If I do find Mikel, how am I meant to stop him?' Maldwyn couldn't work out how he was meant to do what Jerrik was asking. 'How am I meant to know if the king is cursed or if Mikel gave King Viktor any information?'

'Mikel is an arrogant man. He won't lie to you. He will boast about anything he has achieved.' Anton clicked his tongue. 'That's also why we're giving you the book.'

Maldwyn wondered how the book would be of help to him, thinking that he had been getting better at using his power on his own. Since leaving Dresden, Maldwyn had used his magic several times and gotten away with it. He had become better at focusing his abilities and, with time, felt he might be able to control it. The real question was: could he continue to get away with it once he was back in Dresden, where he could not use his power so freely?

'If I agree to help you, you will free the prince?'

'Yes.' The sovereign sounded sly. 'He has his role to play and without him, you might never get back inside the palace.'

Maldwyn noted that Anton had a cunning expression. Thinking about the sovereign's comment about the prince's role to play, Maldwyn remembered the Valuwan Prophecy.

'What is the Valuwan Prophecy?'

'It's not something you need to worry about for quite some time,' Anton reassured. 'There are a great many prophecies about Firebird—and the Lynx—and the Valuwan Prophecy might just be the last in the sequence.'

The Lynx had been mentioned as a figure in the Quandiallan Prophecy Maldwyn had learned of when tending to the sorcerer in the dungeons of Dresden. Maldwyn also considered the prince's armour having the lynx rampant on his chest. He pondered what that might mean.

Having a feeling that they weren't going to share any more information about the prophecies, especially judging by the way they gave such a cryptic answer to Maldwyn's question, he turned his mind back to the deal they were offering: Prince Harlan and their freedom, in exchange for Mikel and the knowledge of the draconite.

'I'll do it,' Maldwyn answered, striving to free the prince from that awful cell.

Knowing that the prince wouldn't be on board with this offer, and recognising that he didn't want to put the prince in a position where he would have to go along with breaking his father's laws, Maldwyn wondered how the sovereign would spin this.

'But as this has to do with magic, it is in all of our interests not to tell Prince Harlan. The prince will be suspicious if you just let us go. How do you plan on giving us our freedom?'

The sovereign sat back coolly and wiggled down into his seat. 'Don't worry, I have a plan.'

Maldwyn was worried, he hated being in the dark. At that, the conversation was over and Anton led Maldwyn back to the healing room. He laid back on the soft bed, the chiffon drapes swaying from the roof around him. Closing his eyes, he missed the prince's warmth beside him.

CHAPTER SIXTEEN

Free from Chains

MALDWYN WAS SITTING ON THE BED, running his fingers over the leather-bound book, feeling the inscriptions on the cover. He had thumbed through the aged, crinkled pages, which crunched as he turned them over. The ancient, musty parchment had a smell that reminded Maldwyn of a mixture of vanilla beans and freshly cut grass. He had tried to make sense of the words written inside, but found Kvasir's convoluted use of language to be overly frustrating, making the text difficult to follow and to draw any meaning from.

Irritated, Maldwyn rubbed along his eyebrows with his index finger and thumb of one hand, relieving the tension that had built up along his forehead. He had begun to feel a headache coming on and let out an exhausted breath.

So far, all Maldwyn had gathered from the book was that magic was an ever-present force, which was the final mark of divinity in the world of mankind, singing all around as if calling to the gods. According to Kvasir, this power originated from a place of equally intense cold and heat, where the two opposing energies intertwined into a frozen, molten pool in the Yawning Void.

This place was an impossible, silent abyss, that was empty of all senses and exploded with pure, raw, power, birthing the cosmos into being. The power that burst forth was primordial, even more ancient than the gods themselves. Maldwyn scratched his cheek as he thought about magic being older than the gods for a moment.

The soft, leather cover of the book was worn and slightly cracked in places. Taking a break from reading the rambling text, Maldwyn looked over at the ordered benchtop. By now, he had learned every facet of the healing room.

The floating chiffon was whimsical, having either a bothering or calming effect depending on Maldwyn's mood. The colourful, plump, silk pillows on the bench seat were perfectly arranged. Anton was always checking that everything was in its place.

In his time here, Maldwyn had inspected the countertop, learning the labels on the shimmering vials that were stored in a timber stand. There were also a number of other extracts and tinctures that did not fit inside the stand and were lined up along the benchtop, including a small phial of bilberry extract, a round bottle of dried yarrow leaves, a larger container of yellow bulbous flowers which was labelled bitter buttons, and a pastel lavender coloured tincture of valerian root. The glazed, teal amphorae were smooth and glossy to the touch, and held a variety of liquids, ranging from fresh water to rich, boozy substances for sterilising and cleaning wounds.

Maldwyn was conflicted, he both disliked and appreciated this place. Its beauty was unrivalled, but it had been tainted by his capture. He sighed.

The door blew open. Anton strutted into the room. The autumn-coloured draperies swung freely from the roof.

'Maldwyn... come with me!' Anton's baritone voice reverberated off the pale sand-coloured stone walls. He was walking tall, with his chest pushed out. Maldwyn could tell he was in a good mood.

'Where are we going?'

Maldwyn placed the book on the bed beside him and stood up, scratching his wrists where the metal cuffs itched his skin. Lately, the shackles were troubling him.

'Outside,' Anton answered, rushing back out the door. Having not breathed in the fresh air for so long, Maldwyn was quick to follow him.

Guided through some familiar halls, Maldwyn was brought to a grand spiral staircase that wound higher and higher up the mountainous city. The marble, paved steps were wide and rose on a gentle incline. There was a humungous candelabra that hung overhead, with delicate, clear crystals dangling down from the fixture, casting white reflections on the surrounding tiles. The roof—high above them—was domed, and had a swirling, tiled pattern that watched over them.

Reaching out with his hands, Maldwyn touched the perfect, velvety surface of the spectacular balustrade, which was sculpted out of an almost colourless stone. Its geometric patterns repeated up the entire length of the staircase.

Leading the way, Anton would glance back and smile at Maldwyn every now and again. Maldwyn, busy taking in the incredible architecture, barely noticed that Anton was checking on him.

When they arrived at the top of the great set of stairs, Tiana stood with her hands resting over the railing, waiting for them to join her. Tiana's long, dark locks were swept over one shoulder, and her eyes were heavily made-up.

'Maldwyn, it's good to see you again.' Her raspy voice carried the lyrical accent of the people from this region. She held her hip out to one side. Her white and gold flowery dress was fitted, hugging the lines of her body. There was something about her confidence that irked him. She verged on the edge of cocky, perhaps even a little conceited. 'Anton, thank you for bringing him here.'

Grinning, Anton gestured for Maldwyn to follow her as she headed toward two massive, carved doors. Placing a hand on each door, she pushed them open and stepped outside. A cold wind swept in from the door, giving Maldwyn a shiver.

Stepping over the threshold, Maldwyn realised this was a sort of outdoor platform, like a balcony, that overlooked the wooded ranges from the mount's peak. Below, the mountain seemed to drop.

The slope was so steep that, if it weren't for the dense layer of trees, Maldwyn might have thought it was the face of a cliff. Many of the trees had dropped their multicoloured coats, covering the ground in a carpet of leaves that were—in the evening's moonlight—a range of grey tones. In the light of day, Maldwyn knew these leaves would be a variety of red, orange, and yellow hues.

Looking around the sandstone-paved platform, Maldwyn noted that there was no balustrade. The edge of the space fell away with the mountain.

Above them, the crescent moon beamed, curling up into a comfortable foetal position. The stars were twinkling like glittering diamonds.

Tiana breathed in the cold night air, arms out at her sides, palms facing up at the night sky. Maldwyn too took in the cleansing pine-scented air, letting it fill his lungs. It had been so long since he had been outside, that Maldwyn almost forgot what fresh air smelled like, or the way the night sky hummed with shimmering stars, like a gentle harp making no sound at all, soothing the world with its silent unsung lullaby.

Tiana moved off to the left and gracefully sat down on a stone bench that looked out overland as far as the eye could see.

'Sit down,' she commanded. Maldwyn hesitated, not trusting her since he had first met her in the baths. 'Please... I only want to talk.'

Maldwyn's shoes clacked as he made his way over to where Tiana was seated. A cold wind could be felt through the sleeves of his silky tunic. He placed himself down on the bench beside the beautiful concubine.

Tiana straightened her gown, flattening the creases over her knees. 'I wanted to take the opportunity to speak with you one on one, before you are freed from custody.'

'Then, you are aware of the agreement between the sovereign and me?'

'I am.' Tiana stroked her skirt, fixing its placement again. 'I am also aware of the offer he is going to make the prince.'

'Really?' Sitting up taller, Maldwyn wedged his ankles together. 'Can you tell me about the offer?'

'We're not here to talk about that.' Tiana turned her gaze back up to the stars. Maldwyn considered what she wanted to discuss. 'We're a lot alike... you and me.'

Maldwyn made a perplexed expression, pursing his lips, scrunching his nose and bringing his brows together. He couldn't begin to imagine what Tiana was implying. 'I don't know about that.'

Tiana laughed. 'That's okay.' She brushed her hair behind her ear. 'What I am trying to say is: we are both less than the people we serve.'

'Ah.' Maldwyn dropped his gaze. He felt his power simmering, and thought of how Anton and the sovereign were convinced he was Firebird.

Maldwyn had always feared his abilities, viewing his magic as some sort of wicked abomination, just as his mother had taught him. Wanting so much to believe that he wasn't awful, Maldwyn wished Anton was right, and that there was some benevolent reason for his powers, but he knew the truth: he was worthless. Good things didn't happen to people like him.

Ashamed, Maldwyn held his head in his hands. The shackles about his wrists sounded, reminding him that, even among people who believed him to be important, he was at the bottom of society. He was a prisoner in his class.

Stroking her hair, Tiana gathered it back over her shoulder. 'I am a concubine Maldwyn. A role I was born into. I was raised in the art of desire and seduction, and—when I came of age—I began serving my masters.' She twisted on the seat to better face Maldwyn. 'I may be Erendil, but I can't wear the robes of my people.' She pulled his hands away from his face. 'My oppression is more subtle than yours in Dresden, but the feeling of being invisible, that is the same.'

Maldwyn looked up at the stars that sparkled above them, like the rest of society. 'Why am I here? Why are you telling me this?'

'Because I want to apologise. I didn't know what Anton and the sovereign believed of you the other night. The sovereign told us to drug you and to bring you along as a part of the evening's entertainment.' Tiana smirked. 'Knowing what I know now, I suppose he felt you might be more likely to use your magic if your inhibitions were lowered. He wanted to confirm that you did indeed have your own power. That you were Firebird.'

'Why would he want to do that?'

Tiana paused. 'The sovereign has his reasons.' Maldwyn noted that she was careful not to betray Jerrik. 'I wanted to take the time to remind you of something… something Anton and the sovereign couldn't possibly understand that you struggle with. Something that will get in your way if you let it.'

'What might that be?' Maldwyn clenched his jaw.

'That you have value. That you are what you do, not what you think, or what some other people might even tell you.'

Maldwyn laughed in a nervous way. 'Is this the part where you tell me I matter because I'm Firebird?'

'It could be.' Tiana scrunched up her nose. 'But, I'm not Anton, or the sovereign. Firebird doesn't matter that much to me. You, on the other hand, do.'

Maldwyn rubbed the skin around his eye, feeling the bone of his eye socket. Tiana crossed her legs.

'Let me explain it to you like this: the past doesn't matter anymore, it's over, it can't be changed; and the future isn't here yet, so who knows what happens along the way, who knows how we get there. Even seers are making educated guesses. It's the present that is important... the here and now. It's the only thing we can truly do anything about. Right now, that is you, not Firebird.'

Maldwyn softened and slackened his perfect posture. The cool evening air was purifying. 'Then you might be the only one who thinks that.'

Tiana tilted her head to the side. 'I don't agree. I think your prince feels the same. It's his father that is consumed with the prophecies, trying to prove they can be averted. Prince Harlan is not his father. He showed that when he decided you were worth saving.'

A lump clogged Maldwyn's throat as he thought about the prince, carefully considering what his views on magic and the prophecies were. Maldwyn took into account Anton's suggestion that the prince was likely the product of King Viktor's hatred. He looked at the floor, remembering the execution he had witnessed, and pondered whether the prince would see him burn for his power.

'He would have me executed if he knew about my abilities.' Maldwyn heard that his own voice was resolved as though what he had said was a well-known fact.

'Do you really believe that?' Tiana leaned closer. She rested her head on her hand, waiting for his answer.

'Sometimes, I do.'

Maldwyn swallowed the lump in his throat. He thought of all the reasons that Prince Harlan would want him dead if he ever learned of Maldwyn's power. Maldwyn was a nobody, a servant at the bottom of the scrapheap of the populace, a man infected with the depravity of magic, a fiendish perversion he had woven so deep into the fabric of his being, that Maldwyn did not believe he could ever be separated from it.

He was a man without value.

Or was he? Tiana believed Maldwyn was a good person who mattered. Anton and the sovereign believed Maldwyn was an awesome figure from prophecy, and that his power was a gift from the gods. Prince Harlan believed that, despite his status, Maldwyn was worth saving. Maldwyn scratched his head.

'Sometimes, I don't.' Conjuring up the fantasy of his imagined kiss with the prince, Maldwyn smirked. 'So, I guess it depends on the day you ask me.'

'Maybe one day you'll find out the truth… what Prince Harlan really thinks about magic, the world and his father. For what it's worth, I believe you will achieve extraordinary things, and that the prince will make a fine king someday.'

An owl hooted from somewhere far away. A moth flew by them as a gentle breeze told Maldwyn to shiver. Footsteps echoed inside.

'Remember, you are more than your thoughts. Don't let your fears hold you back, or we might never really meet Firebird.' Tiana stood. 'One last thing… it seems congratulations are in order, you're about to be a free man.'

Tiana turned and walked off, gliding through the wide-open doors, and disappearing back down the hall. The footsteps in the corridor halted, probably to acknowledge Tiana. Figuring it would be Anton coming to bring Maldwyn back to the healing room, he leaned forward, resting his forearms on his knees.

Maldwyn watched over the swaying silhouettes of the naked trees; their limbs were tickling the stars. A wolf howled at the moon. Leaves rustled as something dashed through the bushes, scurrying away from the predatory sound. A gust whipped around Maldwyn, carrying the tangy scent of the woods.

Reflective, Maldwyn took no notice of the figure that moved through the doorway, joining him on the expansive platform. A shaded nightjar soared across the night sky, wings spread wide as it glided, churring its evening song. Its trilling rose and fell, lilting like the accents of the Erendil. Maldwyn smiled to one side as he watched its flight.

A hand wrapped around Maldwyn's cuffs, then pulled away. He noted that it was more tender than anticipated. Maldwyn turned, expecting to see Anton.

His crystal, blue eyes stared back at Maldwyn.

'Your Grace?' Maldwyn murmured, jaw dropping at the sight of Prince Harlan.

Prince Harlan smiled, mouth parted, just showing his white teeth. His faultless face was smooth and unblemished, more perfect than a portrait. His blonde hair seemed silver under the moonlight. His broad, square shoulders were pushed back, and his unrestrained hands relaxed by his side.

Prince Harlan crouched down in front of the seated Maldwyn. 'You look full of thought.' His voice was low and hushed.

Speechless, Maldwyn failed to produce anything beyond the sound of his tongue smacking against the roof of his mouth. The prince's right hand was closed. He was holding something small. Opening his hand, he revealed a petite, decorative key in his grasp.

Prince Harlan turned the key over in his palm and pushed it into the little lock on Maldwyn's trinket cuffs. The ornamental shackles fell from his wrists. The prince took the handcuffs and placed them on the bench beside Maldwyn.

Maldwyn rubbed his wrists, glad to have the restraints removed. 'I guess being held captive does that to me,' he offered in response to the prince's observation.

Prince Harlan's face saddened. 'I know what you mean.' The prince sat close beside Maldwyn.

'I see your hands are still free, sire.' The world fell away as Maldwyn watched the prince grin. 'How did you get the key?'

'I bargained with the sovereign for it.' The prince tried to mask his pride as he touched the side of his head. 'He's agreed to let us go free.'

Maldwyn raised his brows, surprised that the sovereign's plan to keep the prince from being suspicious about their release was to make another deal. He was also amazed that an agreement between them had been reached so quickly. He had not expected them to be given their freedom so soon, nor had he expected the prince to bear the key to his cuffs.

'Your Grace, what did you have to trade for it? Sire, did you concede that the mine remains under the Erendil's control?'

Shaking his head, the prince said, 'No, I don't have that authority.' He crossed his arms over his chest. 'I agreed to return something which is in my father's possession. Well, actually, it was in my mother's, but my father has kept her things close since she passed. It is something that belongs to the Erendil.'

'You're not going to tell me what that is, are you, sire?'

The prince cleared his throat.

'No.' He turned the angle of his head ever so slightly. The moon's light glinted in Prince Harlan's grey-blue eyes. 'Rest assured that, first thing tomorrow morning, we'll leave this place behind.'

Maldwyn studied the veined pavers. 'I understand, Your Grace.'

Prince Harlan lowered his voice to an almost whisper. 'Maldwyn, I'm not trying to keep you in the dark, or to shut you out.' The cold night air settled around Maldwyn's bare neck. 'I'm trying to keep you safe. The less you know, the less my father can do to you when we're back in Dresden.'

Maldwyn frowned as he glared at the prince. 'Sire, with all due respect, you kept me in the dark about the mission your father sent us on, and I don't recall that going too well for either one of us. Your Grace, if I'm going to be in danger, then I would prefer to know why.'

Dumbfounded the prince turned away thoughtfully. Maldwyn knew he had overstepped the boundaries, questioning his prince and speaking out of turn. Despite that, Maldwyn felt that he had a right to know why he might be in danger, and, that he deserved the prince's honesty, even if his rank in society required the opposite.

'Alright,' the prince agreed, rubbing his hands together. Maldwyn guessed the prince was fighting the effects of the cold night air. 'But, not here.'

'That's okay, sire.' Maldwyn reminded himself that he was the prince's servant. He wasn't owed any explanation. 'I shouldn't have questioned you, sire. You don't have to say anything. I'm sorry, I suppose I just needed to let out some frustration.'

'No, don't apologise. I owe you my life, which is more than my honesty.' Prince Harlan was pensive, fingers pressed to his mouth. 'I will tell you everything, but not until we're on the road… when there are fewer people around listening to our every word.'

Staring into the prince's thoughtful eyes, Maldwyn felt his heart pound. 'No need to worry, Your Grace. When we're on the road, you can tell me.'

The prince's fingertips slipped from his mouth as he looked up at Maldwyn, his expression was wistful. Maldwyn held his breath. He wanted to lean closer, and know the way the prince's soft lips would feel pressed against his. He wanted his dream to become his reality. Instead, he looked away and shivered, this time more from his nerves.

'Are you cold?'

'A little,' Maldwyn answered as he shifted on the hard bench, raking his fingers through his thick hair.

Prince Harlan stood, holding his hand out for Maldwyn to grab. Captivated, Maldwyn hesitated. The prince remained still as he waited.

Reaching up, Maldwyn took Prince Harlan's hand, letting the prince's taut hold pull him up to his feet. His hand was snug, heating Maldwyn's icy palms. Sensing the space between them close, Maldwyn hovered anxiously, lingering in the prince's presence.

'Follow me,' Prince Harlan told him, stepping back on his heels. His hand slid out from beneath Maldwyn's hold.

Taking in a final breath of the cool night air, Maldwyn set his thoughts about the prince aside. The owl in the trees hooted goodnight. The prince scuffed his shoes as he halted in the doorway, waiting for Maldwyn to catch up.

＊　＊　＊　＊　＊

The prince took Maldwyn to Tolamin, who waited for them in a nook not far from the grand staircase. His silvery robes seemed to glow against the warmth of the golden-toned walls.

Tolamin greeted them kindly, bowing to Prince Harlan and offering Maldwyn a sly smile. After a few pleasant exchanges between the prince and the priest, Tolamin led them through a number of vast luxurious halls to an expansive overly adorned set of chambers.

The room was wide with a humungous four-post bed, and transparent white chiffon curtains hanging delicately from the frame. There was a fire blazing from the baroque carved hearth, crackling ever so often to remind them that it was bursting with warmth, battling the autumn cool air.

The golden walls were bright and led Maldwyn's gaze up to the tiled coffered ceiling, sculpting a series of square geometric patterns into the beautiful roof. The floor was crafted with gentle, ivory, veined marble tile. Sandalwood incense burned nearby, filling the room with a pleasant balsam scent.

'Your Grace,' Tolamin said, seeming to sing the words. 'As prized guests of the Erendil, this shall be the room for your servant.' Maldwyn stood still, stunned. 'Is this sufficient? May I tell the sovereign you approve of his lodging?'

Wearing his royal veneer, Prince Harlan's face remained stoic. He gazed around, assessing the room. 'This will do.'

'I am pleased to hear that, Your Grace.' Tolamin smirked. 'Shall we leave your servant to settle in for the night? Perhaps I can take you to your quarters for the evening?'

'Thank you, Tolamin.' The prince nonchalantly stepped further into the room. 'I will meet you in the hall in a moment,'

Prince Harlan said, pointing to the door and dismissing the priest from his presence.

Tolamin wrapped his fingers around the ring hanging from the chain about his neck and bowed respectfully. 'Uller's blessings,' he offered before he left the room, shutting the door behind him.

Astounded, Maldwyn swayed as he turned around, taking in his surroundings. 'Your Grace, I must confess, I am a little confused.'

Prince Harlan seemed particularly tall in the dimly lit room. His muscular arms hanging loosely by his sides. His intense blue eyes shone with contentment.

The prince grinned and guided Maldwyn over to the cracking fire. 'We're not prisoners tonight, Maldwyn.' The prince reassured, his tone was smooth and relaxing. 'This room is one of many rooms for the guests of the Erendil.'

'But, I'm a servant, not a guest.'

The prince cocked his head, confused by Maldwyn's statement. 'Maybe so, but I am their guest for tonight, and you are here with me.'

Maldwyn looked around the space. The bed had a mountain of pillows laying on top.

'The Erendil are big on their hospitality when you're not a prisoner. It's yours… for tonight.' Prince Harlan stepped a fraction closer. 'How's your head?'

'Fine, sire. Why?'

Prince Harlan slackened his upright posture, and moistened his lips. 'Well… the last time I saw you, you had been drugged.'

Maldwyn recalled visiting the prince in the dungeon and falling asleep under his comfortable, soothing grip. The way

Prince Harlan had run his hand along Maldwyn's forearm had made him tremble. Maldwyn had been filled with longing as the prince tenderly pulled him to rest on his shoulder. When Maldwyn had woken, the prince had been tucked in behind him, arm draped over Maldwyn's side.

'Right, sire. Well, I slept that off.' Maldwyn felt a little embarrassed about the way he had been the last time he saw Prince Harlan. The smell of the nearby sandalwood filled Maldwyn's nostrils. The prince inched closer.

'I'm glad.' The warmth of the flames billowed from the hearth. 'When I woke up, you were gone, and I was worried.'

'I'm sorry, Your Grace. You were asleep when they came for me.'

'I understand.' The prince took in a deep breath. 'I know what my bringing you on this mission has put you through, and—tomorrow—I'm getting us out of here. I just want you to know that—when we get out of here—I'm going to keep you safe.'

Maldwyn gulped as the prince turned and left the room. He wondered what the prince meant, and why he wanted to keep him safe. The door banged closed and Maldwyn noted that he had been holding his breath.

Maldwyn went and slumped on the bed. He threw his head in his hands. As Maldwyn ran his fingers through his hair, he sniffed, and saw that the book the Erendil had given him had been brought to the room and placed on the table by the bed's side.

He picked up the book and stroked the cover, figuring he might get some reading done before resting. It would distract him from the feelings the prince brought out in him, feelings that could never be spoken aloud or acknowledged.

CHAPTER SEVENTEEN

Journey Through the Woods

MALDWYN FELT HE HAD DOZED most of the night, drifting in and out of sleep. He woke to the brilliant buttery walls, and the gold and ivory tiled coffered ceiling which sheltered him as he slept. Lying on his side, his hand rested on the pillow beside him in the giant white bed that had cradled him in his slumber. His dreams had been broken, like his sleep.

For the most part, Maldwyn didn't remember his dreams, but there was one moment he recalled with perfect clarity. Prince Harlan had stood with Maldwyn in this room, yet looking around Maldwyn could tell the room was different in his mind. The room had seemed smaller and there had been a window to the outside, painting the sky with stars where—in the waking world—there was a blank wall.

In this dream, Prince Harlan's expression had been fierce and his intense eyes were fixed on Maldwyn's. The prince had sat on the bed, placed a hand on Maldwyn's bare chest and woke him to the dreamland. Maldwyn had been surprised to see him there.

Your Grace? What are you doing here? Maldwyn pushed himself halfway up, unsure about what was going on. The candle on the table beside the bed flickered.

You can stop him.

Bewildered, Maldwyn sat up taller, shaking his head at the prince. *What are you talking about?*

You have the power. The prince's hand rested on the side of Maldwyn's ribcage. *You need to use it.*

I don't understand, Maldwyn uttered, looking for some understanding in the prince's expression. There was no hint of his meaning.

Prince Harlan's hand fell from his side. *You will.* He dropped his gaze and left the room. Maldwyn had called to his back, but before he knew it, the prince was gone.

Then, Maldwyn awoke to his empty bed, feeling awfully restless and confused. After that, he tossed and turned, mind jumping from one calamitous thought to the next. Maldwyn was worried about what awaited them when they returned to Dresden. He wondered whether Mikel had made a move on his plans and how Princess Cassara's training with Erik was going.

Rolling over, Maldwyn rubbed his forehead. He was exhausted and craved a decent rest, but he needed to pull himself out of the bed and ready himself for the journey back to Dresden. Maldwyn sat fully upright on the bed, his legs outstretched and pushed back the warm duvet, sheets balled up untidily beneath the cover.

He stood and used the pan beneath his bed. The sandalwood had finished burning overnight and the candles that were all about the room had burned down. There was a deep, wide pewter bowl over by the lowline dresser with a cloth hanging over the side. Beside the bowl was a large, teal, glazed amphora. There were small bottles lined up next to the ceramic jug.

Maldwyn walked over to the dresser and raised one of the vials to his nose, smelling the gentle flowery-scented oil that had undertones of cinnamon. He filled the bowl with water from the amphora and poured in a few drops of the oil. Maldwyn wetted the cloth and began washing himself, preparing for the day ahead.

He pulled on the fresh clothes that had been folded into a neat pile by the dresser. The black trousers were fitted and the deep, navy-blue tunic was woven out of a thick thread and had long sleeves to keep him warm in the cooler autumn weather.

Eventually, Anton came for Maldwyn, bringing him some breakfast before handing Maldwyn a heavy backpack, stuffed full of all the supplies he and the prince might need on their journey. There had been just enough room for Maldwyn to slide the book he had been given inside.

Swinging the pack over his shoulders, Maldwyn slouched a little under the weight. Fixing the placement of the pack, he straightened his back.

Anton left the room and escorted Maldwyn through the underground city, winding back down the grand staircase and meandering through the immense corridors. As they made their way, Maldwyn took in the remarkable architecture for a final time. He smiled up at the glistening, glazed mosaic tiles and the bright colours that burst from every surface.

Anton took Maldwyn to a massive, heavily guarded iron gate. The doors were open wide, and beyond was the dense forest of the greater Anhalt Mountains. The air was fresh and had a bitter, frosty edge. The sky was hidden behind the trees, which were huddled tightly together watching over them.

The sovereign waited with his arms folded across his chest. His robes billowed in the wind and the hood about his head flapped quietly, protecting his face from the icy breeze. His dark eyes were calculating.

Tiana and Tolamin stood on either side of Jerrik. Erendil rangers were spread about the entrance. Some of the rangers were high up in the trees, bows at the ready. The tiniest touch of red silk was visible beneath the leather belts about their chestnut-coloured robes, hoods hiding their faces. Maldwyn searched for the prince. He wasn't in the area.

'The prince will be here shortly, Eminence,' the sovereign told Maldwyn as he lowered his head out of respect. A bird chirped from the trees.

Caught off guard by the way in which the sovereign had addressed him, Maldwyn dipped his head and tightened his forehead. 'Eminence?'

'Yes, Maldwyn.' The sovereign's hood blew further down his face, darkening his features. 'You may not believe that you are Firebird, but I believe that you are. Moving forward, I shall address you as such.'

'Eminence is the title by which Firebird is addressed by those who worship the gods and their power.' Anton motioned his hands as he talked. His crooked nose was more bulbous in the sunlight. 'It is the formal way of addressing you, Maldwyn.'

Maldwyn opened his mouth, ready to make a case about not being Firebird, but, by the look on each of their faces, and the way Tolamin kissed the ring on the chain around his neck, figured his protests would be wasted, and let it go. Tiana smiled at him in a reassuring way that told him she would not hang the burden of prophecy over his shoulders.

'Have you read anything from the book I gave you?' The sovereign asked, changing the subject. Maldwyn welcomed the change.

'A little,' Maldwyn answered. He locked his thumb under the strap of the backpack over his shoulder. 'Although, I must confess, I won't be able to read any more for a while.' The sovereign's stern face corrugated his forehead. 'A book about magic might concern Prince Harlan. Magic may be permitted here, but it is still forbidden in Dresden.'

'I see,' the sovereign yielded. 'Well, you should know that you are always welcome here, Eminence.'

'If you need any help with magic,' Anton started as he stepped in line with the others, 'I will always help you. You have my loyalty, Eminence.'

Marching footsteps beat on the earth. 'Here comes the prince,' Tiana announced. Her accent made the words seem more important.

A knot formed in Maldwyn's gut. He turned. Prince Harlan was walking tall, escorted by a group of graceful rangers. His leather armour had been restored and buffed. The lynx on his chest stood on one foot with its forefeet in the air, ready for battle. The nearer Prince Harlan got, the clearer he came into Maldwyn's view.

His expression was blank to those who barely knew him, but Maldwyn recognised the subtle signifiers of his triumphant face. A twitch in the corner of the prince's mouth was a well-disguised satisfied smile, as his eyes passed carefully over Maldwyn. The prince halted in front of him. His presence commanded Maldwyn's complete attention.

Maldwyn's throat blocked and his stomach twisted. Words left him. He almost forgot to bow, and hurried into the correct pose as soon as he remembered their people's customs.

Prince Harlan waved his hand to acknowledge his bow. Maldwyn raised himself to stand.

'You know the conditions of your release Your Grace,' the sovereign reminded the prince in his lyrical voice.

'I give you my word, I will honour the deal.'

The sovereign lifted his chin. 'We'll see about that.' He stepped aside. 'Your servant has all the supplies you will need for your journey back to Dresden. You and your servant are free to go.'

'Thank you,' the prince said hesitantly, bowing out of respect to the leader of the Erendil. Prince Harlan strode past Jerrik, nodding back at Maldwyn, signalling for him to follow.

'Until we meet again,' Jerrik called.

Tolamin held his ring and whispered an oath to the bowman god, Uller. The sovereign smirked as Maldwyn followed in Prince Harlan's footsteps. Anton grinned, hands clasped together, hiding his raven mark from the passing prince. Tiana winked at Maldwyn in an encouraging manner.

The two walked wordlessly into the woods. The crisp leaves and dried twigs crunched beneath their boots. The wind whipped about them in sudden gusts, creating swarming gyres amongst the leaves on the forest floor.

* * * * *

Birds hopped from the branches poking out of the masses of trees, springing delicately on their feet and warbling as they sang their sweet tune. A red squirrel with a dark bushy tail scurried up a fat, crinkled tree. The sun's beams broke through the cracks of the leafy canopy, lighting up the path of fallen leaves ahead. Bulging roots hugged the earth. Hours went by slowly as they walked in silence.

After what felt like an abnormal amount of time, the day ended, banishing the sun's radiant light from the sky as the moon made its return to guard the night. Maldwyn set up camp, laying out the bedrolls, lighting the warm campfire and breaking up the rations provided by the Erendil. He passed a piece of bread to the prince.

'You've been very quiet.' Prince Harlan twisted his mouth to the side and picked at the crumbly bread.

'Have I, sire?' Maldwyn sat himself down on the rough ground, leaning his back against a fallen tree, fuzzy moss covering its surface. 'I've just been thinking about what will happen when we get back to Dresden.'

'I understand. I've been thinking about the same thing.' The prince tore his bread in half and stared at the flames. 'I wonder what might have changed, what my sister has been told about what happened to me, or whether anyone else survived the attack.'

The prince took a small bite, chewing quietly.

'You don't wonder whether the sovereign lied about your father, sire?' Maldwyn rested his elbows on the bend of his knees, interested in Prince Harlan's answer.

'No.' Prince Harlan let out a breath and shook his head. 'My whole life, my father has made every choice a test, every manoeuvre a lesson, always quizzing me on politics, power and control. He taught me that there can only ever be one winner in all wars, and that all disputes were wars in their own way. Everything in life is a battle, some are just more cutthroat than others. Compassion is a weakness and you should trust no one.' Prince Harlan stared blankly into the bouncing flames. 'These are the lessons my father passed on to me. Leaving me with the Erendil was a test. Either I passed, or I didn't.'

In the dim evening glow, Prince Harlan's deep azure eyes twinkled ever so slightly, catching Maldwyn by surprise. The minute nuances in his facial expression hinted at the prince's inner sorrow from his harsh upbringing. Maldwyn thought about how perfect he appeared.

'Did you pass, Your Grace?'

'We're free, aren't we?' Prince Harlan tossed a piece of the crust into the blazing fire. 'Although… I'm sure my father will tell me it took too long to negotiate my release. There will be something for him to critique.'

Maldwyn stretched his legs toward the fire. He lifted one foot and placed it on top of the other, crossing his feet. 'I guess we will have our answers soon enough, Your Grace.'

The prince's steely gaze brightened as he looked through the flames and locked eyes with Maldwyn. 'Speaking of answers… I owe you some.'

Maldwyn placed a hand on his cheek and wove his brows together. 'Answers to what, sire?'

'My deal with the Erendil.' The prince waved the bread at Maldwyn and lifted a knee to his chest. His other leg was kicked out in front of him. 'I promised to tell you the deal I made with the sovereign once we were out of there.'

'Oh, right… I'm sorry, sire. It must have slipped my mind.'

'That's not like you,' the prince commented. Maldwyn's mind had been busy with other worries, such that he had forgotten Prince Harlan's promise. Maldwyn shook his head and shrugged, not knowing what to say. 'Well… you've been through a lot. The sovereign offered to release us both if I agreed to return Kristian Sadler's ring to them.'

'Kristian Sadler? Wasn't that—'

'My mother's lover.' Prince Harlan rubbed along his eye with his free hand. He picked at his bread some more. The flames wisped in the wind.

Maldwyn didn't want to pressure the prince for more answers, so he waited. He watched the prince's faraway stare as he slowly ate his food. Maldwyn could see Prince Harlan's wrists were still reddened from the ropes that had been used to bind his hands.

'Apparently, he was an Erendil priest, like Tolamin, and he was acting as a liaison to my father. Kristian had been sent to advise my father on magical matters. After he was executed, tensions between the Erendil and Dresden reignited.'

Something rustled in the trees above their camp. Maldwyn paid no attention as he listened to the prince's hushed, smooth, deep voice, calming his mind that had been busy all day. Somehow listening to Prince Harlan speak freed him from the concerns that had kept him awake most of the prior night. The cold wind stirred the flames, making them crack. Maldwyn shivered and hugged his arms across his chest.

Prince Harlan let out a breath. 'Uller worshippers wear rings to honour him. They swear oaths on the rings and use them to bless objects or people.' A twig snapped as the prince shifted his foot. 'After Kristian was executed, his things were never returned to the Erendil, and his ashes would have been swept from the street like dirt.' The prince tilted his head slightly and lifted his brows just a touch. 'The sovereign wants Kristian's ring so that they can finally honour his soul to Uller.'

Maldwyn mulled over the prince's words, considering Prince Harlan's deal with the sovereign. 'Where will you look for the ring, Your Grace?'

The prince rubbed behind his ear. 'My mother's jewellery box. Kristian would have been stripped of all his things when being taken into custody. I have a feeling she would have kept his ring as some kind of a memento.'

Maldwyn was growing tired. He pushed himself up a little more to sit taller, trying to stay alert and show the prince that he was interested. His gritty eyes scraped the back of his eyelids.

'How will you know it is Kristian's ring?' Maldwyn threw a hand forward defensively, as if his question might have offended Prince Harlan. 'Sire, I only mean that Tolamin wore several rings. How will you know you have found the right one?'

'You're right, of course.' The prince made a contented face. 'The ring they want is the one that he would have worn on a chain. If my mother loved him, I think she would have kept it.' His voice softened as his words drifted away. 'I bet it's still on the chain.' Prince Harlan's expression grew solemn. 'In any case, the sovereign gave me a description of the ring. I'll know when I find it.'

Maldwyn leaned toward the fire and held his hands out, soaking up the warmth. 'How come you think your mother would have kept his ring?'

A droplet of water landed on the flesh of Maldwyn's hand. 'That's what I would have done.' The prince ran his fingers through his short, thick, yellow hair. 'I would have kept something to mourn over.'

Maldwyn's heart skipped at the prince's sincerity. In the flickering light of the flame, the prince's jawline looked to be sculpted out of smooth marble.

'I'm surprised you agreed to help them.'

'It's just a ring,' the prince replied. 'All they want is to set him to rest. The Erendil just want closure and to know his soul can find peace.' Maldwyn analysed the slight changes in the traces of Prince Harlan's face. There was something more he wanted to say. Maldwyn waited for the prince to find the words. 'I suppose that's what I want too… closure.'

Maldwyn wanted to go over to the prince and hold him close, comforting him through the pain of never really knowing his mother and the hurt he had experienced at the hands of his cruel, loveless father. He felt a fluttery sensation in the pit of his stomach at the mere thought of clutching him tightly.

Another raindrop fell onto Maldwyn's cheek. He wiped the wet spot on the side of his face with the back of his hand. The air was filled with the powerfully sweet, fresh-smelling scent of rain. The waxy leaves clapped together on the gust of wind, cheering the coming downpour.

Maldwyn had done his best to find a spot in the woods with decent shelter for the night. There was a nook beneath a protruding rock face that had been deep enough to take their bedrolls and supplies. They would be dry enough for the night once they retired for the evening, leaving the warmth of the burning fire.

'Seems like the rain is going to settle in, sire,' Maldwyn told the prince.

Prince Harlan nodded. 'Seems like,' he agreed. 'We should probably get some rest anyway. We have a long journey ahead of us.'

Maldwyn paused and waited for the prince to make himself comfortable in his bedroll before following his lead. He was tired, his eyelids were heavy and his energy had been completely sapped, but his mind was active. Maldwyn worried that he would have another broken sleep and that his restlessness might keep the prince awake.

* * * * *

Maldwyn awoke to the steady patter of rain upon the glossy leaves clinging to the trees, droplets soaking the crisp carpet of dried fallen foliage. The sound of the gentle trickling raindrops had brought a calmness to his mind, easing him throughout the night with their soft lullaby. A mild sweetness accompanied by the strong pine scent filled the fresh morning air. The sun's beams tried returning to the world, bringing with them the light of day, but the grey rain clouds merely brightened as they kept the dazzling rays hidden.

Maldwyn rolled from his side onto his back, readjusting the rough blanket laying over him. Prince Harlan was facing him, eyes firmly shut, his head resting on his hand. The prince had pulled his blanket tight up under his chin. His breaths were slow and even.

Maldwyn sighed, it had been a cold night and it hadn't taken long for the fire to be snuffed out by the persistent drizzle.

Maldwyn noted that the prince had scooted closer toward him beneath the rocky chasm, probably seeking out the warmth of lying next to him.

Maldwyn pushed the blanket back, rolling up his bedroll and gathering their supplies in his pack, readying their things for the journey ahead. The prince was slow to wake, yawning and stretching as he leisurely sat up. The rain was still falling lightly like snow. They talked about waiting for the rain to stop before continuing to Dresden, but decided to press on due to the steadiness of the fall that gave no hint of ceasing any time soon.

After everything was packed, they went on again, heading south-eastwards down the mountain and through the thick woods. There wasn't much of a path to follow and they struggled to see the woods ahead of them through the misty rain, keeping them guessing that they were still moving in the right direction. The way the mountains and hills steeply rose and fell made it difficult to keep track of where they were going.

The rain lasted for days, and it was difficult for them to find shelter to rest under. There were a few nights that they huddled together beneath the cover of thick branches that caught most of the droplets. Every time Prince Harlan would sleep against Maldwyn, a feeling inside him would stir and it seemed as if every ounce of air escaped his lungs.

They spoke very little, mostly concerned with trying to stay dry and warm. Maldwyn couldn't stop worrying about what would happen when they made it back to the palace. All the things he didn't know circled his mind, jumping from one concern to the next. Maldwyn strained to distract himself from his thoughts by focusing on the path, finding their way through the forest.

Maldwyn crouched down to tie the lace on the side of his boot that had come undone. The leaves were mashed into the muddy ground in a squelching mess. Rushing water could be heard racing along a river bed. The rain had been heavy throughout the day, but had begun to ease since the sun started setting, grey clouds with pink and purple hues covered the sky. They hadn't found decent cover for some time.

Maldwyn guessed they were nearing the border, but they were still too far northwest. The prince had continued on a few paces ahead while Maldwyn fixed the laces on his shoe. He could just make him out in the distance through the trees.

As he fastened the laces of his boots, a snapping sound came from somewhere in the vicinity. Maldwyn shot his head up to the noise. Prince Harlan continued walking carelessly in the rain, head down towards the ground, one hand resting on the hilt of his sword, the other swinging back and forth by his side. His broad shoulders were slouched forward.

Another sound came through the brush, this time sweeping steadily through the carpet of soaked leaves. Prince Harlan stopped in his tracks, studying their surroundings and casting a glance back at Maldwyn, checking he was alright.

A tall man, wearing the brown and blue lightweight leather body armour of Dresden stepped through the soaked, dead bushes. A sheathed ornate sword hung from his belt. Maldwyn recognised Ser Theodor, relieved that it was him and not some kind of dangerous forest predator, like a bear.

'Your Grace!' The knight exclaimed, bowing before Prince Harlan.

Behind Ser Theodor were a few other men, all wearing the same leather armour from Dresden and showing their respect for the prince. Maldwyn began to make his way over to the group.

'It's great to see you! We were never sent word that you had been released!'

'Theodor?' Prince Harlan dropped his hand from the hilt of his sword, leaning back a little. He was shocked, yet pleased, to find the knight in the woods. 'What are you doing here?'

'Your father sent us here to protect the way along the border. He's had a messenger travelling between Dresden and a meeting point further up in the Anhalt Mountains.'

Prince Harlan squinted the corners of his eyes a fraction, trying to conceal his disgust with his father's false attempts at negotiating his release. The messenger would have been little more than a front for public relations. A father trying to protect his son and see him safely home was nothing more than a fake projection to the world. The truth was, King Viktor had refused all attempts to negotiate.

'Of course,' Prince Harlan said under his breath. The rain was still misting gently through the sparse canopy. 'Did anyone make it back to Dresden after the attack?'

'Just Nicholas, sire.' Theodor scratched the back of his head. 'He told the king that you had escaped the attack. Maybe three days later we got word that you had been captured in the woods and imprisoned.' Theodor gawked awkwardly at Maldwyn, as if he had just noticed him standing there. Maldwyn locked his thumb under the strap of his bag, his shoulders ached from the weight of the pack. 'I'm glad to see your servant made it, Your Grace.'

The prince let a subtle smirk touch the corner of his mouth as he avoided looking over at Maldwyn, who mostly kept his gaze downturned. The presence of others meant he could no longer glance freely upon the prince. Royalty was protected from the shame that was Maldwyn's class.

One of the other knights who had dark hair and a mole on his jaw stepped out of line, looking down on Maldwyn. 'The king won't be pleased to see the servant.' Maldwyn gulped and blinked. 'He lost some good men in the woods when you were captured. He won't be happy to see that you're bringing the servant back with you.'

Prince Harlan folded his arms and stepped between Maldwyn and the knight. 'I've decided to reassess my father's authority on that matter.' The prince neared the knight in a threatening stance, his buff arms tightening beneath the sleeves of his armour. 'This man is my servant. If you have a problem with him, you come to me. Do you understand?'

Maldwyn's pulse raced, flattered by the prince defending him. He fought the desire to smile and look over at Prince Harlan. A heavy droplet fell from the tree standing above him, splashing onto his cheek.

The man bowed deeply in submission. 'Of course, sire.' Prince Harlan pursed his lips as he glared at the knight prostrating before him.

'Good.' The prince's voice was cold and flat. He waved at the knight, signalling for him to get up. 'How far are we from Dresden?' Prince Harlan turned back to Ser Theodor.

'About two days from the city's border, Your Grace.'

Nodding, Prince Harlan returned his hand to rest on the hilt of his sword. 'It'll be night soon and it's been raining for days, is there somewhere with good shelter to rest for the evening?'

Ser Theodor pointed over his shoulder with his thumb. 'There's a waterfall a short walk from here. Near the falls is a cave. We should be safe and dry if we camp there for the night.'

The prince waited for Ser Theodor to lead the way through the rough terrain. All wildlife had retreated from the world, avoiding the pouring rain. Only the pattering of the heavy droplets sounded as they fell onto the trees and thick brush. The fallen leaves crunched beneath their boots, scrunching into the muddy ground.

After some time, rushing water beckoned them, guiding them through the trees. White water cascaded down a slippery, rocky wall. The water flowed gently at the fall's base, moving in a nonchalant fashion, as if the drop had been nothing more than a bump in its path.

There was a wide, tall, dark hollow in the rocky wall by the water's edge, leading into the dry cave. The knights waited for Maldwyn to collect wood and set up the camp, not lifting a finger to help now that there was a servant in their midst. There was a lot of chatter by the campfire, but Maldwyn had been excluded, drafted to sit on his own near the cave's entrance. He was glad to be free of the weight of his pack.

When the knights were all asleep and dawn was soon to break on the horizon out of view, Maldwyn walked out into the night. The rain had stopped, leaving the air with a sweet, wet, fresh tangy scent. He smiled as an owl hooted, glad to know that birds had returned to the woods from their hiding places.

Standing by the stream, he watched the rippling water surface. The moon and stars glimmered, reflected in the charming pool, which roared as the water plunged into the brook.

Maldwyn gritted his teeth and tucked his hands into his pockets, bothered by the harsh reality of returning to his life as a servant. On his first meeting with the knights of Dresden, his station had been made abundantly clear. In a strange way, he felt that he had been treated better as a prisoner by the Erendil. He sighed.

'What is it?' The prince's voice called to him.

Maldwyn turned to see Prince Harlan a few paces from where he stood. He moved closer, standing proudly in front of him. Maldwyn kept his gaze down; in case anyone should follow him.

'Your Grace?'

'You're upset, I can tell.' The prince ran his fingers along Maldwyn's chin, pulling his face up until their eyes met. 'What's on your mind?'

'It's nothing, sire.'

Prince Harlan wetted his lips with the tip of his tongue. 'We'll be back in Dresden in a few days.'

'We will, Your Grace,' Maldwyn replied, turning his gaze back to the ground. 'You must be glad that we're almost back.'

'Well, it will be nice to be out of the weather again.' Prince Harlan was grinning, trying to lift Maldwyn's mood. His face soured when he could see it didn't work. 'I'm sorry about earlier.'

'Sorry, sire?'

'Yes, for what Ser Gerard said about you when he was talking about my father.' The prince tentatively lifted a hand as if to grab Maldwyn, but let it fall back by his side.

'That's not your fault.' Lifting his brows, Maldwyn gave the prince a resigned countenance. This was hardly the first time the knights had condemned him for existing. Prince Harlan was not to blame. Maldwyn knew that. 'I should say thank you, sire, for defending me.' Maldwyn took in a deep breath.

Prince Harlan smiled and bit his lower lip. 'It was the least I could do, especially after everything we've been through.' His face grew more serious. The dim moonlight highlighted the prince's strong jaw and high cheekbones. 'I'm not looking forward to it though, being back in Dresden.'

Maldwyn angled his head a tad. 'Really, Your Grace?'

'To return to a place where I am the Crown Prince and I have the pressures of an entire kingdom on me doesn't excite me. There's also my father's disappointment and disdain. No doubt he has already scripted a list of criticisms about the mission, my capture and our release.' Prince Harlan rubbed the back of his neck and inched forward. 'I've kind of enjoyed the quiet we've had in the last while.'

Maldwyn felt his chest hammering as the prince got closer. 'I know what you mean,' he agreed, growing very aware of the shallowness of the prince's breath that matched his own.

Prince Harlan locked his thumbs in his belt behind him, edging closer. The water hushed them in the background.

'I like the quiet.'

The world fell away as Maldwyn stared into the prince's twinkling, fierce, grey-blue eyes. The prince looked down as if shy and placed his hand on Maldwyn's torso, running his hand along his ribs.

Maldwyn shivered.

A cold breeze swept all around them. Prince Harlan rested his hand on Maldwyn's neck, thumb passing over Maldwyn's jawline. Tense, Maldwyn's chest tightened.

Cupping Maldwyn's jaw, the prince slowly leaned in as if to kiss Maldwyn on the mouth. Pulse racing, Maldwyn went with the moment, unbelieving of what was about to happen.

Something scraped behind the prince and he pulled away, hand slipping from Maldwyn's neck as he watched the cave's entrance. Ser Theodor walked towards them from the rock opening. Maldwyn sucked his lower lip as he hoped the knight hadn't seen anything unfolding between him and Prince Harlan.

'Your Grace, it will be morning soon.' Ser Theodor blurted to them, making a coy, presumptive expression. 'We should move out while we have the weather on our side.'

CHAPTER EIGHTEEN

Homecoming

THE CASTLE LAY UPON the gentle, grass-covered rolling hills like an old man sitting on a boulder in a thoughtful pose. The grey and charcoal stone walls stood mute in the distance between the dense woods and the crashing water on the shores of the faraway beach. The fierce towers shot up from the ground as if they were an army of giants guarding the city. The mild salty sea breeze grabbed Maldwyn's attention.

Since that tender night in the woods, when Prince Harlan and Maldwyn had reunited with the knights of Dresden, Maldwyn and the prince had spoken very little, barely able to get a moment free of the watchful guards. Maldwyn longed to find a moment where he would be alone with the prince, but Prince Harlan had been avoiding him, hardly uttering a word. The silence had left Maldwyn isolated, somehow making the journey alone despite the group accompanying him. The final days had seemed to drag.

Maldwyn was glad to see Dresden on the horizon. It was a cold, beautiful day. The sun was shining brightly overhead, and the blue skies were crystal clear, welcoming the crisp icy day. The pack Maldwyn carried had some added weight from the knight's supplies. He had been careful to ensure the book the sovereign had given him wouldn't be crushed by the extra items. He sighed, glad to know they would reach the castle by midday.

They kept a fast pace, reinvigorated by the promise of arrival from the vision of the city ahead. As they reached the village, passing by the farms on the outskirts of the city, the people gaped at the return of the prince, whispering to each other as they gossiped. Poised, Prince Harlan walked through the leering crowds, wearing his royal unreadable veneer.

The chorus of sweet birds was drowned out by the sounds of boots pounding on the ground. Word of the prince's homecoming had reached the castle and an escort had been sent to welcome him home. The heavily armoured soldiers marched in formation. The captain of the guard bowed, paying his respects to the prince.

They exchanged a few pleasantries, and then the escort formed around their group, leading them through the cobbled city streets. Passing the many timber and stucco houses, Maldwyn smiled at the way the evergreen, leafy vines hung like velvety curtains. The sails of the sea vessels could be seen rising from the port as the group rose higher and higher through the city.

When they reached the open square before the palace, they made their way to stand on the palace steps as King Viktor walked out onto the grand balcony that hung off the front of the rugged castle. Their escort stopped them by the palace doors, directing their attention to the king who was about to make a speech. Glossy, green vines climbed the stone walls of the palace.

The king raised his hands to the crowd, waving at the peasants gathering to see the prince's return. The crowd cheered, hooraying their prince and king. Heavy guards fanned out along the balcony behind King Viktor, followed by the demure Princess Cassara. The black streak in the king's greying hair ripped up to the laurel crown atop his head.

'Thank you. Thank you.' The king yelled, gesturing for the growing crowd to settle. 'For a long time, the people from the mountains have troubled our great kingdom, making claims to lands and resources that don't belong to them. They would have us live in a meritocracy that favours sorcery, where the rest of us, the weak and the poor, would be left behind.' The king's voice bellowed across the square and the pauses in between the king's sentences kept the audience tense, anxious about the rumours of the disputes at the kingdom's border. 'As most of you know, my son was taken prisoner by the wretched magic-worshipping squatters in the Anhalt Mountains.'

Angered, the throngs mumbled to each other, fists pounding in the air as some people shouted offensive slurs about the inhabitants in the mountains. Hatred seeped forth from the citizens of Dresden like a leaching infection having a contagious effect, contaminating their otherwise kind hearts.

'After much negotiating with the enemy, I am glad to report that my son has made it home safely.' The crowd cheered and applauded. 'I would like you all to join me in welcoming our prince home. Long live the crown!' The swarming assembly roared, arms waving victoriously at the sky.

Princess Cassara clapped along with the people filling the square. The sleeves of her royal blue gown draped from her wrists. Her black curls were pulled into a half-updo, and loose tresses bounced around her face, framing her prominent cheekbones. Maldwyn noted that, like her brother, she was very good at putting on a royal veneer, one that hid her disgust for the king's speech.

Maldwyn stole a look at the prince and noted the glint of anger in his eyes, for there had been no negotiations on his father's part. He yearned to console Prince Harlan, but stayed back, scanning the growing masses that were pushed away by the guards at the base of the tall stone steps.

Across the court, Maldwyn spied a suspicious man leaning against the speckled rock wall of the square, wearing a loose-fitting cloak. Beneath the hood, Maldwyn recognised the slimy sneer of Mikel, the man Maldwyn now knew to be the prince's cousin on his mother's side.

'The recent events have solidified my resolve in eradicating magic from the land.' The king paused, looking over his people with a cruel expression. The people quietened down, hanging onto the moments between King Viktor's announcements. 'From this day forward, I declare that raids will be ordered throughout the kingdom where sorcerers and their sympathisers will be rounded up and executed.'

Maldwyn's heart pounded. This news terrified him. The crowd too fell silent, afraid of what this invasion of privacy might mean for themselves, their families and their friends.

'If you, or anyone you know, has anything to do with magic, remember… you're in our sights.'

The corners of Prince Harlan's eyes creased ever so slightly. A minute shift in his façade revealed both his disapproval and curiosity, as though his father was about to do something more, perhaps something worse.

'As my conviction on this matter is unyielding, I cannot ignore recent developments within the castle.' Many of the people cocked their heads, glancing around as though their neighbours might be able to explain what the king was talking about. 'I regret to inform you that magic has made its way into the palace, spawning new followers to the craft as thoughts give life to actions.' Maldwyn's palms began sweating. His breaths shortened, terrified by this statement. 'I stand before you, openly and honestly, to announce that I am ashamed of the actions of members of my court.'

The princess's eyes shot from watching the crowd below, to glaring at her father. No longer applauding, her hands were held together in front of her chest.

'As I pride myself on my honour, I will be conducting a full review of my court, rooting out magic wherever it may reside.' King Viktor looked over at his daughter, cold and calm. 'Which is why, as I welcome home my son, I must place my own daughter under arrest.'

Shocked and horrified, Princess Cassara cupped a hand to her gaping mouth. Her other hand rested on her stomach, sickened by the betrayal as she backed away from her father. The crowds gasped, heads darting about in confusion as the guards on the balcony surrounded the princess. She was paralysed with fear.

Prince Harlan stepped forward. His attentive eyes raged at his father. Maldwyn could tell from the prince's tightened jaw that his teeth were gritted.

Noting that the crowds' focus was on the balcony, Maldwyn reached for the prince's hand, just catching the tip of one of his fingers. Prince Harlan turned his head to face him. Maldwyn shook his head, trying to convince him that now was not the time to act. He indicated to the cloaked figure across the square and mouthed the knight's name to the prince.

Prince Harlan breathed in and nodded. He stayed fixed on the steps. He bit his cheek, torn between defending his sister and stopping the foe across the court.

'The princess was caught practising magic and, under the laws of the land, shall be put to death.'

The king was saying something to the princess who was begging and pleading helplessly on display for the kingdom as guards grabbed her arms. Princess Cassara was dragged from the platform.

'May Dresden one day be free from the dangers of magic!'

The king retreated from the balcony. Guards tailing him closely. Hands on heads, the people in the crowd were gasping in horror at the news.

Prince Harlan leaned over to Ser Theodor and said something that Maldwyn couldn't quite catch. The knight was standing to attention with his legs together, angled toward the prince, trying to conceal his distressed face. Maldwyn heard the knight accept an order, lowering his head to royalty. Ser Theodor turned and made his way down the steps.

The knight muttered orders to the guards along the steps. The sentries raised their shields and moved down the stairs, pushing back the people to clear a path through the hordes.

Ser Theodor and the group that had been their escort, moved through the mob, making their way toward Mikel. No longer cocky, Mikel pushed himself off the wall, unfolded his arms that had been crossed and turned away, heading away from the square.

Maldwyn's power fumed.

He examined the courtyard, searching for a way to use his power to stop Mikel from escaping. The attention of the masses was on the chase that was about to begin.

The prince's eyes were fixed on Mikel. Ser Theodor stomped through the throngs, hand pulling out the sword at his hip, steel ringing in the air.

Mikel hurried away, racing along the castle walls, rushing for an exit. Mikel shoved people out of the way as he went for a side alley.

Maldwyn looked up and saw one of the stone-carved spouts in the wall, shaped like the head of a growling wolf with teeth bared, designed to direct the rainwater away from the masonry walls and through the statue's mouth. Mikel was running below the sculpture.

With no one looking his way Maldwyn focused his power on the spout, willing it to break off the castle wall. The heavy stone figure fell down, breaking into pieces over Mikel's head, knocking him to the ground.

People jumped out of the way of the falling rocks. Ser Theodor and the knights pressed through the commotion, taking the catatonic Mikel into custody. Prince Harlan's wide eyes ignored their surroundings and shot straight at Maldwyn, who remained fixed beside him, acting as shocked as everyone else in the square.

'Sorcery!' One of the peasants shouted. 'There's a sorcerer!'

The crowd erupted into chaos, people darting in every direction, climbing vines up the walls and trampling each other to escape the square. The guards secured the palace steps forming a defensive perimeter to protect Prince Harlan. Ser Theodor and the escort fought the disorder, pulling Mikel through the insanity towards the main entrance of the castle.

Ser Theodor stopped on the steps, guards dragging Mikel behind him. 'Your Grace, you need to get inside the palace.'

'What happened?' Prince Harlan's suspicious expression analysed the anarchy, as if he might spot the person who had cast the spell.

Relieved that the prince had discounted him as the sorcerer, Maldwyn watched the hurrying, frightened citizens of Dresden throw themselves into disarray in their fear.

'I have no idea, sire,' Ser Theodor answered honestly, lowering his head and sharing in the prince's wariness. 'It's not safe here now, Your Grace. You need to get inside.'

Ser Theodor led the group dragging Mikel inside through the massive reinforced doors, which creaked to welcome them. Their boots echoed on the stone ground inside the foyer. Prince Harlan lingered a moment on the stairs, carefully watching his panicked people. Maldwyn waited for Prince Harlan to move first, then followed him inside the palace.

In that fraction of an instant, Maldwyn saw the prince's prejudice. His apprehension over what had happened made it clear that he agreed with his father's views on magic. The prince may not have been as outspoken, or as dangerous in his beliefs, but he had been raised to fear magic, and that's exactly what he did.

As Maldwyn heard the huge doors bang shut behind them, shocking him into the realisation of what it meant to be back in Dresden, he recalled the shame he felt from life in the city. In this place, he was destined to hide. His thoughts of the prince, his place as a servant, his abilities, and every facet of who he was, belonged in the shadows.

* * * * *

The prince's boots clacked on the charcoal-coloured paved floor in the expansive throne room. Pillars stood like staves lining either side of the hall, holding the massive vaulted ceiling up above them. Yellow beams of sunlight poured through the large pointed windows, shaped like upside-down, gigantic, transparent, crystal shields.

Maldwyn saw the leafy vines dangling atop the windows through the glass on the outside of the palace. From a distance, huge bricks formed smooth grey walls but, up close, the blocks were a range of different shades of grey. The hall had a mild peppery odour and was cold despite the gleaming sun. It was obvious winter was approaching.

King Viktor sat menacingly, his fingers steepled together, on the far side of the hall on a fine chestnut-coloured throne carved from a rich timber. The throne rested on a podium at the top of a set of wide steps. Jewels were crested in the decorative metalwork that swirled the length of the arms of the chair. Although it was an impressive throne in a wistfully striking hall, it was a far cry from the luxury of the imperial hall of the Erendil.

'Your Majesty.' Prince Harlan addressed his father and bowed at the base of the stairs. Maldwyn watched the perfect lines of his muscular form as he lowered himself to the proper angle. Maldwyn too bowed before the king.

'I see you brought the servant with you.' The king pointed at Maldwyn. Maldwyn was not permitted in these halls under normal circumstances, but the prince had instructed Maldwyn to follow him through the palace.

Maldwyn had assumed the proper posture: head lowered and his hands clasped before him. He knew better than to gaze up or utter a word in the king's presence. Maldwyn's being there was already an irritation for King Viktor. He considered that this was why Prince Harlan had ordered him to follow.

'You just started a witch hunt and sentenced my sister to die!' Prince Harlan accused, shouting at his father. His deep voice filled the hall that was empty of guards. They were the only three people inside the throne room. 'Don't do this!'

King Viktor flicked off the prince's request. 'These are dangerous times son. Sorcery must be stopped wherever it finds roots.'

'Spare me the archaic spiel about the dangers of magic!'

'I understand that you're angry... but you will be a better king for the lessons I give you.' King Viktor raised his hand to hush his ranting son. 'Don't let your emotions get the better of you.'

'Sure, I'll calm down. We'll have a nice father-son chat!' The prince began stalking up the steps toward the throne. His father rolled his eyes at Prince Harlan's anger. 'Let's talk about how you sent me on a pointless mission without so much as looking into the source of your information! The Erendil don't have Iluvitar! They never did.' King Viktor's face sparked with vexation. 'Or about how you left me prisoner with the Erendil! Or how you've just arrested my sister and sentenced her to be executed!' Prince Harlan placed a hand on the arm of the throne and leaned forward, threateningly. 'Tell me this father… are you determined to have your entire family killed or just the women?'

'You watch your mouth!' King Viktor burst from the throne and shoved the smirking prince back, who was gladdened to have struck a nerve. 'Iluvitar is crucial in the prophecies and there was reason to believe it was in the Erendil's possession. As for your sister, she sealed her fate when she began dabbling in sorcery.'

Prince Harlan's face was a mixture of emotions, morphing from disbelief, through disgust, to complete rage. Standing still at the base of the steps, Maldwyn didn't know what to do. His role was one of invisibility.

Once upon a time, before he had come to know the prince, Maldwyn might have witnessed something like this remaining completely poised. Now, he wished to jump to the prince's defence, and it took everything he had to stop himself from using his magic or rushing up the steps.

Maldwyn knew the prince could never care for him, especially if Prince Harlan ever learned of his powers, but, for him, it was too late. The prince had already become something more to Maldwyn than he could explain.

'Did you ever ask yourself, father, why Mikel handed you this information about the Erendil?'

Confused, King Viktor made a strange face. 'Mikel? He's been missing for months!'

'Not anymore.' Prince Harlan gave his father a cold, self-satisfied smile. 'I just saw him in the square. Ser Theodor should be making him comfortable in our dungeons by now.'

'Dungeons?' The king's brows came together as he reached out and grabbed the prince's arms, yanking him forward a step. 'Why would you do that?'

Prince Harlan swiftly threw his father's hands off him, pushing the king backward against the throne. King Viktor rolled his shoulder, bothered by the jolt. His face was incredulous that the prince would fight back, and at his son's strength. Maldwyn supposed this might have been the first time his father had seen this side of him.

'Lord Darius betrayed you, father. He manoeuvred you like a puppet. He sent Mikel to you with a lie. Mikel was an imposter.' Prince Harlan rubbed his eyebrow, backing off. 'He's from Mordiallok, father. He's a member of the royal family and was sent by King Filip to infiltrate our court. I don't know what his plans are, but he's been reporting back to the king since before he arrived in Dresden.'

King Viktor straightened himself, still recovering from the prince's forceful thrust. Interested, he leaned forward. 'How do you know this is true?'

'Who do you think told me about my mother's execution?' The prince sneered, mocking sympathy. 'There's also what Jerrik Taramae said, father... the Sovereign of the Erendil.' The prince walked back down the steps toward where Maldwyn was standing. The leathery scent from his armour wafted Maldwyn's way as he moved down the steps. 'Mikel stole from the Erendil before he made it to Karana Downs. They're after him, and I intend to find out why.'

Maldwyn gulped at the prince's statement. He knew that Mikel had stolen the draconite, and that this was what the Erendil sought. More than that, this was the information he had promised the sovereign that he would keep the king from learning. The prince could never learn what Mikel had in his possession. Maldwyn couldn't risk it.

King Viktor came around to the front of the throne, staring down the steps at his son, seeing him in a new light. 'And what did the sovereign think of Firebird and the prophecies?'

The prince shrugged indifferently. 'Your theories were news to them.' Prince Harlan turned and, dismissing himself, he signalled for Maldwyn to follow. As they reached the doors out of the hall, the prince stopped and looked back at his father. 'Oh… and, father, I will fight you on your decision to have Cassara executed, no matter the reason.'

Surprised that the prince would choose to protect his sister despite the magic, Maldwyn became filled with hope. It was strange. Moments ago he had thought the prince hated magic, now Maldwyn considered that his opinions about sorcery were secondary to his desire to protect his family.

The prince walked with Maldwyn to a quiet nook where he apologised for what had happened in the throne room. This was the first time they had been alone since the waterfall and Maldwyn yearned to feel close to him again. Prince Harlan said nothing of what had almost happened between them in the woods, or of their time as captives with the Erendil.

He checked that Maldwyn was alright, and dismissed him, sending him back to the servant halls. As Maldwyn walked toward the dusty, dark corridors, he felt Prince Harlan watching him depart. Maldwyn considered gazing back but thought that would make it more difficult to leave.

* * * * *

As he walked through the servant halls, Maldwyn felt oddly claustrophobic. He had forgotten that these corridors were quite so musty and dark. He went straight to his sleeping quarters to drop off his pack before planning on looking for Ailaya and Erik. When Maldwyn opened the small door to his room, he saw Ailaya waiting for him inside.

Her deep red tresses delicately fell down her back that faced toward the door. She was wearing a simple pale blue dress, and stood with one hand resting on her hip, the other rubbing her forehead. She spun around when he opened the door and threw herself into his arms. The waft of her lavender perfume filled his nostrils. Maldwyn felt at home being held by his closest friend. The closest thing he had to family in the palace.

As Maldwyn held her tight, he saw that his room was exactly as he had left it. There was a small sleeping pallet against the wall with a rough, thin blanket; a deep, plain wooden chest at the end of his bed; and a table beside the bed that had a candle that had burned halfway down.

Pulling back, she smiled at him, delighted to see him return safely to the castle. Maldwyn pushed back a lock of hair that fell in her eye. She lifted her hands to her cheeks and stepped back, taking him in completely.

Ailaya jabbed him in the shoulder. Maldwyn flinched at the gentle whack. 'Never do that again,' she scolded. Maldwyn smiled, glad to see she hadn't changed. 'I'm glad you're back, Mal. I was so afraid I'd never see you again when we were told that you and the prince were missing.'

'Believe me, there was a while I thought I wouldn't make it back to Dresden.' He ran his hand through his hair and pulled the pack off his shoulders, placing it on the bed. 'I almost died.'

'Ser Nicholas returned and said you had been shot.' Ailaya was close to tears as she crossed her arms. 'He also said the prince pulled you out of the fight. Everyone assumed you would have died, but I didn't want to give up hope.'

'I promised to make it back, didn't I?' Maldwyn placed his hands on her shoulders as a comforting gesture, telling her everything was alright.

Ailaya nodded, sniffing back the tears in her eyes.

'You did.' Maldwyn hugged her again, making sure she knew he was alright. 'So, the prince saved you?' Her voice was muffled by his shoulder.

'He did.' Maldwyn stepped away, considering exactly how much he should tell Ailaya about his rescue and their capture. He made a flippant gesture with his hands. 'He pulled me to safety and treated my wound. When I came to, we were with the Erendil.'

'That must have been awful.'

'It was strange.' Ailaya looked up at him with eyes that glinted with curiosity. 'I don't really want to talk about it all right now.' Maldwyn sat on the hard bed.

'Of course,' Ailaya agreed, sitting beside him. 'What would you like to talk about?'

'Tell me what I've missed.' Maldwyn rested his arms on his knees. 'Why does the king think the princess was using magic?'

Ailaya looked at the floor and shrugged. 'Well, a few months ago the rumours were that she was spotted one night with a man in the sacred grove. They were making yellow orbs of light glow all around them. The knight recognised the princess and reported it to the king. No one knows who the man was.' Scrunching her nose, Ailaya shook her head. 'Everyone thought it was just a rumour when nothing happened. I guess not.' Her voice trailed off.

A low knock pounded on the door. Maldwyn scratched his chin, got up and opened the door. A small servant boy wearing basic clothes that had rips and stains waited outside the door. His hair was messy, and he had a patch of dirt on his cheek. The smell of horse on the stableboy was overpowering.

'Master Damyan is gathering the servants in the undercroft. He wants to brief everyone on the king's speech earlier.'

'Thank you,' Maldwyn told the boy, rubbing behind his ear. 'We'll head down there right away.'

Maldwyn gestured for Ailaya to follow him and the two of them filed into the halls, which were packed with the palace staff, marching toward the cellars as mindless sleepwalkers. Each of them funnelled through the halls in unison, twisting down the flights of steps.

The air was stuffy in the undercroft, and there was a strong earthy smell from the dirt ground beneath them. The ceiling was vaulted, built from masses of stones of a range of shapes and sizes, creating a patchwork of bricks and mortar. At a distance, the rocks appeared to be the same shade of grey but, up close, Maldwyn noted the range of neutral shades and colours in the rocks.

Master Damyan waited for them under the archways. His silver hair shone in the darkness. The servants gathered about him in a large semicircle. 'Gather round, gather round.' Master

Damyan instructed, insisting that the staff bunch closely together.

A hand touched Maldwyn's shoulder. Maldwyn turned and saw Erik standing beside him, his scar ripping through his brow. 'Meet me by the door to the royal courtyard at nightfall?'

Ailaya was standing at Maldwyn's side and looked intrigued by the hunter's request. 'Yeah, of course,' Maldwyn replied, keeping his voice low.

Once all the servants were assembled, Master Damyan made a gesture, signalling that he was about to begin speaking. 'Can everyone hear me?' Master Damyan checked, his voice carried easily through the room, echoing off the rounded ceilings. 'I know how alarming the king's speech earlier must have seemed, but I assure you that you are in no danger. As per the king's words, searches will be conducted throughout the castle ensuring that there are no lawbreakers in our midst.'

Maldwyn's stomach turned, and he realised he had left the book the Erendil had given him in the pack on his bed. It was likely enough evidence to incriminate him as a magic sympathiser. Depending on the full contents of the book it could even implicate him as a sorcerer.

'The guards are commencing the searches today and will sweep through every room in the castle over the coming days to ensure the safety of the royal family. You have nothing to fear.'

Maldwyn glanced at Erik who was nervously fidgeting with his fingers. Maldwyn brushed the tip of his nose.

'In regards to the princess's arrest, she was witnessed using magic by one of the king's trusted knights. The king is an honourable man who does not hold himself above the laws he sets for the kingdom. Please, do not whisper and spread rumours about the princess's pending execution. I expect that if you have any further questions about the recent events you will come to me.'

Master Damyan proceeded to remind the staff of their duties to the court, making sure they were not to be seen where possible and checking they have the necessary permission before entering rooms beyond the servant halls.

Once the meeting was over, Master Damyan instructed the staff to return to work. The crowd slowly scattered. Maldwyn and Ailaya continued to talk as they walked back through the cold, damp servant halls, returning to their duties.

*   *   *   *   *

Erik stood alone on the steps that led up to a small timber door, with twirling iron that decorated the slats. He was slouched with his hands in his pockets. His stubbled jaw was more shadowed in the dark of the night.

There were no guards by the servant entrance to the royal courtyard. They would be patrolling outside as always. The place was silent apart from the crackling flames of the torches on the walls.

'Mal, I'm glad to see you're back.' Erik's speech shuddered. Nervous, Erik looked up and down the hall. He rubbed around his mouth, anxious about something.

Seeing that Erik was troubled by something, Maldwyn chose not to waste time with pleasantries. 'Erik, what happened?'

Erik's lower lip trembled. 'I made a mistake, Mal.' He ran his fingers through his dark, lank hair. 'We weren't... I wasn't careful enough.' Erik gritted his teeth as he straightened his thoughts. 'The princess and I were meeting in the woods for her training. It was night and I thought it was the perfect place to show her how to create light. It's a relatively simple spell. I didn't know someone was watching us.'

'Then what?' Maldwyn pushed.

'Then there were rumours for a while about that night, but nothing happened.' Erik shrugged. 'We figured someone must have seen something, but we had been lucky enough to get away with it. We stopped meeting for a while after that. We were more careful when we recommenced her training.'

Maldwyn folded his arms. 'So, you had no idea that the princess was about to be arrested?'

'No.' Footsteps sounded up the corridor as a matronly servant woman carried a basket of clean linen from the laundry room to the residential area of the castle. Erik and Maldwyn both smiled as she passed and waited for her to disappear before continuing their conversation. 'And, with the rooms being searched, it's only a matter of time before I am arrested too.'

'What are you going to do?'

'I'm leaving, Mal. Tonight.' Maldwyn let out a breath at the news and raised a hand to his face. 'I can't stay to watch the princess die. I don't have enough spells or magical supplies to break her out of the dungeons without getting caught myself. My people are sworn never to kill. That's all I have left from them. I won't take a life. I just wanted to let you know before I left. You helped me feel reconnected with magic... I really am grateful.'

'Where will you go?'

'Ellinor. Magic is still allowed in that kingdom and they're not about to go to war with Dresden, like Mordiallok.'

Maldwyn checked the halls were still empty. 'Don't go to Ellinor. Find the Erendil in the Anhalt Mountains.' Erik frowned at him. 'There's a man there, Anton. He's one of your people. He bears the raven mark.'

Erik's eyebrows shot up, making the scar more obvious. 'You met one of my people?' He moved closer. His expression was one of amazement.

'I did. You'll be safe with the Erendil and you won't be alone there.'

Erik smiled. 'Thank you, Mal. For everything.'

Erik offered Maldwyn his hand to shake. Maldwyn pulled him into a friendly embrace, wishing him luck for the road ahead.

CHAPTER NINETEEN

Chained

THE DUNGEONS WERE AS bad as Maldwyn remembered. The stench was worse than horse stables, and caught at the back of his throat making him gag. Strands of hay and clumps of muck covered the ground. The corridor was dark and cramped. Heavy timber doors lined the walls several feet apart.

The guards waved him through, guiding him from cell to cell as he carried a pile of bowls in one hand and a bucket of sloppy, plain stew in the other. A huge metal ladle hung from its curved handle over the side of the pail.

Maldwyn had swapped shifts with one of the other servants so that he could get in to see Mikel. The servant he had taken the shift from had been more than happy to trade places for the evening.

For every door Maldwyn reached, the guard would pause and give him any required instructions before opening the cells. When Maldwyn reached the cell at the end of the hall, the guard gave him specific instructions not to touch the prisoner's shackles. He was also reminded of his duty to keep any and all information related to the dungeons confidential. He was not to participate in the spreading of rumours.

As the door opened, Maldwyn saw Princess Cassara curled up in a foetal position on the ground. The chains about her hands and feet were marked with spelled runic inscriptions. The princess had been stripped of all her belongings. All she had was a stained brown sack covering her body.

'I know you,' she mumbled, pushing herself up as the door closed behind him. 'You're that servant who introduced me to Erik.'

Maldwyn clenched his jaw, worried that the guard may have heard her remark. As the guard failed to thrust the door open and arrest him, Maldwyn assumed the doors were thick enough to mask their chatter.

'I am, Your Grace' he answered.

'You shouldn't call me that anymore.' The princess pushed a lock of hair behind her ear. 'I'm not exactly what you could call very graceful right now.' She hung her head in shame.

'I'm sorry this happened to you princess.' Maldwyn placed down the bucket and filled a bowl with the slop. 'I had hoped knowing about your gift would make the king more open to magic.' A wave of guilt washed over him, seeing how broken and helpless she had become as she wrapped her arms tight around herself. 'I feel responsible, Your Grace. I introduced you to Erik.'

Princess Cassara's arched brows met, creasing above her nose. 'This was always my destiny. It was only a matter of time before my father would learn the truth of my power. He was never going to let me live.' The princess let out a breath that was a sort of sad laugh. 'Being his daughter isn't enough.'

Maldwyn offered the princess the warm bowl. She took it, cupping it in both her hands. Lifting the bowl to her mouth she took a sip of the broth. There were no utensils that were to be offered with this stew, it was more of a lumpy soup.

'You didn't see this coming?' He asked, assuming that someone with her gift should have been able to predict her arrest. 'I mean before it happened?'

Princess Cassara raised a single brow. 'In a way I did. I dreamt of it a thousand times, in a thousand different ways. This always happens... there was no escaping it. Running could not save me from that moment.'

The princess had a sort of faraway look in her eyes, staring at the blank walls. He wondered what it must have been like to see her father's betrayal in her mind's eye, knowing that whatever she tried, he would always react to her power the same way. As a seer, she knew better than anyone that destiny was not something that could be outrun. It is inevitable.

'But no. I did not see it well enough to understand when it would come to pass.'

Maldwyn knelt on the floor. He kept his head lowered and rested his hands on his knees. 'I wish I could help you.'

The princess gave him an encouraging expression as she placed her bowl on the floor beside her. 'You can... by helping

Erik.' Her glassy eyes sparkled, even in this dark room, and she sniffed.

Nodding, Maldwyn felt that he might cry for her. He felt connected to her. He knew what it was to be born with a gift that no one else could understand.

There were times when Maldwyn wondered if it was possible to distinguish between himself as a person and the power that existed within him. He had asked himself many times, where did one end and the other begin? Was it possible to distinguish one from the other? He considered that he was his magic, as she was her dreams. In this way, he and the princess were the same.

'I've done what I can for Erik.' Maldwyn lifted his head, speaking to her with direct eye contact for the first time. 'I found his kin.'

Mouth twitching, the princess attempted to smile at her teacher and friend. Tears streamed softly down her face.

'That's good,' she told him; her voice choked. 'You should go, before the guard gets suspicious. Take this.' The princess passed back the bowl that she had hardly touched. 'Besides, I've lost my appetite.'

Maldwyn took back the bowl and bowed as a final sign of respect to the princess. Saddened for her, his chest felt heavy and he noted how dark this room felt. If it were possible, it appeared dimmer than when he had stepped through the door.

Maldwyn knocked on the door for the guard to come and let him out. 'It's strange,' she called to his back as he waited. 'In my dreams, you don't exist.'

Alarmed by her statement, Maldwyn tilted his head and turned back slightly. He wondered what that could mean, but did not have the time now to ask her.

'Maybe that just means I'm insignificant.'

The princess squinted up at him. Her eyes were dark, and her face inquisitive as she stared at him. Her chains rattled as she brought up a hand to her cheek. She didn't speak another word. The door creaked open and Maldwyn slipped through.

* * * * *

Maldwyn was brought in and out of a number of other cells before he reached Mikel's. When he entered the imposter's cell, Maldwyn saw him lurking in the shadows with a smug expression on his face. Mikel's eyes were dark and his hair was as slick as his hideous grin.

'Ah, it's you!' Mikel waved his hands in the air as if he were welcoming Maldwyn to his cell. Maldwyn noted that the chains about his wrists did not have the runic markings that had been on the princess's cuffs. 'I should have known.'

Maldwyn's skin crawled. 'I've brought your dinner.' The door banged shut behind him. There was an indescribable, heavy stench in this cell. Maldwyn tried to hold his breath.

'You really do get used to the smell.' Mikel reassured as if reading Maldwyn's thoughts. Maldwyn placed the bucket on the floor, used the ladle to fill a bowl with the sloppy mess and held it close before himself, as if ransoming it to the fraud. 'What's this? A servant trying to have some sort of power over someone like me? Face it, even when I'm in the dungeons, in this kingdom, you're beneath me.'

Maldwyn pursed his mouth, making a smacking sound with his lips, dangling the bowl in front of Mikel just out of his reach. 'If you want your dinner, then I want something from you.' Mikel glared at Maldwyn. His eyes were dark with purple rims encircling them. 'It's only fair after the way you used me.'

Mikel sat back and spread his hands, resigning himself to Maldwyn's request. 'The draconite. Where is it?'

Mikel laughed, donning a false, yet knowing, smile. 'The draconite? I'm sorry, I have no idea what you're talking about.' His mocking tone was grating.

Crouching down to level with the prisoner, Maldwyn gestured to the food. Mikel licked his lips and turned his head away.

'I recently was taken hostage where I spent some time with the Erendil, and they told me some pretty interesting things about you.'

'Oh?'

'They told me you're the prince's cousin.' Maldwyn noted that his eyes were a little bloodshot. 'They said that you're so unimportant to the royal family in Mordiallok, that you were considered expendable and sent on a fool's errand.'

Mikel scowled.

'That, is a lie.' His upper lip scrunched up into a jagged line. His voice was brazened and intimidating.

'Is it?' Maldwyn shrugged. 'I can't say I would know.'

Hovering the bowl near Mikel, close enough that he would catch a whiff, Maldwyn noticed that he had lost a fair amount of weight since becoming a drifter on the run. The sack he wore hung off his bony shoulders.

'My family sent me here for retribution.' Irritated, Mikel leaned forward and pulled on his chains. They clattered, fixed to the wall. 'Stopping in the Anhalt Mountains was meant to be nothing more than a fact-finding mission before continuing to Dresden. You won't believe how trusting they are of enemies to King Viktor.' His persona was deflated and diffused despite his perpetual grin. 'They practically handed me everything I wanted to know.'

'If all you want is revenge, then why not just kill the king and leave?'

'I thought about it… but it didn't seem like justice. King Viktor is a cruel man.' When Mikel spoke, his face morphed into a repulsed expression and his eyes would not meet with Maldwyn's. 'I've seen things you could not possibly understand or imagine. When I was a boy, I saw the bodies of men piled into a heap and set alight for the flames to destroy them. The corpses of King Viktor's victims in a senseless war, and the bodies of people whose only crime was practising sorcery—a practice once carried out by highly respected people who the King of Dresden has systematically hunted and killed. Women and children dead, on his orders.' Mikel wiped his mouth and leaned forward, wagging a finger at Maldwyn. 'Every time, I would swear to myself, never again would I stand idly back while the bodies of innocents amassed on our doorstep. Never would I turn a blind eye to his cruelty.'

Footsteps in the hall beyond the door suggested that one of the guards was on the move. Mikel hunched, slumping weakly against the wall.

'All those times, I never actually believed I would get an opportunity to stand by my beliefs.' Mikel scratched his face, nails scraping against his stubbled chin. 'Then, I decided the only way I could do anything about King Viktor, was to do it myself. So, I asked my grandfather if he would allow me to travel here and infiltrate the court in Dresden. He accepted my proposal, and here I am.'

It was strange, Maldwyn had always hated Mikel, but now he could see that Mikel saw himself as a hero, determined to stop the king's tyranny. In a weird way, Maldwyn understood his point of view, he even sympathised with his desire to protect sorcerers from the king's laws to eradicate their existence. If he were in Mikel's position, Maldwyn considered that he might have acted in the same way.

Thinking of all the ways Mikel had plagued him while being among the court in Dresden, stalking and hurting Maldwyn to learn about the royal family, Maldwyn found it difficult to forgive the imposter. For one who saw himself as so different from the king, Mikel had acted in ways that were a lot more like the king than he would ever care to admit. He had no real regard for the people beneath him.

'You think you can save the world from the king... but, who will save the people like me, the lower class, from the people like you?'

Not expecting that question, Mikel dropped his head, possibly a little ashamed. 'I admit, I may not have treated you fairly, but you had information... information that I needed.'

Sighing, Maldwyn accepted his answer as honest.

The truth was, to Mikel, Maldwyn had been nothing more than a pawn in his plans. Struck by the memory of the first time Mikel had used him, Maldwyn recalled the fateful letter which informed Prince Harlan of the queen's execution.

'Why did you tell the prince about the queen's execution?'

'Because, if Harlan knows what sort of a man his father really is... then, maybe he won't become him.' Mikel swatted the air, as if Maldwyn couldn't possibly understand. 'King Viktor is the sort of man that would sentence his own wife and daughter to death.'

The warmth of the bowl began to overheat Maldwyn's tight hold. Slackening his clutch Maldwyn, readjusted his grip.

'Dying is too good for a man like that,' Mikel mumbled with a distant and dark stare. The wicked grin still touched his cheeks. 'King Viktor killed my aunt. For that, he deserves exactly what he's going to get.'

A feeling of deep concern stirred within Maldwyn. His chest tightened. 'What do you mean by that? What have you done?'

'The draconite you're looking for… it's gone—destroyed in the spell. You see, I've already used it.' Mikel laughed under his breath. It was a low-sounding, echoing sort of giggle. 'You're already too late.'

'What did you do?'

'I cursed the king!' The imposter clapped his hands together as if it was a wonderful notion to behold. 'Actually, I had to get a sorcerer to do it for me, but I had my aunt's pendant cursed. I hear it is precious to King Viktor. The only thing he mourns over… perhaps reflecting on her death like any true murderer. A token for him to relive the moments.'

Maldwyn felt as though the walls were closing in on him. Trying to stay calm, he steadied his hands that were holding the hot bowl of stew. He had run out of time to stop Mikel. The draconite was destroyed and the curse that had come to Princess Cassara as a warning had already been put into play.

'Who helped you?'

'That's my business.' Mikel gazed off to his side and sighed. 'I've waited my whole life for the opportunity to avenge my aunt, and I'm not about to fail by giving in to questioning so easily.'

'How does the curse work?'

'All the king has to do is touch the pendant once and he will be subject to the curse's ruling until his death… but, don't worry, the pendant can't harm anyone other than the king.'

'What does it do?'

Mikel slithered closer like a snake. His smarmy expression made Maldwyn's skin crawl.

'The curse is poetic justice.' Mikel sneered, holding out a long, slender finger. 'Once cursed, King Viktor will eventually die… at the hands of his own children.' Smiling widely at the mastery of his idea, Mikel held out his hands to take the bowl.

'So… you've orchestrated the king's death as justice for your aunt's execution and the people murdered by the king, and you plan on having his children deal out this sentence.' Maldwyn passed the prisoner the scalding bowl of stew. 'And, up until now, you've painted yourself as a hero. Someone acting to protect the people.' Mikel took the bowl, finally making eye contact with his lesser. 'Seems to me like you're just a madman, obsessed with destroying a tyrant king, trying to justify his own cruel deeds by comparing lists.'

Bringing the soupy stew up to his mouth to take a sip, Mikel watched Maldwyn over the top of the rim of the carved timber bowl. Maldwyn returned his greasy grin and slapped the bowl. The boiling hot broth poured over Mikel who gasped in surprise.

'You know, you really should be more kind to the people that serve your food.'

Mikel held his hands out wide, assessing the mess. The bowl had landed upside down in his lap. The stained sack was now soaked and would reek of the stew.

Mikel scowled at Maldwyn.

'You'll regret that.' Maldwyn moved to the door and knocked for the guard. 'Wait! I'm hungry, you owe me my dinner!'

Maldwyn shot him an uncaring look.

'I'm sorry. It's one bowl per prisoner.' The lock began to turn over. 'You really shouldn't be so clumsy,' Maldwyn told him as the door yanked open. He left Mikel shouting at the blank walls that suffered him.

He considered that it was possible that the king had yet to touch the pendant, that he may not yet be cursed. He needed to get to the king's chambers while they would be unoccupied. At this time of evening, the king would be in the dining hall with his son, probably trading words about Princess Cassara's arrest over an exquisite feast.

Maldwyn slowed as he passed the princess's cell. It was not fair that she should die for how she was born, being condemned for something about herself that she could not change.

He felt his power and called it forth. One word came to mind as he focused on her shackles beyond the door: release.

He heard a metallic jangling inside the cell and the door's lock clicked. Hoping that she would be able to escape on her own, Maldwyn continued to follow the guard down the hall.

CHAPTER TWENTY

The Tides of Life

THE SOFT HUES OF THE EVENING moon and the glittering stars shone through the tall windows, curtains still drawn back, lighting King Viktor's personal chambers and highlighting the shadows in the variegated timber floors. Maldwyn had knocked and, as expected, there had been no answer. He glanced around the room; it was dark.

A warming fire battled the freezing night air. Winter was on the horizon; Maldwyn could tell from the frost building on the glass. The huge four-post bed was made up with clean white sheets and a finely sewn embossed royal blue quilt. A thick fur blanket was folded neatly, and arranged along the end of the bed.

Before the fireplace was a set of high-backed armchairs and a rectangular rug. On the far side of the room was a dais with a desk, covered in the king's paperwork. To Maldwyn's right, was the king's wardrobe and dressing table.

Decorative boxes of the king's finery were lined up on the dresser. Large, richly coloured jewels spilt out of the boxes, propping the lids open. Delicate buckles sculpted from metal into gentle swirls were falling out of one of the cases. A variety of crowns were displayed on soft pillows. Some were more decorative for formal occasions, while others were more subtle and practical. Bottles of gently scented perfumes were collected on the dresser to one side. In the centre, was Queen Sonia's jewellery box, a lock fastened over the latch.

Maldwyn moved over to the dresser. Reaching out, he held the padlock in his hand. He closed his eyes and focused on his ever-present power. Clicking open, the lock fell into Maldwyn's palm.

He opened his eyes.

His heart raced, hoping that he would be the first to touch the queen's pendant since it was cursed. There was no way to know for sure whether the king would already be subject to the curse's ruling. It was possible that Maldwyn could spare the king's life.

Lifting the lid, he weighed up whether he should let the curse do its work. Mikel did have one point: the king deserved it.

Still, Maldwyn couldn't be complicit in murder, nor could he let the guilt of the death of King Viktor hang over Prince

Harlan or Princess Cassara's destinies. If he could spare them that feeling, then he would.

Queen Sonia's triple horn pendant sat on top of the stack of jewels inside the case. The three interlocking horns were elegant and had a swirling pattern inscribed into the surface. Maldwyn held up the queen's pendant.

It was such a little thing. He hesitated and contemplated how odd it was that he worried over such a delicate object, but the curse could ruin the lives of people who deserved better fates.

He considered how he had no idea how to unmake a curse, especially when the Erendil had suggested to him that draconite was such a powerful source for curses. Was it even possible to break a curse? He thought about how he might be able to ensure the curse was not able to harm anyone other than King Viktor.

Mikel had said the curse was intended to harm the king only, but Maldwyn wasn't sure he could trust Mikel, and thought it best to take precautions. Figuring that if he could encase the pendant in stone and throw it away where it could never be rediscovered, then disaster would be averted. Maldwyn held the pendant in both hands and closed his eyes.

He focused his breathing and felt his power course through his hands into the pendant. A sound creaked behind him and a draught swept around where he stood. When he opened his eyes, Maldwyn pulled his hand back and saw a solid layer of rock encasing what had moments ago been a pendant. Its surface was now rugged and black squiggles marked the layers of stone.

'By the divinity's grace!' A familiar voice behind Maldwyn said. 'You're a sorcerer!'

Maldwyn spun to see Ser Theodor standing behind him, hand resting on the hilt of the sword at his hip. The door to the grand hall beyond the king's chambers was wide open. Maldwyn swallowed. His heart pounded in his chest.

This was it.

The moment when he would be turned in to the king as a sorcerer and executed had finally arrived. His mother had tried to warn him what using his magic could mean. He had ignored her cautions, choosing to protect the man that would kill him.

'Ser Theodor, I can explain,' Maldwyn said, although that wasn't exactly true. Unable to think of a solution to what the knight might have witnessed, Maldwyn turned more fully to face Ser Theodor, holding his hands up to try and calm him.

'How did you do that?' Ser Theodor's hand left the hilt of his sword. He stepped forward, brows weaving together. His forehead creased. 'I didn't see or hear you cast any spells.'

'I don't know what you're talking about.' Maldwyn couldn't think of anything else to do other than to play dumb.

'I saw you turn the queen's pendant to stone.' Ser Theodor pointed at the pendant-shaped rock in Maldwyn's hand. 'How did you do that?'

'I don't know exactly.' Maldwyn said softly, still trying to calm the troubled knight. 'Sometimes, I can just do things. I don't know how, or why.'

Ser Theodor's face was questioning Maldwyn's statement as he gave him an odd sort of side-eyed expression. 'You don't use spells?'

Maldwyn shook his head.

'You have your own magic… your own power?'

'I do,' Maldwyn confessed, running out of options.

He hoped to convince the knight that executing him for his power would be no different from executing someone for being born with green eyes instead of brown.

Ser Theodor held his head back and straightened his posture, as if being struck with some sort of sudden realisation. 'So, it's true?' Ser Theodor neared him. 'Firebird is alive. It's you!'

Maldwyn felt his mouth drop as he hushed the knight. 'No, I'm not Firebird.' For some reason, Ser Theodor did not seem afraid of him, despite learning what he can do. 'I'm just a man, trying to stop the king from being cursed.'

Maldwyn held the stone pendant forward for Ser Theodor to assess. The knight bent forward and examined the rock. His face was amazed.

'Cursed? How so?'

'Mikel.' Maldwyn said matter-of-factly. 'He used something to curse the queen's pendant. I'm just trying to spare the king's life.'

Ser Theodor's brows shot up with surprise. 'Why?' He scratched the side of his head. 'The king would have you executed. Why would you protect him?'

'I guess I don't want to be a part of someone's plan to commit murder.' Stepping back, Ser Theodor let out a hefty breath and ran his hand over his chin. 'Are you going to turn me in?' Maldwyn asked, starting to get the feeling that Ser Theodor might let him go.

'To be executed? No. I don't believe in executing innocent people.' Ser Theodor gave him an admiring expression. 'What do you plan to do with the pendant?'

'I've encased it in stone to stop it from harming the king—that is, if he hasn't already touched it.'

Ser Theodor watched Maldwyn for a few seconds, hands hanging by his side. When he didn't offer any words, Maldwyn felt he should explain himself further.

'I figure, if the king can't touch the surface of the pendant, then it can't hurt him.'

'But you can't leave it here... the king will notice what has happened.'

'I'll cast it into the ocean. From the weight of it now, it should sink to the bottom and be too heavy to easily wash ashore.'

Leaning his head to the side, he assessed the knight who continued to soften toward Maldwyn. His racing pulse finally began to ease.

'Can I ask, why you won't turn me over to the guards?'

A little edgy, Ser Theodor looked back at the door checking they were still alone and that no one was listening by the open door.

'I have been known to help sorcerers escape Dresden unscathed.' He had lowered his voice to a whisper.

'You're Master Damyan's accomplice.'

'You know?'

'Only what the prince told me in the Anhalt Mountains. Apparently, he learned about Master Damyan's actions from the sorcerer that was executed not long before we departed Dresden. The prince kept the knowledge to blackmail Damyan for information about his mother.'

A look of horror washed over the knight's face. 'Does he know about my involvement?'

Shaking his head, Maldwyn too checked the open door. 'I don't believe so.' Maldwyn shrugged. 'Maybe this sorcerer didn't know about you.'

Relieved, Ser Theodor rubbed his temples. Footsteps sounded in the hall. They shared worried expressions, neither of them was meant to be here rummaging through the king's personal possessions.

'You need to get out of here now. Put the lock back on that, and take that thing with you. Go!'

'You really won't tell anyone?'

'I swear on my honour and my life... I will keep your secret.'

Ser Theodor smiled back at Maldwyn, slipped through the main entrance to the king's chambers and shut the door. Maldwyn hurried to reseal the jewellery box, holding the queen's stone pendant firm in his grip.

He heard talking outside.

Ser Theodor was stalling for Maldwyn to make it out of the room unscathed. He too darted from the king's private chambers, rushing out the servants' entrance.

* * * * *

In the encroaching darkness of the servant halls, Maldwyn strode through the quiet corridors of the palace toward the exit, through the city and the beach that waited at the base of the mount. The strangeness of the encounter he had with Ser Theodor had been set aside as he resumed his mission to stop King Viktor from being cursed and learning of the draconite. Maldwyn had made a promise to the Erendil that he would do this, and that was exactly what he intended to do.

Turning up a corner, Maldwyn saw a servant donned in the plain attire of the staff running up the corridor. His face was ghostly white with fear.

'The princess has escaped!' The man's arms were waving erratically. He took no notice of Maldwyn as he sped by. 'The princess has escaped!' Maldwyn tried to hide his smile as he stood out of the way, both proud and gladdened to hear she had escaped the palace dungeons. Maldwyn turned to continue down the corridor. 'She's taken the knight with her! The princess and Ser Mikel have escaped!'

Maldwyn stopped dead in his tracks. The man continued shouting as he bolted through the castle raising the alarm. This was not what he had intended. Maldwyn had hoped the princess would escape, but he had no intention of seeing Mikel go free. At least he would not be around for the king to question him and learn of the draconite. Still, Maldwyn worried who else he might share this knowledge with.

With two escaped prisoners, Maldwyn knew it would not be long before the city's bells would sound. He needed to hurry out of the palace before all exits were blocked and he was found with the stolen pendant. Someone had been coming into the king's chambers when Maldwyn left. It may be that the king already knew the queen's pendant was missing.

Jumping into action, Maldwyn sprinted through the halls. He whisked around the corners, skidding along the stone, and dashing down the stairs two at a time. He didn't stop to look at the other servants he passed on his way. The patrolling guards in the courtyard all ignored him. Hurrying servants were a common occurrence.

As Maldwyn made it through the gatehouse, out of the palace grounds and into the city, he heard the bells toll, ringing loudly throughout the capital. The people in the city streets all fretted at the sound of the bells, dropping baskets and rushing indoors in a state of panic. They wouldn't yet know that the bells were tolling for the escaped princess, but they knew that it meant danger was imminent and to get off the streets and hide.

Maldwyn flew across the docks, boots beating on the wooden panels. Massive anchored vessels with huge, ballooning sails and long oars sticking out of their bellies, lined the coastline, unable to sail any closer without becoming banked in the sand. Rowboats of a variety of intricacies were tied to the wharves. The simpler lowline boats belonged to the city's fishermen who were rowing back to shore at the sound of the calling bells. The larger more detailed ferries were manned by the city's navy and moved supplies from the shore to the distant ships on the horizon, unfazed by the ringing.

At the end of the docks was a set of wooden steps that led down to the beach. The black sand glittered, sticking to Maldwyn's boots. The dusky water picked up the shining stars and sparkled in the dim evening light.

He slowed as he approached the water, taking a moment to catch his breath. He leaned forward, hands on his knees, still holding the heavy stone pendant between his fingers. Maldwyn stood and walked over to the water.

Taking one final look at the pendant which—even in its rough state—was beautifully crafted with fine markings, Maldwyn considered that he may have been too late. Perhaps the king had already touched the unassuming piece of jewellery. Maldwyn wished he knew if he were too late, but could only hope that he had made it in time to stop the curse. He walked into the water a little, the gentle tide lapping at the base of his boots.

He couldn't risk the cursed item washing up, or being picked up by someone swimming in the sea. He needed it to go far enough that it would be in deeper waters.

Stepping back and bending his legs slightly at the knee, Maldwyn put his weight on the leg behind him. He took a deep breath and called forth his power. He pushed forward and threw the pendant, letting it be carried by his force, watching as it flew through the air into the blackness. He heard it plop into the water many hundred feet from where he stood.

He let out a heavy breath, there weren't many sandbanks along this shore. It would be far enough that it would remain on the base of the seafloor for an eternity. Maldwyn raked his hand through his thick hair and walked out of the water, glad to see the deed was done. Making his way back up the dock, he headed back to the castle where the bells were calling him home.

* * * * *

The next morning, when all the commotion was over and the city had returned to its normal level of chaos, Maldwyn went to complete his usual duties in the prince's chambers. He knocked on the familiar, simple door.

'Enter,' the prince's voice called. Maldwyn hadn't expected him to be inside. Placing his hand on the cold metal door handle, he opened the door. 'I'm glad you're here.' Prince Harlan sounded miserable seated behind his desk, which was covered in papers. His head rested in his hands. Maldwyn felt sad to see the prince so down.

Maldwyn closed the doors and clasped his hands. Now that they were back in Dresden, Maldwyn felt it was only appropriate for him to resume formalities.

'Are you alright, Your Grace?'

'I'm fine.' The prince slumped back in his seat, stroking his jawline. Maldwyn knew that, although he wasn't looking at the prince, he was giving him a disbelieving expression. He was doing it on purpose.

'Are you upset about your sister, or your father?'

'Both.'

Maldwyn walked closer to where Prince Harlan was sitting. The papers on the table were muddled into senseless piles. He noted that there was something in the prince's hands. It was something small, fitting in the palm of his hand and able to be well disguised by the fist he had formed around it.

'I wish Cassara had told me she was a seer, and I'm mad that my father sentenced her to death.'

'If she had told you, what would you have done?' Maldwyn asked to satisfy his own curiosity about the prince. He unclasped his hands, better matching the informality of the conversation.

Prince Harlan pulled a baffled face.

'I don't know.' Placing his elbows on the table, the prince put his head back in his hands. 'My father raised me to believe that all magic is a corrupting power. It's dangerous and can't be trusted.'

Maldwyn was a little hurt to hear the truth spoken aloud. He had imagined that the prince might hold different views from the ones his father placed in his head.

'Then, that's why she didn't tell you, sire.' Prince Harlan looked up at Maldwyn as though he had said something that should make him feel guilty. 'She couldn't be sure of how you would react.' Maldwyn placed his fingers on the table, glancing over the mess of papers.

'You're right… of course.' Prince Harlan waved a hand as if that were a given. Some sort of fact that Maldwyn was always right. His blue eyes were particularly bright as the sun's beams gleamed through the windows. 'But I do know that I wouldn't have executed her.'

Maldwyn bit his cheek and smiled, holding out hope for the prince to change. The bigger the rift between Prince Harlan and his father got, the more he opened his mind and thought for himself.

The prince brought his fist down from under his chin. 'What's in your hand?' Maldwyn asked, curious about what he had been hiding.

Opening his fist, Prince Harlan revealed the ring that was in his grasp. The ring had a wide band with red jewels crested in it, and swirling patterns that were so tightly woven together it was difficult to discern where one ended and another began. There was an open linked chain about the ring.

'Is that what I think that is?'

'It's Kristian's ring.' The prince watched Maldwyn with an intense expression. 'It was right where I thought it was… in my mother's jewellery box.'

'When did you find it?' Maldwyn considered that it had been the prince's shoes he had heard coming up the hall to the king's chambers the prior evening.

'Last night.' Prince Harlan's face flashed with a self-satisfied expression. 'My father had business to attend to after dinner, so I thought it was a good opportunity to search through my mother's things.'

Smiling at the confirmation, Maldwyn fumbled his fingers on the table slightly, as if he wanted to reach forward to touch the ring, amazed at its seamless artistry. The prince held his smooth hand out for Maldwyn to have a look. Maldwyn didn't dare to touch it.

A sound pounded on the servant door. The prince formed a fist again. Maldwyn stood tall and reassumed the proper stance: back straight, hands clasped and eyes downcast. The prince called to the door. Master Damyan stepped through the door.

'I apologise, Your Grace, but there is an urgent message for Maldwyn from Alander.' The silver streaks in his hair were fairer in the sunlight. Maldwyn lifted his head to meet his master's gaze. 'It's your mother, Maldwyn.'

Maldwyn's heart jumped. His mother had been unwell for some time. By the sympathetic look on Master Damyan's face, the news was not good.

'Sire, I was hoping that it would be alright for me to take Maldwyn with me and to have another servant tend to your chambers for the time being.'

'Of course.'

Maldwyn felt strange, as if he were watching himself walk through the door, following his master from a distance. It was like his body was somehow not his own.

As he moved, he felt the prince watching him closely. He yearned to look back, but continued onwards, having what seemed like no control over his movements at all.

ACKNOWLEDGEMENTS

Originally this book was intended to be a series of short stories, but, as I began writing the stories of Maldwyn and Harlan, the events took unexpected turns and grew into something larger than I had initially planned. I would like to take the time to thank my dear family, friends and colleagues over the years, especially whilst working in retail as I worked to complete my degree at university. These were some of the most personally challenging days of my life, and you all kept me smiling and laughing through many dramas. You all taught me a strength of character that I can't explain, and without your support through many tear-filled days, I would never have gotten the courage to share my work with anyone, and my piles of notes would have lived in a box away in some cupboard. Thank you all for teaching me so much.

To my long list of friends and family, who have always accepted me and made me feel normal when I couldn't yet accept myself. I am who I am today because of each and every one of you. In a way, this book has ended up being an ode to my many inner turmoils over the years. Because of all of you, I have been able to create a book such as this one.

Tormented Dreams wouldn't exist without the amazing efforts of my mother and my sister, who put in countless hours editing every chapter as I finished drafting them. They supported me, encouraged me and pushed me to always better my writing. I cannot thank them enough for their careful guidance and honest feedback. Imagine where the commas might have ended up if it weren't for the two of you. I hate to think of it!

I would like to give a special thanks to the many stories in my life which have inspired me in so many ways. There are too many to list in full, but here are a few that I would like to mention. *Harry Potter* by J.K. Rowling created one of the most incredible magical realms on paper. I grew up with these books, and faced many perils alongside this infamous trio. These stories helped me to think outside of the box. *Lord of the Rings* by J.R.R Tolkien. I don't think I need to explain the incredible ways these books build a completely epic world, nor the impact his writing has had on so many people. *Lud-in-the-Mist* by Hope Mirrlees is one of the most beautiful and whimsical stories I believe I have read. And last, but absolutely not least, *Xena Warrior Princess* by Renaissance Pictures and portrayed by Lucy Lawless. This TV series taught me how to be a strong, independent woman from a young age. This quirky show inspired me to dream big, to believe that the greater good will always win in the end, and to stand up for myself.

I cannot get through this brief list without giving a special thanks to my characters whose voices told the story for me. In many ways, I felt like their interpreter. Maldwyn, Harlan, may we find a happy end to this series and all your troubles together.

The list of people who have supported and encouraged me on this journey is very long, and I could not possibly mention them all by name. You all know who you are, and I thank you!

ABOUT THE AUTHOR

Maddison Greer's long-lasting love of fantasy and Norse mythology began at a young age while living in Sweden. The richness of the lore and the beauty of the Scandinavian landscape inspired her to begin writing. Having written several short stories, drafted novels and growing piles of scribbled notes about characters and worlds throughout her adolescence, Maddison began writing her debut novel, *Tormented Dreams*, when she moved to Melbourne, Australia.

You can find out more about Maddison, *Tormented Dreams* and the latest news about the Maldwyn & Harlan series at:

www.maddisongreer.com

www.ingramcontent.com/pod-product-compliance
Lightning Source LLC
Chambersburg PA
CBHW030602120726
47904CB00006B/1746